PENGUIN BOOKS

THE SECRET HISTORY OF LAS VEGAS

Chris Abani is the acclaimed author of *GraceLand* and *The Virgin of Flames*. He is the recipient of a Guggenheim Fellowship, the Hemingway/PEN Prize, the PEN Beyond the Margins Award, the Hurston Wright Award, and a Lannan Literary Fellowship, among many honors. Born in Nigeria, he is currently Board of Trustees Professor of English at Northwestern University. He lives in Chicago.

ALSO BY CHRIS ABANI

PROSE

Masters of the Board
Graceland
Becoming Abigail
The Virgin of Flames
Song for Night

POETRY

Kalakuta Republic
Daphne's Lot
Dog Woman
Hands Washing Water
There Are No Names for Red
Sanctificum

THE SECRET
HISTORY
OF
LAS VEGAS

A Novel

CHRIS ABANI

PENGUIN BOOKS

PENGUIN BOOKS
Published by the Penguin Group
Penguin Group (USA) LLC
375 Hudson Street
New York, New York 10014

USA | Canada | UK | Ireland | Australia | New Zealand | India | South Africa | China
penguin.com
A Penguin Random House Company

First published in Penguin Books 2014

LIBRARY OF CONGRESS CATALOGING-IN-PUBLICATION DATA
Abani, Chris.
The secret history of Las Vegas : a novel / Chris Abani.
pages cm
ISBN 978-0-14-312495-5
1. Las Vegas (Nev.)—History—Fiction. 2. Secrets—Fiction. 1. Title.
PR9387.9.A23S43 2014
823'.914—dc23
2013033496

Printed in the United States of America
1 3 5 7 9 10 8 6 4 2

Set in Bembo Std
Designed by Sabrina Bowers

This is a work of fiction. Names, characters, places, and incidents either are the product
of the author's imagination or are used fictitiously, and any resemblance to actual persons,
living or dead, businesses, companies, events, or locales is entirely coincidental

For
My siblings who allow me
to be a crazed animal: I love you all.
and
Sarah
Who taught me grace.

There is no refuge from memory
and remorse in this world. The
spirits of our foolish deeds haunt us,
with or without repentance.

—GILBERT PARKER

History is a nightmare from which
I am trying to awake.

—JAMES JOYCE

ACKNOWLEDGMENTS

The popular myth is that writers create books in isolation, locked in a garret; that all novels are the product of singular work. While it may be true that the vision of a novel is singular, the best writers know that without a community of helpers, this vision will remain at best locked up in their heads. This is not an exhaustive list of those I need to thank for helping this book become a reality:

Sarah Valentine for reading multiple drafts and for generously giving me the title for this book. For reading and feedback, also: Cristina Garcia, Peter Orner, Kathleen Blackburn, Matthew Shenoda, Kwame Dawes, Colin Channer, David Mura, Traise Yamamoto, Vorris Nunley, Pumla Gqola (who cannot be blamed for the South African inaccuracies—those are all mine), Kathryn Court (best editor in the world and my champion), Benjamin George, Ellen Levine (my incredible agent), Lucy Stille (whose feedback on my screenplays helped me formulate this novel), Junot Díaz, Dave Eggers, Scott Cohen, and Brad Kessler.

Since there is no real separation between my art and my living, I must thank the following people:

Adrian Awopitan Ifabiyi Castro, who continues to help me shape the craft with which I sail into mystery: priceless.

Kolawole Oshitola, whose very life is the miracle that infuses so many, giving shape and purpose.

Percival Everett, David St. John, Viet Nguyen, Daniel Tiffany, T.C. Boyle, Carol "Trukina" Muske Dukes, Johnny Temple, David Rose, John Moser, and Eloise Klein Healy—just because.

And thank you to Tezira Nabongo for the gift of possibilities.

THE SECRET
HISTORY
OF
LAS VEGAS

BRISTLE-
CONE

This hands cannot do.

Even interlaced across a pregnant woman's stomach, even if the will that webs the fingers desires nothing more than to protect the unborn in her—not even this is sufficient to form a barrier against the flash of light and a cloud that grows not into a mushroom, but rather into a thick tree with a dense plume; a tree to shame Odin's, a tree to make Adam cover the inadequacies of his, a tree even Shiva would stand back from in awe.

And bright.

A constellation? No, a rogue star, a renegade sun, the very face of awe, and if there are true names for divinity, then that too.

As Selah watched the cloud mushroom up, she wondered if the babies in her womb were lit by the incandescence before her. Had they beheld all this glory? And what would it shape in them when they were born? A penetrating insight into mystery? A desire for a life untinged by the fear of death? Or eyes that see only constellations? Only truth?

But the warnings led in other directions.

The oracles spoke mostly of death. Of darkness. Of eclipse.

But could she mold even this cloud into a defiant sign? A promise of good things?

Perhaps the tone seems heavy, Old Testament–weighted, but

until you have seen this power bloom in a desert, you can never fully understand the truths that made Elijah weep, or Elisha wail in despair for his people; you cannot know the terrible loneliness of Moses, the cry in Gethsemane. But sometimes simpler words can do the same work, and watching the explosion of a nuclear bomb in the Nevada desert from a spot less than two miles from its sky-obliterating epicenter, Selah said:

Shit, I'm fucked!

And she was.

Her babies were born fused, like the glass formed by the chattering of sand jinn.

We cannot operate here, the doctor said as he placed the bundle of limbs in her arms. But we could ask the doctors on the army base. They have the best minds and equipment.

The idea of it, an unspeakable insult, that those who did this should be begged to undo it, curdled the milk in her.

No, she said. No. They were born this way for a reason.

And she named one Water, for the living waters from the throne, and the other one Fire, because his very existence was the curse she would use to end them.

The boys were still young, barely seven, when the sickness began.

Leukemia.

The word itself conjured up only a deep royal blue in her mind; beautiful like a Nile lotus, which she couldn't know because she had never seen one. But blue; like the angle of light on Lake Mead at a certain time and place on a certain summer day.

Terminal.

The word rattled like the gates of a crypt, all rust and the smell of decay, but also conjuring adventure. A train pulling into a station on an evening in Casablanca, or roaring through a dark desert, its lit carriages pulling through the night like a spell, an affirmation that it can all mean something.

Then her job at the diner, precarious as it was with the slow onset of decrepitude, which announced that their town, Gabriel, named for that indomitable angel of light, was waning into a ghost as the government moved the freeway, came to an abrupt end. Only the most adventurous tourists came through anymore. Even the steady flow of Indians from the reservation dried up like a desert creek in high summer when a Denny's made its way resolutely, if reluctantly, onto the outskirts of the res.

The small strip of land her people had tried to grow artichokes and dates on when they moved north—because, as her father said, you came along, my love, my Selah—had failed to yield anything but more dirt. The truth was that her father was already caught in a pause, in a moment of rest, before the courage to move had come upon him. That was why he named her Selah, the Hebrew word that marks a pause in a psalm, a moment to consider the music. And so they moved north and had lived here in Gabriel since. That is, until her father was shot by a sheriff too excited to see that the gun the black man was holding was actually just a pipe he was packing with tobacco before sucking on it.

Selah had just turned four when it happened and never fully understood his death.

Her mother did her best until she died shortly after.

Heart attack was the official reason, but Selah knew it was really heartbreak.

At eighteen she got pregnant from a boy on the nearby army base who promised to marry her but who shipped off soon after her belly began to show. She never heard from him again.

Many people have come back from worse, so Selah, like everyone in the dusty town of Gabriel, soldiered on, but her leukemia, and the closing of the diner sealed everything into a premature death.

Now there was nothing left for Selah but the glass case. The display that old Dan the mechanic had built her from the scraps he could spare. It was a curious thing, this glass box more terrarium than fish tank, four feet tall and four feet wide. Glass bolted together as though by Dr. Frankenstein, with a sluggish fan, powered by a car battery, cut into the back panel, struggling to move the hot Nevada air.

Selah sat with that box every day, dressed like a carnival gypsy, under a large 7 Up beach umbrella, the terrarium by the table, a deck of tarot cards before her, offering readings for a dollar and for three dollars, the chance to look under the velvet cloth draped over the terrarium at the monster inside.

More often than not, people chose the terrarium, and she would slowly peel back the green velvet drape to reveal the conjoined seven-year-old twins, sitting or sometimes standing in the tank, one reading, the other holding court loudly until, annoyed by a particularly careless onlooker, he would crawl under his caul and hide.

That was how the years went by, she getting sicker, the twins getting bigger until Water couldn't stand in the tank anymore but sat cross-legged at the bottom, still reading, always reading. Fire held rapid-fire philosophical debates with customers while Water read, pausing only occasionally, when prodded to engage, to look up and speak in simple facts like: cats cannot taste sweet things, or, cold water weighs more than hot.

Their fame, if one can call this fame, spread, and soon tourists were stopping over just to see them. It wasn't long before a traveling circus came by, more sideshow than circus, truth be told. The owner, a Mr. Jacobs, paid a hundred dollars to see the twins.

It's more than you need to pay, Selah said.

As you can see, we are alike, Mr. Jacobs said. You and I, parents to what some might call freaks but which I tend to think of as marvels of the Lord's creativity. And in my sideshow, all the marvels are natural, he boasted. Why, that's why we travel under that name, Jacob and the Lord's Marvels, he explained, himself a man with what looked like lobster claws where his hands should be. And we are all like a family, he added.

We are, the midget with him said. We are a family.

Selah thought the midget had the saddest eyes she had ever seen.

Mr. Jacobs offered Selah a very good deal. To take the boys and look after them, teach them how to have a life in his show. In exchange he would pay for her to live in a hospice until she passed in her sleep. She demurred and coughed blood into a handkerchief, a clump of her hair falling out disgracefully as she did.

If you won't have the money, what will you have?

Selah glanced at the blood in her handkerchief. The boys were twelve and Water was smarter than she would ever be.

Swear on this blood to treat them like your own, she said.

I sure will, Mr. Jacobs said, offering a lobster claw. And here is my own daughter so you may see that I am true.

And a tall girl, slender as a wisp of smoke, walked forward.

How old are you, Selah asked.

Twelve, the girl said.

And your name?

Fred.

That seemed to cement it for her. Although to confirm, Selah drew a card and laid it faceup.

The Hanged Man.

She sighed, a sound of infinite sadness.

Come by my house tomorrow, she said. It's five miles from town, under the blue-barked bristlecone.

Mr. Jacobs nodded.

That night, through bouts of hacking coughs and much

blood spat into handkerchiefs, Selah sang the boys to sleep with their favorite lullaby.

Then, kissing them on the cheek, she let herself out just before dawn, when the mist was still upon the ground and dragging a length of rope behind her, walked up the slight rise behind the house to the bristlecone tree.

FRIDAY

One

A desert wind rippled across Lake Mead and through the tamarisk on the shore. Dotting the reedy grass, the ghostly foundations of the sunken Mormon town of St. Thomas returned with the water level falling, like a rude reminder of all the secrets this place kept.

Detective Salazar was taken by the quiet of the ghost town. He liked that the only sound was the wind through the needle-leaved shrubs, the occasional birdcall, and the crunch of shells underfoot. He went there as often as he could, but not for the scenery or the quiet. It was his habit to visit crime scenes, long after the evidence had been tagged, bagged, and collected. He came to this site where, two years before, dead homeless men had begun appearing in dumps of ten, sometimes twelve, occasionally fewer, in an untidy pile. He combed over it again and again, convinced there was something he had overlooked, something that would break the case. Other times it was just to sit with the spirits of the place, as he liked to explain to his former—now retired—partner, Vines.

Shitload of good it does, Vines had told him.

But Salazar was convinced it did.

Maybe Vines was right, though. Even with increased patrols, they hadn't been able to apprehend the killer. The local police had called in the FBI and even psychiatrists and specialists in psychopathy from a local institute, the Desert Palms, all to no avail.

Then one day the killings stopped, but not before Salazar
came upon the body of a teenager in the last dump. It wasn't
only her age that marked her apart, or the fact that she was the
only girl who had ever shown up at the body dumps. It was
something else, something about her eyes, about the serenity
that shone from them belying the thick finger bruises around
her neck. That girl haunted him, kept him returning to the
different dump sites around the lake for the last year. He was
determined to find her killer.

Two months ago, at the end of summer, the body dumps
had begun again, and this time Salazar didn't wait for the case
to be assigned to him. He asked for it. Demanded it. He was
due to retire soon, anytime he wanted to, as Human Resources put it. This would be his swan song, his last good
thing. The only part he truly regretted about being a homi-
cide detective was that he never arrived in time to save anyone. This would change that for him.

But it was now Halloween and he had no leads, was no
closer to solving the murders. He looked down at his watch—
4:00 p.m. If he was going to leave, he had to do it soon; otherwise he'd be stuck in traffic. But still, he didn't move. He
looked out across the water.

Across the lake, unknown to Salazar, a park ranger had come
across a man taking a dip in the blue water. To be fair, Ranger
Green had first come across an old sedan with a bad paint job
at the edge of the lake and, following the line of the car, a
man in the water.

Sir, he called on his bullhorn. Sir, you have to get out of
the water. This area of the lake is off-limits to the public.
Overton Beach is a mile from here; there are signs.

The man was still, like he might have been carved out of

driftwood, torso bent at a near ninety-degree angle, left side submerged under the water.

Sir, the ranger called.

The man in the water turned to the ranger, mouth moving, as though he were arguing with himself. He stood up straight and Green saw something attached to the man's left side, something that had previously been submerged under the water, something flailing. Green thought it looked like a baby or, at the very least, a small child. But that didn't make sense; surely the man couldn't be drowning a baby. He reached for his radio and called the police. Looking up, he saw that the man in the water was hesitating in the shallows. Green returned the horn to his mouth.

Sir, get out of the water now. The police are on their way.

Whatever internal debate the man seemed to be having ceased at this information and as he advanced rather rapidly toward the ranger, he gave off an air of quiet threat. Green stepped back, realizing now that the man was in front of him, shirtless, that there had been no baby. In one glance he took in the second man, though to call him that was a stretch, hanging as he was like an appendage off the first one's side.

Your name, sir, was the only thing he could think to say.

Fire, the appendage said. And this is Water, the appendage added in a high-pitched wheeze, pointing to the man Green had seen in the water.

A group of twelve or more cows is called a flink, Water said.

Come with me, Green said to Water, careful not to look at Fire.

Attached as he was, and measuring just over twelve inches long, Fire appeared to be little more than a head with two arms projecting out of Water's chest. He had no legs or feet, but he did have one toe, and that was attached to Water's torso. He was bald, and a large skin caul, like a turkey wattle, drooped down one side of his head. His left eyelid was swollen and misshapen, almost as if he had been punched there. His nose was squished nearly flat against his face and the nostrils flared with every breath he took, although he seemed to do most of his breathing through his mouth, a rattling harsh wheeze, and with each one his surprisingly generous lips curled back to reveal caninelike teeth. Only his bright and gentle eyes gave any indication of the intelligence behind them.

Water, at six feet, had a muscular, lean body and a face so perfectly proportioned that he seemed like a cruel joke at Fire's expense. He was quite simply beautiful. And this made Fire seem all the more shocking and alien.

The ranger pulled a blanket out of the back of his truck and offered it to Water, averting his gaze from Fire. He was glad when the blanket covered him.

It was getting dark, and the ranger's truck, roof lights flashing, idled next to the hunched sedan whose slender back tires were sunk a little into the soft mud by the lakeshore. The sedan's door bore the legend KING KONGO: AFRICAN WITCHDOCTOR.

This is too fucking much, the ranger muttered, and walked a little up the trail to look out for the police cruiser.

Water, a stoic and perhaps even otherworldly look on his face, gazed off to the hills in the distance behind which the Hoover Dam sat like an alien ship anchored to the walls of the Black Canyon. Left of the dam, just a few weeks before, a magician had walked across the lake, stopping in the middle to sink from sight, down to the wreck of the B-29 bomber that had crashed there in 1948. To the right of his line of sight, the Valley of Fire, also known as the playground of the gods, named for the spectacular red sandstone rock formations that flickered like grainy flames against the sky, spread like a red rash on the landscape. Behind the twins, snaking up through the tall tamarisk like a green tunnel, was a path of shells.

Fire, hanging from Water's side, was getting cold and irritated.

Is this a citizen's arrest, he asked. You can't keep us here.

But he had swallowed so much water from the lake that his voice was raspier than usual and, muffled by the blanket, he wasn't audible.

The ranger didn't respond but kept glancing over at the twins with a very disturbed look, somewhere between open curiosity and repulsion. An unmarked police cruiser winding down the trail, dust cloud in tow, brought a tight smile to his face.

Salazar, in a gray suit, stepped out and walked over to the ranger.

Fire moved the blanket from his face and blinked in the sudden light.

You really have no right to keep us here, he shouted.

Salazar, his gleaming gold badge on a chain around his neck, glanced at Fire, not quite believing his eyes.

Some fucking Halloween costume, he said to Green.

I'm afraid it's no costume, Green said.

No shit?

No shit.

Fuck, Salazar said under his breath, approaching the twins. I'm Detective Salazar, he said, looking at them with a little unease.

Salazar took the call because he was only five minutes away when it came in. This could be the killer he had been looking for. He hoped it was; that way this case would finally be over. Salazar was a twenty-year veteran of the Vegas police and nothing fazed him much. Still, he was a little unsettled by the twins in front of him.

What the fuck are you, he asked.

People, Fire said.

You don't look much like people, Salazar said. He does, he

added, pointing to Water. But not you, he said to Fire, and turned to spit.

Only humans and horses have hymens, Water said.

That's some fucked-up shit to say, Salazar said to him. Who the fuck talks like that?

Leave him alone, Fire said.

Are you Siamese twins?

There is no Siam, Fire said.

Feisty, Salazar said to Green, who looked unhappy. To the twins, he said: Listen, I don't usually respond to these calls. It's more for the uniforms, you know? I just happened to be in the area, and quite frankly I don't appreciate your shit, understand?

Water smiled serenely while Fire glowered.

Listen, I need you to turn around and put your arms behind you, Salazar said.

What the fuck, Fire said.

Come on, freaks like you, I can't be the first policeman who has cuffed you. Turn the fuck around.

Water turned. Salazar approached and, careful not to touch Fire, put cuffs on him.

Now, he said, which one of you fucks is King Kong?

King Kongo, Fire corrected.

Salazar squinted at the sign on the car door. Whatever, he muttered, not like I give a fuck. Then to Water: ID?

Water shook his head.

See, that's a problem, Salazar said. You're supposed to have your ID on you.

Is this a police state, Fire demanded.

Shut the fuck up, Salazar said to Fire. Names?

Water shook his head.

Water Esau Grimes and Fire Jacob Grimes, Fire said.

For real?

Water shrugged, which sent Fire into spasms, and Salazar looked away again.

Address?

We have no fixed abode, Fire said.

Occupation?

Fire waved at the car: We are King Kongo.

Didn't I tell you to shut the fuck up, Salazar said. Fire was confused because while clearly addressing him, Salazar's gaze never left Water's face.

Water shrugged, causing Fire to jiggle up and down again. Salazar looked away once more.

I can see the look in your eyes, Detective. You look like you've just seen the devil, Fire said.

Only if the devil is a fat man in a pink dress, Salazar shot back. Jesus, you've got me talking like a freak too. Is King Kong the name of some kind of act?

Yes, Fire said. *King Kongo* is our act.

And what are you doing out here?

Enjoying the ruins, Fire said. Is that illegal?

It is illegal to be in an area prohibited to the public, Salazar said, pointing to a sign leaning at a forty-five-degree angle.

It is illegal to ride a camel on the freeway in Nevada, Water said.

Cut that out, Salazar said to him. Why would you be out here on Halloween? That is, unless you are up to something strange. You know anything about the bodies that we've been finding around here?

Water had a serene look, but Fire was getting visibly agitated.

Come on, Freak Show, Salazar said. Tell me why you're really here.

We're here to sightsee, Fire said.

Do I look that fucking stupid, Salazar asked.

The twins were quiet.

The ranger says you were out in the lake. Says you were drowning that thing on your side. Says it was submerged under water, Salazar said. He was back to addressing only Water.

We have rights, Fire yelled. You can't treat us this way. We've done nothing wrong.

In Idaho you may not fish on a camel's back, Water said.

You're fucking with me, right?

There are feral camels in the southwest United States, Water said.

Shut the fuck up, Salazar said.

Hadji Ali was the lead camel driver for the U.S. Army Camel Corps. He died in 1902 and is buried in Quartzite, Arizona, where a metal camel on a pyramid marks his grave that bears his name as Hi Jolly.

Salazar looked intently at Water. Don't push me, he said. Where are the rest of your clothes, he asked, waving at Water's bare midriff.

On the hood of our car, Fire said.

Wait here, Salazar said, and walked over to their sedan. There was a baggy shirt and jacket on the hood.

A little big for you, Salazar said to Water.

I need space to breathe, Fire said.

I am searching your clothing for drugs and weapons, Salazar said to Water. Tell me if there are any sharp objects in the pockets.

There are no sharp objects, Fire said. Why would you think we have drugs or weapons?

Salazar ignored him.

You're really going to pretend I'm not here, Fire asked.

Saint Maximilian Mary Kolbe is the patron saint of drug addicts, Water said.

Fuckhead, Salazar said to Water. To Green he said: Get the

digital camera out of my glove compartment and photograph the scene for me, will you, while I run their ID.

The scene, Green asked, a little confused.

The damn scene, Salazar said, waving around him. I'm going to go run them on my computer.

Sure, Green said, trailing Salazar, who was heading back to his cruiser.

Could you push our car out of the mud, Fire asked.

Tow truck's coming, Salazar threw over his shoulder. Your car's headed for impound.

This is a shakedown, Fire said. We are Americans.

Uh-huh, Salazar said. Keep talking and I'll arrest you.

For what, Fire asked.

You know, I'll get a camera from my trunk, Green said, wanting to put some distance between himself, the twins, and Salazar, whom he found abrasive.

Knock yourself out, Salazar said, continuing to his cruiser.

Green retrieved the camera and walked to the twins' sedan. Approaching from the rear, he noticed that the grass to the left was soaked in blood. He examined the spread of blood and found it coming from a plastic five-gallon drum lying on its side. The leak was slow, the blood coagulating. From what Green could make out, the drum was still about half full.

Detective, he called.

Yes, Salazar yelled back from his cruiser. He was about to settle himself into it and boot up the computer.

I think there's blood.

What?

Blood.

Salazar ran to the sedan. He took in the drum of blood quickly.

No body, he asked Green.

Green shook his head and turned to puke in the grass.

Don't fuck up my crime scene, Salazar growled at him. Turning to the twins, he said: I knew you freaks were up to something.

He had his gun trained on them.

Isn't that overkill, Fire asked. We haven't moved in a while.

You shut the fuck up, Salazar said, reaching for his radio.

Two

Thirty apes shot in the head with a butcher's bolt gun is not promising by any standards.

Sunil stared at the phrase used for the executions: "humane endpoint." A contradiction in terms, surely. The cost of sacrifice, the weight of absolution, or something more mundane and necessary—the killing of nonviable laboratory test subjects. The term had no doubt been coined by an ethically challenged researcher, or worse, an administrator. Sunil wasn't skilled in the delicacy of finding the right language for obscuring the intersection of death and scientific distance, and he had a grudging respect for those who were. At least it was nearly five, and while the institute didn't run regular hours, it was still close to the end of the day.

He sighed and rubbed his eyes, staring at the results of the tests graphing neatly across the squared paper in blue, green, and red hills. He willed them to change, to be different, to have the data reevaluate itself. But this was the beauty of science—most times the evidence was irrefutable, especially if the tests had been run with the kind of strict controls that he had implemented. Doubly so if they had been repeated as often as these had.

Such a waste, Sunil muttered, thinking not only in terms of lives and resources but also in terms of time. He looked over the termination order that was attached to the data, grateful that he wouldn't have to deal with the tedious task of drafting the paperwork.

He hadn't authorized this test, which meant that his boss, Brewster, must have. No one else had the authority. The last test that Sunil authorized used capuchins, but these test subjects were apes, bonobos to be exact, and they were more than 99 percent genetically similar to humans. That seemed like a significant line, not one Sunil would have crossed lightly. He was no stranger to experiments with lower primates and would never authorize a test that could result in this many deaths unless he was sure that it would be worth it.

There had been many such experiments when he worked in South Africa, in Vlakplaas, a notorious apartheid death camp. To test the limits of endurance, they would put a female baboon and her baby in a cage. Then they would start a fire under the metal floor, slowly turning up the heat, calculating how long the mother would endure the pain before putting the baby down and standing on it. It never took that long, usually less than thirty minutes. Sunil never told anyone at Vlakplaas, especially not his boss Eugene, that the screams of the dying infant kept him up at night. He couldn't show that kind of weakness, so instead he stuffed his ears with cotton wool while the experiments were being conducted. That sound, a muffled gurgle, like a distant brook, became the soundtrack of his denial, a white noise that successfully obliterated every last bit of conscience when he needed it. In this way he was no different from any South African: they all had their soundtracks.

The problem with primate tests was that sooner or later, apes weren't enough. The first human trial at Vlakplaas of the heat test was a woman called Beatrice. No last name. Her baby didn't even get a name in the file. Just Baby.

Flicking through these results, he found nothing remarkable in them; nothing he didn't already know, and, by extension, since he shared everything he knew with him, nothing that Brewster didn't know either. So why had Brewster autho-rized this, and why was he hijacking Sunil's experiments when he had access to all his data? Of course, the bigger ques-tion was what else had Brewster done behind his back?

Sunil had three labs, and each one was under video surveil-lance, and the footage fed live to his laptop and was stored on a hard drive he took everywhere. But there was no evidence of the test anywhere in the footage. Sunil cross-checked the time stamps. All in order, so it wasn't that. There was only one other explanation: the tests were not conducted in any of his labs. So why was Brewster keen for him to sign these papers? Why not one of the interns? Why was it being brought to his attention? What was going on? Fuck, Sunil thought. His best move was to sign the form and say nothing to Brewster.

He held his pen over the paper, nib poised, hesitating, un-able to shake the feeling that beyond the mere fact of his sig-nature, beyond this moment, everything would change. It was a clammy feeling, but feelings have no place in science, in the rational, and that was perhaps the real problem—that be-yond his denial, he knew exactly where this feeling was com-ing from. He knew the power of saying the wrong thing, of taking the truth on a detour.

Fuck, Sunil muttered, I have become more American than I thought.

He too, it seemed, had come to believe that he could some-how escape history. That it was possible, and even desirable, to live in a perpetual present. When had that happened? He hadn't been here long enough, it seemed, a mere seven years, and yet like the almost imperceptible, if inevitable, creep of sand in the desert, it had happened.

With a sigh he scratched his signature across the form and crossed the room to the coffee machine. Through the win-dow behind him the sun was beginning to dim on Las Vegas.

Three

Less than twenty minutes after Salazar called it in, the lakeside was crawling with police cars and an ambulance. Crime scene investigators were in everything, taking samples and photographing, and cataloging and sniffing.

Terry Jones, the CSI shift leader, stood next to Salazar and scratched his head.

So, no body, huh, he said.

No, Salazar said.

But you went ahead and called us all in, Terry said, indicating the uniforms with a sweep of his coffee cup.

Already a team of divers had arrived to look for the body in the lake.

I mean, it's almost six thirty, Terry said. Shift change is at seven. You couldn't wait?

What the fuck are you implying, Salazar asked. That I'm wasting your time?

You're too close to this case, he said. Maybe you're not thinking straight.

Fuck you, Salazar said.

Yeah, well, Terry said.

Yeah, well, fucking find the body, Salazar said.

If this is connected to the case from two years ago, shouldn't there be more bodies, Terry asked.

Fuck you, Salazar said.

Terry nodded. We're not likely to find anything soon, he said.

Why not, Salazar asked.

Big lake, Terry said. A lot of undercurrents. The body, if there was one, and with that amount of blood you'd need several, could be in Arizona by now. Or washed up somewhere where the lake meets the river and the river the desert. The desert gives nothing back.

Salazar liked Terry, they went back a ways and Salazar respected that Terry, a beat cop, had taken night classes at UNLV to qualify as a forensic expert. It took guts to go for a thing you wanted, at least that was how Salazar saw it. Still, he thought Terry talked a lot of shit sometimes.

Fuck, Salazar said.

I hear you. But there's more. There's no blood on the twins. I mean, if there had been a body, with that much blood, they would be covered in it. Nothing on them, not even a trace. And with all that blood, we would be looking for a lot more than one body.

How many?

Fuck if I know, Terry said.

But it's definitely human blood?

Yep, Terry said. Very human.

Shit. Could they have at least transported the drums of blood and dumped them here?

Nope. No blood in the car, either, Terry said.

Shit, Salazar said.

I know, Terry said.

They could have washed off in the lake.

Trace would still show up under the black light. There was an awkward pause. You know we have to move on soon, Terry continued.

Why?

Well, there's no body, so this isn't an active crime scene, Terry said. Half a five-gallon drum full of human blood is disturbing, but budget cuts and all mean we need an actual body, you know?

Salazar wanted to scream. Instead he said: I have to take the freaks in.

If they lawyer up, you'll have nothing, Terry said.

Yeah, Salazar sighed. I guess I have to break them. You remember how that goes?

Terry smiled. I sure do, he said. Listen, didn't you work closely with a psychiatrist a couple of years ago when the bodies first began to turn up? Singh, right? Take the twins to County. Before you go, call Dr. Singh and ask him to meet you at County to perform a psychological evaluation. You'd have them for seventy-two hours.

Salazar smiled. They do look kind of sick, he said.

Shortly after Salazar took the twins, the crime scene crew and the rest of the police left. Even the divers gave up the search for the night. The lakeshore returned to its normal quiet. An animal rustled in the tamarisk. A bird landed on the water. The wind threw some dust from the road onto the foundations of the houses that sat in the mud like the ruins of an ancient culture. On the shore, only the ranger's truck remained, lights still flashing in the gloom.

Four

The dying sun burnished the copper ingot of the Mandalay Bay. Next to it was the pyramid of the Luxor and, reclining in front, the light catching the gold paint of its headdress, the Sphinx. Farther to Sunil's left, the Bellagio and the tip of the Eiffel Tower rose above Paris Las Vegas. The Venetian, his favorite, was obscured.

He loved this moment when the sun was on a slow decline, just before the abruptness of night that seemed exclusive to deserts and plains. It reminded him of the light on the South African veld. One moment bright and full, the next, gone. The veld was just like its name, a stubby felt of grass and trees and small hills that seemed to break only when the green and brown rim of it touched the sky.

For one magical summer as a seven-year-old, he'd left Soweto behind on a summer trip to see his grandmother, Marie. She lived in KwaZulu, a homeland—one of those odd geographies created arbitrarily by the apartheid state as all black enclaves within South Africa. Not unlike Native American reservations, homelands were corrals, ways to contain and further impoverish native populations: entire settlements made up of shanties leaning unevenly into the wind.

Grandma Marie lived in the foothills, and as Sunil and his mother, Dorothy, traveled higher into the old Zulu territory, the shanties disappeared. Up there, everything felt different— the pace moved only as fast as the swaying fields of corn, or the lumbering herds of zebu that roamed everywhere, horns curved like arms raised in prayer. Each cow was marked so distinctively, in so many variations of red, white, black, brown, rust, and dun, that from a distance they looked like flocks of birds littering the grass on the hillsides.

The frenetic mood of Soweto seemed then like a bad taste spat from the mouth, and the air smelled fresh and sometimes heavy with rain. There was hardly a white person to be seen, and the blacks were less suspicious of one another. The only anger was the gossip—how Lindiwe Mabena had slept with Blessing Nkosi's husband a week after she died. How Catechist Brown was never the same after Father John passed, though no one would admit they'd been lovers. How Doreen Duduzile always miscarried because she'd had an abortion as a young woman in Cape Town, and how though she'd renounced the world and followed the Lord, she couldn't find any respite until she confessed to the murder of her unborn child, but as his mother told Grandma Marie, there are no words for some things. Everything else was pure scent. The smell of the toffees his grandmother pressed into his palms that melted in the heat of his clutched fingers, the drying grass and herd animals that filled the air with dust and delight. And something else—butterflies—everywhere, butterflies. And at dusk, the soft purple pastel of sky blurred into the darkening grass and then, before he could count to a hundred, night.

Sunil knew that his memory was faulty, that it was so tempered by nostalgia it could offer nothing concrete, but that knowledge did nothing to diminish his joy in the recollection.

The sun in his eye brought him back to the moment, to his body standing at the window of his sixth-floor office in the nondescript building in the nondescript business park east of the strip that was home to the Desert Palms Institute. His reflection in the glass made him uncomfortable, the way the honesty of shop windows makes fat women flinch. His hair was kinky and thick like a wool cap—not quite an Afro, but close enough—his nose clearly his mother's, the soft mouth that he believed he'd inherited from his father, and skin so dark, he could be black. His eyes were the only thing he liked about himself, soft and warm, and honey-colored flecked with green; his father's eyes, Brahmin eyes, a strange thing for a Sikh, stranger still in an African. Sighing, he took a sip from his coffee cup and focused on the view.

Sunil loved to watch the city from his office window, high up, tracking every little change in the landscape. He knew very well the illusion of chronology, the way it gave the impression that everything moved onward, expanding on a straight line, heading toward epiphany. But events weren't linear, they moved in circular loops that made little sense, and this disjointed reality was the only truth. Chronology, he believed, was a pattern grafted over the past to claim control and understanding, to pretend meaning. It was all shit, though, in the end. He felt people were made of little more than this: history, myth, and ritual. When he remembered his past, he remembered his father with the distance of myth.

He drew with his forefinger on the glass to connect the hotels with invisible lines, reading some esoteric Masonic notions in the pattern. Even from this far away, he could see the extravagance of it all, an extravagance that was as old as the city itself. A history buff, he knew the Jewish-Irish-Sicilian mob syndicate that built the mirage of Vegas opened grandiose hotels early. In 1952, the Sahara was designed to mimic the movie romanticism of North Africa. In 1955, the Dunes, with waitresses dressed like DeMille extras in an Arabian Nights production, and a thirty-foot-tall turbaned black sultan with crossed arms guarding the doors, appeared almost overnight. And in 1956, in the new Fremont, twelve-year-old Wayne Newton rose to fame singing "Danke Schoen."

Vegas is really an African city, Sunil thought. What other imagination would build such a grandiose tomb to itself? And just like in every major city across Africa, from Cairo to his hometown of Johannesburg, the palatial exteriors of the city architecture barely screened the seething poverty, the home-lessness, and the despair that spread in townships and shanty-towns as far as the eye could see. But just as there, here in Vegas the glamour beguiled and blinded all but those truly intent on seeing, and in this way the tinsel of it mocked the obsessive hope of those who flocked there.

In Johannesburg there had been the allure of gold and un-told monies to be made in the mines. Gold so plentiful, there were hills of it. No one bothered to explain to the obsessed that the glittering hills were just a trick of the light—mounds of yellow sand dug up for the gold, the silicate glowing in the sun with false promise. No wonder he felt at home here.

He hadn't lived in Johannesburg since White Alice left, shortly after his mother was taken to the madhouse, and he had returned only once in the years since, just after apartheid officially came to an end. He'd been shocked then to see that the once vibrant city center had turned into a ghost town. In-dians and whites had emptied out, fleeing either abroad or to the suburbs. What surprised Sunil, though, was that in the wake of that flight, the city hadn't been filled by South Afri-can blacks leaving the townships for more salubrious digs, but by Nigerian and Senegalese businessmen selling everything from the popular Nollywood movies to phone cards. The feeling of racial camaraderie hadn't been extended to these in-vading blacks, who the more gentle South Africans thought were worse than Zulus, which was saying something.

Now Sunil thought of Las Vegas as home. That's the thing about having always been a displaced person; home was not a physical space but rather an internal landscape, a feeling that he could anchor to different places. Some took easier than others, and although it was always hard work, he was good at it.

He had come to Vegas from Cape Town seven years ago to codirect a new research project at the Desert Palms Institute, which, among its many government contracts and research projects with no oversight, was studying psychopathic behavior. This was the project Sunil had come here to work on. He had expected to enjoy the work, but what he had not expected was that he would fall in love with the city.

His attention returned to the coming night and the darkness that held nothing but what was projected. Was night the same everywhere? In the Soweto of his childhood the darkness was a contradiction of lights, noise, and an absolute stillness that held only police cars cockroaching through. Here in Las Vegas, near the Strip, where it never really got dark, could anything be revealed in the bright neon? He often tried to read the faces teeming there but quickly realized that everything was obscured, even in revelation; the brightness was its own kind of night.

Noticing that the coffee had run in a tiny rivulet down the side of the cup, Sunil frowned and reached for his monogrammed handkerchief, a throwback to his childhood, to the older men in Soweto who always seemed to have a clean handkerchief on them, no matter how threadbare and patched. He wiped the rivulet away, brows furrowed in concentration.

There was an exactness to Sunil that spilled out into the world and was reflected in his sense of order: the neat row of very sharp pencils in the carved ebony holder on his desk, upright and ranked by use like soldiers on a parade ground; the sharp diagonal line connecting the brushed aluminum box of multicolored paper clips and the stapler; the small photo, not much bigger than a baseball card, held in a solid block of Perspex, angled so that it was visible to him and anyone sitting across from him.

The photo was of a man with a red turban and a thick black beard and mustache. It was eroded on one side, the man's face disappearing under a mottled furry stain. Sunil still sometimes wondered if it really was his father or a generic photo of a guru that his mother had bought in the market. He'd been too scared to ask and he regretted that.

Against one wall, color photographs of zebu cattle were arranged like the speckled squares of a Rubik's Cube. The riotous color and patterns of the cattle hides contradicted all his control. Like a tarot deck, Asia had said the first and only time she'd come to his office. They'd had sex on the sofa and, walking around nude, she'd stopped by the wall, mentally shuffling the framed cows, trying to read the spread. He'd felt more naked than she was in that moment, more revealed than when they had sex, and though she came to his home often after that, he never asked her back to the office again.

He sighed now and crossed to the sideboard to pour himself some more coffee, wondering if he should call her and see if she was free tonight. It was Halloween, though, and she was no doubt busier tonight than on other nights. Everyone else was.

Five

Eskia was sitting in his car in the parking lot of the Desert Palms Institute, watching Sunil's sixth-floor office. He had followed Sunil from a distance for days, always staying just out of sight, always within touching distance. He couldn't believe how soft America had made Sunil. In the past he would never have been able to get this close to him. Those were the days—days that Eskia both loved and hated. Days that he could never forget, never quite muster the will to leave behind. He said the word, apartheid, under his breath. The way someone says the name of a lover they want to murder and fuck at the same time. His character had been forged in that crucible, in that dysfunctional relationship. Yep, Sunil had become as soft as the police. They were the easiest to follow, they never saw it coming, their sense of complete invincibility made them blind. Eskia laughed at the thought of Sunil being like the police.

There was a small bag of biltong on the seat beside him and he chewed thoughtfully on the cured meat, grateful that he'd been able to get it past customs. The last time he'd had to make do with American jerky. He took a swig from the Dr Pepper that was not as cold as he liked it, and a bite of biltong, and looked up at the window he had seen Sunil standing in. It didn't seem to bother Eskia that he was in plain sight in the parking lot and that the thick-rimmed plastic-framed glasses were the only disguise he wore. It was surprising how people never gave nerds a second glance, how this look always blurred into a generic account if witnesses were pressed to recall who they'd seen.

He'd learned from his years working undercover for the African National Congress, the political party Nelson Mandela led, that this disguise was most effective on white people. Something about a black man in thick Clark Kent glasses threw off their balance and they simply edited him out of their perceptual reality. He even checked into hotels under the name Clark Kent, and no one ever made a joke when he presented his papers, pushing his oversize glasses up his nose. Not at the hotels, not at the airport or in customs or immigration: nowhere. If it worked for Superman, he always said, it was good enough for him. Besides, the security guards at the institute were predictable and not paid well.

What he'd come for would be easier than he thought, but no less fun. He was here to kill Sunil.

He leaned back to wait. He was good at that.

Six

Sunil touched the soft leather of his desk chair. With his forefinger and thumb he rubbed at a line of dust that had become visible in a shaft of light, making a mental note to speak to the cleaner. It would be the third time this week. Really, he sighed, and reached for his phone.

Asia's number rang for a long time, then went to voice mail. As usual there was no outgoing message, just a beep. In her line of work it was pointless, she changed numbers every other week. Occupational hazard. If she wanted to get back to him she would just hit Redial. Still he wished he could say something to her. He hung up and turned on his computer, to return to studying the MRIs his team had taken the week before in the Arizona State Penitentiary.

An e-mail alert pinged up on his screen. He opened the message and scanned it quickly. He didn't know who'd sent it, but it was a photo of a ring; a big silver ring, with a turquoise butterfly wing under resin. His stomach fell away. It was Jan's ring. He had buried her with it, all those years ago in South Africa.

Sunil had been in college on a state scholarship when he met Jan Krige. The first thing he noticed about her was the Bible. She had it with her always, a red pocket-sized leather-bound book with a red five-pointed star and a gold-and-black kudu in the middle stamped on the front: a South African Army Bible. Sunil had loved that there was a meticulousness

to her. To the blond hair pulled back severely into a bun so
tight he could see the blue veins pulse just under her hairline.
To the green eyes carefully shaded by eye shadow and lined in
fine black liner. To the expensive cashmere sweaters buttoned
over newly starched white shirts, and then the white coats
with the pens lined up like little soldiers in the breast pocket:
red, blue, green, and black. Pens she never used, never even
took out of her pocket. She always wrote with a heavy foun-
tain pen—all black body with a gold cap—wielded like a
wand, like a sword. He sat next to her at every opportunity,
mostly because she was the only one who never moved away
from him when he sat. Never shrank or wrinkled her nose as
if he secreted an odor. It intrigued him that she treated him
no different from anyone else, and it wasn't like she couldn't
tell. He was the only black in the room.

He would sit next to her, watch her pull open an old leather
satchel, a man's satchel, worn and fading in brown. She would
select her notebook, a different one for each class, whatever
text they were studying, and her pen. She would line them up
on the desk and then, finally, she would pull out the Bible,
and lay it down. Then, turning to look at him, as though noticing him for the first time, she would smile, her red lips
parting to reveal small white teeth in pink gums. Hello, Sunil,
she said, every day. Hello, he said, and smiled back.

When he finally plucked up the courage to ask her about
the pen and the satchel, she explained that they had belonged
to her father. He died before she was born, on a peace mission
to Mozambique, she explained, to convince the ANC terrorists to give up their attacks on the government.

That was his, she said, pointing to the Bible. It had been a
gift from Mr. Botha to her father. It's signed by Mr. Botha,
she added.

Sunil couldn't tell which Mr. Botha she meant. May I see,
he asked, reaching for it.

She put her hand on his, white on black, small on large, and shook her head gently, sadly even. No, she said, it would be like looking into his soul. I've never even opened it.

Oh, he said, his hand burning under hers, wanting the pressure. My father died before I was born too, he said, lying.

I'm sorry, she said, moving her hand imperceptibly.

He felt it ignite a flame in him, feeling the delight of her, the warmth of her, and yet the conflict of his desire was strong. How could he feel this for a woman whose people were oppressing his? Desire is a fool, he thought then, wondering if it was his thought or something he had read somewhere.

He had never seen a Bible like hers before, so red, and that day it pulsed under his palm like a heart.

But that had all been so long ago. And yet here she was, at least the ghost of her. Material and present; a heavy silver ring with a wing. He touched the computer screen.

Seven

Fire watched keenly as Shiva's eight arms waved dangerously close to Chewbacca's face every time he moved. Chewy, tired of ducking, threatened to pull off Shiva's extra arms if His Royal Blueness didn't sit still.

Fire looked at Water, but Water had his eyes closed. Fire returned to watching, peering out from Water's shirt.

Across the aisle from the ER waiting area, a man, pants down around his ankles, shuffled up to the nurses' desk to find out how much longer he had to wait. The wool sheep attached to his waist kept him at arm's length from the desk and the nurse had to cup her ear to hear him over the noise of the ER.

It was six when I got here, he said, pointing at the clock. Now it's seven thirty. What the fuck is taking so long?

Please sit over there, sir, she said in a tired voice, pointing to the waiting area. The man sighed loudly and shuffled back to sit down next to a woman and her daughter. The woman pulled her child closer.

In the corner a very skinny Spider-Man was being harangued by a three-hundred-pound Wonder Woman wearing her hair in a three-foot updo: Don't rub up against me, pervert, she said, pushing against his chest. The skinny Spider-Man backed away and Fire realized that apart from a leather G-string he was naked, his costume painted on in colored vinyl.

Salazar stood a ways down the hall talking to the duty cop.

Vegas County saw a lot of law enforcement and correctional patients and there were always several cops milling around, in addition to the two officers permanently stationed there to make sure that nobody left unless they wore the appropriate wrist tag. Everyone was issued a tag at check-in: red for convict, blue for supervised (which included mental patients or people not yet processed, like Fire and Water), and green for everyone else. Simple but effective.

In the back row, a teenager wearing the costume from *Scream* bled from a knife embedded in his head. It was hard to tell if the knife was real or fake, and if it was blood or syrup dribbling down his face. A man in a Predator costume, sans face mask, screamed: Shit, I've been shot, shit; all the while holding a thick piece of gauze tight against his alien arm. It's not that bad, the woman next to him said, I only shot you with a BB rifle. It was clear that she was his girlfriend. She wasn't wearing a costume, and for that reason, she looked the weirdest in the room. The man next to the twins wore a gorilla costume with a cage attached to the front. In the cage was a man in jungle fatigues, hands wrapped around the cage's foam bars. The twins didn't immediately realize it was one costume, and that the wearer's head was poking out of the gorilla's chest, becoming the head of the caged man.

Fire undid Water's buttons and pushed out into the open. Staring around with open curiosity, he seemed completely at home in the melee.

Hey, you're not going to the Halloween pageant at the Fremont, are you, the gorilla asked the twins. 'Cause your costume looks even better than mine. The pot is five thousand dollars and frankly, I don't need the competition.

This isn't a costume, Fire said. We are twins.

Right, got you, the gorilla said. Bending down, he added in a conspiratorial whisper: I won't tell.

Before Fire could answer, Salazar came over and led them to an examination stall, screened off but otherwise open to the ward. Fire overheard him say to a nurse: I want a psych consult for the patient.

Why, the nurse asked.

Salazar looked at her name tag: Andrea Hassiba. Listen, Andrea, Salazar said. My assessment of the scene leads me to believe they are a risk to themselves.

Fine, Nurse Hassiba said, I'll call for one. In the meantime, it would help if you go to the admissions desk and fill out all the required paperwork. They will get the duty psychiatrist down here.

I would rather have my own psychiatrist come down, someone who has worked with me before on police business. A Dr. Singh.

Nurse Hassiba shrugged. Work that out with Admissions, she said.

Salazar headed off to take care of things.

Alone with the twins, Nurse Hassiba attempted to wrestle what she thought was a wet doll away from Water. Dressed as she was for Halloween, as a vampire, teeth and all, and having been an ER nurse for twenty years in Vegas, she had seen weirder costumes.

Please unhand me, Fire said, his grip unexpectedly firm, all but immobilizing the nurse.

When she realized that this was no costume, and just before she apologized and let go, a primordial look of disgust crossed her face.

Can you fetch the doctor now, Fire asked.

Yes, Nurse Hassiba said, glad for an excuse to leave the examination stall.

While Water stroked Fire's bald head, Fire rolled his eyes and muttered, Bigot, under his breath. Lost in meditation, the twins waited for the doctor.

Eight

Hello.

Sunil started, looking up. Sheila was standing at his door. Dr. Sheila Jackson was a colleague and one of the smartest and most beautiful women he knew. He liked her but there was something about the way she dressed, like a young Pat Benatar with spiky black hair, dark shaded eyes, boxy '80s tweed jackets with weird lapels, Palestinian neck scarves, and ripped jeans, that made him wary of her. It was Halloween and yet Sheila wasn't in costume. He'd always thought it was an odd way for a black woman to dress, although if pressed to explain what he meant, he wouldn't be able to.

Hello, Sheila, he said. You startled me.

She sat opposite him and put her legs up on his desk. Her shoes were shiny.

So, he said, what's up?

Not much. Just heading out for the day. Thought I'd stop by and warn you to stay out of Brewster's way.

Bruiser Brewster, as the interns called him. Bad mood, Sunil asked.

Worse than usual, Sheila said. How's it going, anyway, Sheila asked.

It's good, he said.

Really, she asked. I'm sorry, Sunil, but all those dead apes and no results can't be good. She paused at the look on his face. It wasn't you? I knew it. Is Brewster hijacking your work?

Why would you say that? Has he ever hijacked your work?

My work is not that interesting, I build robotic insects, she said, sitting up and craning her neck to see the images on his screen. How do you tell anything from these MRIs? I mean, how can you even be sure they are meaningful?

Sunil said nothing. He wouldn't admit it, but Sheila's question had touched a raw nerve. All this time and he still had nothing to show. Putting the thought out of his head, he turned his attention back to the screen and the MRI images.

There were two groups of MRIs, the test subjects and the controls. All the test subjects were inmates of the same prison and the controls were kids from the same university, a fact that seemed important at the time but in retrospect didn't matter at all, as it ended up not affecting the process at all. His prison subjects were all serial offenders. They were the perfect study group because while also having committed many small crimes, they usually had one major crime they returned to over and over. It was the pattern of these major crimes and their triggers that held the most promise for his work.

To generate the MRI images that were meaningful in any way, his test subjects were shown different sets of photographs, sometimes concurrently, sometimes consecutively. The sets included photos of flowers and sunsets and children laughing and also horrific and often bloody images: one moment flashing a flower, the next a mutilated human body. The MRI took scans of the brain, and the accompanying computer program tracked what parts of the brain lit up in response to the images. The variances were what Sunil studied.

Sheila finally broke the silence.

Are you happy with these new MRIs?

Yes, he said.

Compared to your test subjects, mine are harmless, Sheila said.

You're right, Sunil said. My subjects are unsavory and I

must admit many people would find this kind of research difficult.

But not you, she asked.

No, he said. That wasn't entirely true, but he shrugged off the small nag from his subconscious.

Sunil's research was part psychological, part chemical. He was studying the causes of psychopathic and other violent behavior with the aim of harnessing and controlling that behavior. To turn it off and on at will, as it were, with a serum or drug of some kind.

For Sunil, though, the work at its core was redemptive. He wanted to find cures, ways to help.

Brewster laughed at him when he expressed that sentiment. Redemption is easy, Sunil, he said. Restoration, now, there's the kicker.

Sunil hated that Brewster was right. Redemption was easy—that momentary flash of conversion, the road-to-Damascus moment. Turning it into a lived thing was what made it restorative and that was hard.

Don't kid yourself, Sunil, Brewster said. There's a reason only the U.S. Army will fund your research. This serum you're developing is to weaponize the condition.

Is that even a word, Sunil thought. He hated words that ended in "ize." They never led to anything good: weaponize, Africanize, terrorize. Weapons, all of them.

His research, in comparing notes from his control subjects and his prison group, seemed to indicate that at least 5 percent of the general male population of the United States was afflicted with the condition. These were successful psychopaths, successful in the sense that they had found ways to live with the condition, either by sublimating desires or by being smart enough not to get caught.

Like other researchers in the field, Sunil was sure that the condition had its cause in a defect in the paralimbic system, a network of the brain stretching from the orbital frontal cortex to the posterior cingulate cortex. These areas were involved in processing emotion, inhibition, and attention.

The brain scans on his computer were the last step in this new data-collection phase. Next he would have to conduct field studies, which meant triggering the condition in people whose brains showed latent possibilities for it and then waiting to see if the drug he had developed to control the condition was effective.

Two years earlier they had moved into human trials prematurely, with disastrous results. Sunil tried not to think about that time. But he was worried about this new phase of testing.

To be really sure the serum worked, the more advanced stage of testing would have to be conducted outside laboratory conditions—in the real world, so to speak. There was no exit strategy, and neither were there real controls in place to limit the damage. As Brewster said, To see if the product works, we have to see it work.

I'm going away in a few days, Sheila said, changing the subject. This will be my first holiday in five years.

Good for you, Sunil said.

You should get away too, she said.

I do need a break.

Come with me?

You're going to Cape Town, aren't you? I have no interest in going back there. There I'm just a black man.

I thought it was here that you were just a black man, Sheila said.

As black as I am, I am also Indian. Not half, not part, but in equal whole measures. In the new South Africa, there is no room for complications like me. I know there's no real room in the U.S. for the kind of complication I present either, but at least it's big enough to give the illusion that there is. And you, Sunil asked.

And me what?

How much of you has been tainted and fucked up by the racism here? Is that why you dress like a white soft-rock singer from the eighties, he asked.

I'm not sure. I think I'm just a nerd who thinks she looked her best back in the eighties. I think that it's more about being a woman that preoccupies me, she said. You know, the cost of the extensive education I've had, the demands of the work I do, the expectations I have for myself and also for a partner, all these concern me more than race.

You think these things isolate you, as a woman? Lead to a lonelier life?

Of course they do. There are just fewer men in the world who want or can deal with a black woman like me; even fewer that I want.

Funny, I didn't even think about that, Sunil said.

Never thought about me as a woman?

I mean, Sunil began, but stopped.

Yeah, well, it's different for women, Sheila said. Time and all that.

Yes, time and all that, Sunil echoed.

Trying to clear the air, she asked: So—seeing anyone?

It's complicated, Sunil said.

It always is, Sheila said.

Sunil smiled. He crossed the room and refilled his cup, pausing to inhale the fragrant, woody smell. He loved this blend—all wet forest leaves and warm hearth fires. Sheila watched him.

I'm sorry, he said, catching her look. Would you like some coffee?

She shook her head. No, I don't want to be up all night.

Right, he said, of course.

When you were a child, did you imagine your life would ever turn out the way it did? I didn't. I don't really know what

I expected, what I thought it would be like. It's elusive, like the fragment of a song, or a smell or even a taste, all of which come upon me in the least expected places at the least expected times, she said.

I know what you mean, he said. The smell of pipe tobacco and rain will always remind me of my father, of long drives in a car, none of which are mine or true. Yet sometimes the memory is so visceral it makes me want to cry. And it feels like I know what's missing but then it's gone.

In my case, I know exactly what's missing, she said.

You do?

And then he caught that look in her eye. The one he'd seen so many times. The one she had when she thought he wasn't looking. And he loved it, the look, the feeling it gave him, like he could fall into it and be in love. But he was already in love, with Asia. And though it made no sense since she was a prostitute and unable to love him back, he couldn't help it. And what if he gave up Asia and fell for Sheila? What then?

Whatever Sheila saw in his face made her sit up. Look at the time, she said.

Yes, he said.

I must go, she said. I have work.

Yes, me too.

See you tomorrow, then?

Yes, sure.

At the door she paused momentarily, then shut it resolutely behind her.

Nine

Sunil knocked on Brewster's door and entered without waiting. An older, often offensive, and unpleasant man, Brewster had founded the institute thirty years before. His early work had been in the area of group dynamics, a term that was a catchall for all kinds of work and that made Sunil in particular deeply worried. When it came to Brewster, everything sounded like a euphemism for something darker. There were five other projects housed there, all sponsored by the Department of Defense—Psychological Research; Weapons and Applied Tactics; Information Extraction and Analysis; Robotics and Organic Intelligence; and Planetary Resource Management.

Dr. Brewster, Sunil said, I need to talk to you.

As urgent as you might feel that need is, Sunil, you can't just barge in here. Brewster was wheezing a little from the oxygen pumping from the portable tank, not much bigger than a thermos, in his lab-coat pocket. A hose snaked up to his nose, held in each nostril by a discreet clip. Brewster used the oxygen to stay alert for the long hours he put into work, and at seventy-five he probably needed it.

I just got an order to sign for thirty dead apes, Sunil said.

Brewster looked at Sunil with a blank expression.

Bonobos, Sunil said, as though that would jog Brewster's memory.

So what? We run a lot of animal experiments here.

So I didn't authorize any tests on bonobos. I was wondering if you did.

Listen, Sunil, I made it clear when I hired you that you answer to me, did I not?

It's just that thirty bonobos are a lot, and I wasn't consulted on it. I would like to be consulted on experiments that are being signed through my lab.

How long have you been here now, Sunil?

Six, seven years, why?

Wrong answer, Brewster wheezed. You should have said, long enough to know that's just how things run here.

I don't like wading through shit like this. It's too much to ask.

Just hold your breath and swim upstream, Sunil. Don't take it all so personally.

Sunil smiled tightly. He wanted to say that in South Africa it was always personal. But he didn't.

Brewster was watching Sunil closely.

Fine, Sunil said. He was awkward and uncomfortable as any boy would be in the principal's office. Just then Sunil's phone rang.

Take it, Brewster said, waving his approval.

Sunil took out his cell and looked at the caller ID. It was Detective Salazar. He vaguely remembered the man, but he did remember the case from two years ago that had led Salazar to consult him. Dead homeless men dumped out by Lake Mead. Sunil had been brought in as a psychological consultant. But since, unbeknownst to Salazar, the institute had dumped the bodies in the first place, Sunil was really more of a spin doctor. Protecting the institute.

Salazar, he said.

Dr. Singh, so good to get hold of you. I have a problem I think you can help me with.

Listen, now is not a good time—

The bodies have started appearing again.

Sunil looked at Brewster and turned away, thinking, Shit, shit, shit.

I can't really help, Detective, he said.

Yes, you can. I think we've arrested the killer and I need you to come down to County and administer a psychological evaluation.

You caught the killer?

Yes.

So why do you need a psychological evaluation?

It's complicated.

It always is with you, Salazar.

They are Siamese twins.

Conjoined twins?

Yeah. I found them out by Lake Mead and there seems to be some uncertainty as to whether they were committing suicide or covering up a crime scene.

The duty psychiatrist could handle this, Sunil said.

No, Salazar said. I am convinced it's the same case we worked on.

Then surely it's a police matter.

No, I need your help on this.

Okay, look, I'll call you back in an hour.

Can you make it sooner?

I'll do my best, Sunil said, hanging up.

What was that about, Brewster asked.

It's a police matter.

All the more reason I need to know what it's about, Brewster said. Can't have any potential security breaches.

Remember the body dumps from two years ago?

Of course, he said.

The police think they've found the killer and want a psych eval from me, but I don't think I'm going to do it.

What's the matter with you, Sunil? This is perfect for us, and in particular for your project.

The killers are apparently conjoined twins.

Imagine the opportunities. We've never had the chance to study the brain chemistry of a monster before.

Sunil flinched at the medical term for genetic abnormalities. I study psychopaths, he said. Not monsters.

And conjoined twins can't be psychopaths?

They can be, yes. But we have to be careful about finding psychopaths everywhere. My research has to be very focused and free of anything that could devalue its science. Besides, we both know that there is no killer.

There's always a killer, Sunil, Brewster said with a smile.

Sunil hated Brewster. It was Brewster who said what everyone must have been thinking when they first met Sunil: You don't look Indian. You are very dark; you look black.

Which was true. Sunil was very dark, near black, with kinky hair, but still, he was pretty sure he looked Indian enough. After all, there were plenty of dark-skinned Indians.

But when Brewster first said it, Sunil had wondered if he was referring to the fact that he didn't look Native American, and felt his anger rise. But he realized years ago that it never helped to go down that path, so he explained that he didn't look Indian because he was half Zulu, and no, they didn't have Zulus in India, at least not that he knew of, but they did have them in South Africa. And yes, he added, there were a lot of South African Indians. Mostly in Durban, thank you very much, even though Sunil was from Johannesburg. Well, I've never met an Indian like you before, Brewster had insisted. What kind of Indian doesn't have a lilt in their voice or talk with their hands and head? In that moment Sunil had been glad the man was over seventy; otherwise he might have given in to his urge to hit him.

There was something else about Brewster that bothered

Sunil. He reminded him of the old guard of apartheid: privileged and smug in their power, but even worse, carrying a deep conviction in their own rightness. Sunil liked his job, though, so he tempered his response. But that's the thing with fights; if you fold too early, you keep folding.

I don't really know that much about conjoined twins, Sunil said. How their biology might affect their psychology.

That's okay, Brewster said. I will have the research department put a file together for you and have it delivered to your doorman tonight. It'll be there before you finish at the hospital.

Fine, Sunil said. He had to admit to himself that he was curious.

Just make sure to sign the papers so we can have them for at least seventy-two hours, Brewster said. Here, at the Desert Palms, not County.

This isn't the way I like to work.

Just go get me those monsters. With the weekend, we might get away with holding them for five days, Brewster said.

Sunil returned to his office to get his stuff. The elevator took only a moment to get to him.

As he stepped into the lobby and walked briskly to the front door he passed the usual Halloween decorations. There was one new addition this year: a hanging skeleton. He paused for a moment to regard the lynched figure and wondered if it was inappropriate before heading outside, where he heard the peacocks that roamed free through the grounds screeching. He paused by his car and inclined his head up at Brewster's window, throwing a malevolent look in the dark. He never noticed the car seven spaces down, from which Eskia watched his every move.

Ten

Eskia started up his engine and pulled out of the institute's parking lot, tailing Sunil. He had been waiting all day in his car, and he was hot and irritable. He pushed his glasses up on his nose and reached forward to turn up the air and the music. Hugh Masekela's "Grazing in the Grass" filled the car, and Eskia whistled along. Tailing Sunil right now was not really necessary; it was more for the fun of it. Having intercepted Sunil's phone call from Salazar on the cell-cloning software he was running on his laptop, he knew Sunil was heading to County to interview conjoined twins suspected of being serial killers. It would probably be quicker just to meet him there, but Eskia was a dedicated hunter, trained for years to follow his prey until he had secured the kill, and in this case he intended to do just that.

Eskia was an operative of South Africa's Security Services based in a clandestine unit that didn't officially exist. The clandestine units still operated the same as they had under apartheid—assassinations of enemies of the state, spying on politicians, stealing secrets from other countries, starting wars in other countries, carrying out renditions for other governments for a price, and more. But he wasn't here in Vegas in an official capacity. This was personal.

Eskia had joined the security arm of the African National Congress while still in college. You could say it was a family tradition. His father, Isaac, had been a weapons expert for the

ANC. He built bombs and trained others to build bombs. A chemist, and later a chemistry teacher, trained in Moscow, he returned in the '50s to an oppressive state. Six weeks after he came back, he was assigned a house in Soweto and an all-black school to teach in. It seemed he was content to do nothing more than teach young blacks chemistry and try to live a quiet life. That was until the Sharpeville incident when the police had fired on and killed young schoolkids peacefully protesting. As he watched the tear gas fly, the Casspirs tear through the crowds, and the children fall in bloody masses, he felt himself change. A couple of weeks later he joined the ANC and sought out the armed units. While he adored Mandela and believed in the need for a peaceful transition to self-rule, he couldn't stomach what he had seen. His soul ruptured that day, a rupture that would never fully heal. He turned to violence and, in turn, violence turned itself to him.

Eskia's mother was in labor with him the day Isaac decided to build his first bomb. It was an experiment he wasn't sure would work, and he hadn't told anyone about it.

It was 1965 and a mild day in Johannesburg when the gentle mannered Isaac stood on the edge of that downtown street and stared at the small rivulet of water running at the edge of the concrete. Across the street history awaited; taking a deep breath, he stepped off and crossed quickly to the small chemist shop. He emerged a few minutes later with a package wrapped in brown paper: ordinary household chemicals that were harmless on their own but volatile when mixed. They were forbidden in Soweto and it was illegal for a black person to be in possession of them. As he walked, he tried really hard to appear nonchalant. It was the days of the pass laws and he couldn't afford to be stopped by the police. Ahead, two policemen demanded passbooks from a black couple, and Isaac pressed into the shadows of an alley to wait.

Passbooks, known in those days as dompas, controlled everything. They laid out your race, where you lived, where you were allowed to travel. Passbooks, carried only by blacks, Indians, and coloreds (the light-skinned non-whites who were a mix of races, and the Indians), made them guest workers in their own country.

Isaac stepped back onto the pavement. The policemen moved on. Isaac trotted over to the taxi rank and got aboard a taxi bus headed back to Soweto. If he got caught now, he would go to prison for bomb-making, having never made his first bomb. But it was his lucky day.

It was also the last day he built bombs himself, from then on restricting himself to teaching others. But it wasn't enough for him. A veteran of the Second World War, he missed the rust of blood. So he began hunting for Boer, as he put it, laughing at the pun. His old Lee-Enfield rifle was his weapon of choice. And with time, Eskia became its constant companion.

Eskia pulled up to the hospital and studied the façade. Sunil would be in there for much of the night. Eskia hacked into the hospital records. His fingers moved fast over the keyboard of his laptop. Thank God for broadband Internet cards; it made spying such a breeze these days. He didn't know the names of the twins, but it would be easy searching under "conjoined." How many could there be? Sure enough, their record popped up—it was still pretty blank. It had their names and the date. Even their vitals hadn't been added. Eskia was bored.

There was nothing interesting happening here, so he decided he would break into Sunil's office tonight and steal his hard drives. All Sunil's research should be on them and he could sell that for a lot of money. Or at the very least the research could be used as a bargaining chip. What for was not clear yet, but then he'd only arrived a few days ago, plenty of time to get into trouble. He started his car. The only question was whether to stop by his hotel first, so he flipped a coin.

Eskia pulled out of the hospital parking lot, headed back to his hotel: New York, New York. Why was it that Vegas had to wring every last gag out of things? Everything here was a pun on a pun, so many times removed that it was not clear what the original joke had been, or if there had even been one in the first place. As he drove past the ziggurat of the MGM, black and polished, like an ancient Aztec temple cleaned up for a visitation by aliens, he thought of ways to hurt Sunil. He knew just the thing.

Smiling, he turned on his phone and used the voice-dialing function.

Call Asia, he said.

The phone rang.

Hello, Asia said on the second ring.

Eleven

Sunil's drive over to County was slow, and he played with the idea of taking the Strip. Natives always avoided that route, so taking it seemed like a good idea. Going up West Flamingo Drive, he made a right onto Las Vegas Boulevard. As he'd guessed, there was less traffic, although the sidewalks were packed with people.

The Halloween crowds poured up and down the Strip like a thick sludge. Fireworks, set off by the Bellagio, fired straight up and out of its fountains, filling the sky with mushrooms of dazzle. Sunil was reminded of the old bomb parties the casinos used to host back in the '50s, when the U.S. government set off nukes in the nearby desert, sometimes as close as six miles from the city. The casinos sold package tours to see U.S. history in the making: the end of the Commies and the death of the Red Threat. People flocked by the thousands to the dawn parties to watch the mushroom clouds. Minutes after the display, they would return to gambling or turn in to catch some much-needed sleep. Seats on the terrace, where one could watch the explosions while sipping on a cocktail, were fought over. Those unable to afford the parties or terraces drove out to ground zero and hiked as close as possible. The Atomic Energy Commission never turned them away, even when there were families with children.

Sunil watched the light show across his windshield, fireworks ceding to electricity. The radiance gave the impression that the city was a mirage. At a stoplight, where the traffic was held up not so much by the red but by the endless stream of pedestrians in costume, Sunil saw a young woman, a girl really, eating fire. Slowly, with what seemed like reasonable trepidation, she dipped the long-stemmed tapers into a clear fluid and lit each one. Holding the flaming stem delicately, she tilted her head back and pushed the fiery tip into her mouth, where it died with an audible sigh. Something about that girl took Sunil back to a memory of Dorothy, lighting and blowing out votives set at the foot of a statue of Jesus in the corner of her hospital room. Flame. No flame. Flame. No flame.

The duty psychiatrist, a small mousy man, was waiting outside the ER. Sunil recognized him as he approached from the parking lot but couldn't remember the man's name. They'd probably met at a conference; Vegas was the city for that. The doctor snuffed out the cigarette he was smoking in the sand-filled ashtray by the automatic doors.

Dr. Singh, he said.

Hello, good to see you again, Sunil said, holding out his hand.

Dr. Alan, the duty psychiatrist said, taking Sunil's hand limply. Sunil had never gotten used to the fact that American men didn't shake hands as a matter of course.

Of course, Dr. Alan, Sunil said.

Look, I'm not happy with you doing this; I just wanted to express my position.

Noted, Dr. Alan, Sunil said, but you should tell that to the police.

I already did.

Good. Have you seen the twins?

Yes.

Can you tell me anything about them?

Their twinning is rare.

How so?

One twin has only a small torso and head growing out of the side of the other one. Quite disturbing, even from a medical point of view.

That is odd, I've never even heard of a modern case of undifferentiated twins. How old are they?

In their late thirties, I think, much older than you would think. They are also pretty unresponsive.

Well, thank you for letting me interview them. Is the policeman who brought them in still here?

Yes. Just over there, Dr. Alan said, pointing into the ER. I think his name is Salazar.

Thanks again, Sunil said, heading inside toward Salazar.

I'll meet you in Exam Room 3. The twins are there, Dr. Alan said.

Sunil paused: That's okay. I'd rather see them alone. You understand?

Fuck you, Dr. Alan said, turning away.

Sunil ignored him and walked down the hall, tracking Salazar to the snack shop around the corner. Pausing by the door, he took it all in—shelves of chocolate and candy, sugary treats and drinks, and nary a piece of fruit in sight. It was as if the hospital were trying to drum up repeat business. He recognized Salazar straightaway. He looked like every cop Sunil had ever seen, and he'd seen plenty.

Officer Salazar, Sunil said, offering his hand.

Dr. Singh. Thank you for coming. I wasn't sure you would remember me.

Of course I remember you, Sunil said. So tell me what happened exactly.

Well, earlier this evening I received a call to assist a park ranger out by Lake Mead. When I got there, it appeared as though two suspects were trying to commit suicide or murder.

Which is it, Sunil asked, thinking Salazar seemed more

polite than he remembered. He must want something pretty bad, he thought.

I don't know, Salazar said. The suspects were in the water. The tall one, whose name is also Water, was bent over. The smaller one, named Fire, on Water's side, was submerged. The ranger says he had to ask Water to come out of the water—oh, fuck it; he had to ask the suspect to come out of the water several times.

Sounds like the park ranger could have handled it by himself.

Well, he called it in, so I came to his assistance.

All right, Sunil said. But why a psych evaluation, why not just arrest them?

There are no bodies, just drums of blood.

But you said the body dumps had started again, Sunil said.

I had to say something to get you here, Salazar said.

Sunil sighed with relief. So this is not really a straight-ahead psych eval, he said. You want me to help you hold them for seventy-two hours while you search for the body or bodies?

Yes. I'm also hoping you might find out for me where they might have dumped the bodies.

If there still are any, Sunil said.

How do you mean?

A quick memory flashed through Sunil's mind. A hillside with stubby grass, a quickly dug shallow grave. A body. Male. Teeth extracted, ground to powder earlier. Overhead a hawk circling. Heat shimmering. Then powdered lime poured over the body. Then that horrible sizzling, soft almost, like effervescence.

Anyway, he said, to Salazar. If I recall from two years ago, the killer dumped the bodies out in the open. If the twins are the killers, shouldn't there be bodies in plain sight?

Salazar shrugged. Fuck, nothing's ever that easy, he said.

Is there anything else I should know, Sunil asked. Anything you tell me is bound to help, even the slightest thing.

Well, the small one is kind of feisty, but sounds college-educated, and the tall one looks normal but is kind of like Rain Man.

Rain Man?

You know, like the movie. He never says anything directly, only mumbles weird facts, like someone on *Jeopardy!*

Interesting, Sunil said. Anything else?

Just a feeling.

What kind of feeling?

I don't know. They're pretty odd-looking, but there's something else off about them. Look in their eyes.

Sunil nodded as Salazar walked away, down the hallway.

Twelve

Alone with the twins, Sunil drew the green cubicle curtain closed behind him. There was a dark stain on the fabric just below his left elbow that Fire seemed to be staring at.

My name is Dr. Sunil Singh, he said. You must be Fire, he said to Fire, and you must be Water.

Dr. SS, Fire said, and laughed.

Sunil smiled wanly. Please don't call me that, he said. You may call me either Sunil or Dr. Singh. Sitting down, he pinched the crease of his pants between two fingers and smoothed it out.

I'll just call you Doc, Fire said.

I wish you wouldn't, Sunil said, but Fire showed no sign he had heard him. Sunil studied the twins. Water was sitting on the examination table, feet nearly touching the floor. He was wearing pants and a shirt that was unbuttoned but no shoes, and Sunil wondered whether his shoes had been left at the scene. Fire had pushed the left panel of the unbuttoned shirt behind his head and Sunil could make out his caul draped like a thick fleshy scarf. Why hadn't they had it removed, he wondered.

Have you been treated well, he asked.

No worse than usual, Fire said.

Are you used to being treated badly?

Look at us, Doc, Fire said. Of course we are.

And when you say "we," are you speaking for your brother, too?

Yes, Doc.

Is that true, Water, Sunil asked.

Twins have an unusually high incidence of left-handedness, Water said.

Sunil smiled. This must be what Salazar meant; Water avoided direct questions. Sunil tried a different approach. I didn't know that, he said. But did you know that polar bears are left-handed?

Bats always turn left when they exit a cave, Water said.

Don't get him started, Doc, or we'll be here all night, Fire said.

Does Water talk like that often, Sunil asked him, glad to have drawn a response.

Yes, Fire said.

The voices of people settling into the next cubicle came over the curtain. Across the room a baby was crying. Medical personnel walked back and forth; their shadows against the curtain looked like a puppet show. Fire looked Sunil over, taking in his three-hundred-dollar shoes, his gold pen, the Rolex, and the tailored suit pants.

You don't look like a county employee, he said.

I'm not, Sunil said.

Who do you work for?

I'm here to conduct a psychiatric exam, he said. Do you know what that is?

Conjoined twin, Fire said sarcastically, not retarded.

Good, Sunil said, unfazed. Do you mind if I conduct a basic physical? Check your vitals?

"Vital" is from the Latin for "life," Water said.

Yes, Sunil said, careful not to indulge Water. May I examine you?

Fire nodded.

Water?

Water nodded.

Sunil conducted a brief but thorough exam and with the exception of telling them what he was going to do from time to time, and asking them to clamp down on thermometers or open their mouths, the process was conducted in silence and the twins surrendered with ease to Sunil's quiet authority.

I need to take some pictures, he said. Is that okay?

Whatever, Doc, Fire said.

Good, Sunil said, reaching for the Polaroid camera in his coat pocket. Please stand against the wall.

Water shrugged off his shirt and did as he was told. Sunil lifted the camera to his face and took a picture.

Turn to your left, Sunil said to Water, who turned, bringing Fire straight into focus.

Please put your shirt back on and sit, he said to Water.

Water sat and arranged the shirt so Fire was visible, hanging off his side; clearly they had done this before. Sunil waved the Polaroid around to dry, and something in the movement looked like he was fanning away a bad smell.

You don't have to do that anymore, Fire said. They dry by themselves.

Sunil ignored him and took a manila file from his briefcase and flipped it open. With extra care he stapled the photos to a blank sheet of paper.

How odd, Sunil said, rubbing the photo where Water's mouth was. He looked up at Water. Is your mouth always slightly open?

I call him Lizard Mouth sometimes, Fire said. His tongue flicks.

Why is that?

Probably some birth defect, Doc, I mean, look at us.

And what is this tattoo, he asked, pointing in the photo to

Water's chest, over his heart. These lines—looks like a Chinese character.

It's a hexagram, Fire said, from the I-Ching. It means Fire and Water.

A hexagram is a combination of characters for the elements, Sunil said. It can mean many things. Isn't that the point of the I-Ching? Precision is important.

Even at the risk of sounding like an asshole, Fire said.

Even then, Sunil replied, reaching for the hole-punch on a medicine cart. He lined the paper up exactly and punched two clean holes and then threaded the paper onto the metal clasps. When he looked up Fire was studying him intently. Their eyes met; Fire smiled, Sunil flinched. Fire's teeth were rather canine looking.

You should get a tattoo, Fire said.

No, I don't want a chup, Sunil thought, returning in his mind to the slang of his youth.

In Vegas you can get a tattoo on your eyeball, Water volunteered.

Sunil thought about Asia and the tattoo on her shoulder. No, he wouldn't be getting one anytime soon.

I'm just going to ask some questions. May I record the session?

The twins nodded.

Good, Sunil said, setting a digital recorder between them. Full names, please.

Water Esau Grimes and Fire Jacob Grimes.

Date of birth?

December twenty-first, 1969.

Address?

No fixed abode, Fire said.

Where do you live, then, Sunil asked. Did the police not ask for ID?

We live off the grid. Don't believe in IDs, Fire said.

So what did you tell the officer?

He didn't press it. He was too busy trying to get us here.

I see, Sunil said, not seeing at all. You must be staying somewhere.

Motel over by Fourteenth, Fire said.

Sunil asked for and wrote down the address. Maybe he could get Salazar to search it.

Occupation, he asked.

King Kongo the African Witchdoctor, Fire said.

Circus act?

No, Fire said. Sideshow.

Marital status?

Single, Fire said.

Fred loves me, Water said.

What is your sexual orientation, Sunil asked.

Fred is a girl, Fire said.

Are you married to her, Water?

Water shook his head.

I would still like you both to answer the question regarding your sexual orientation.

Water here is straight, Fire said. And I have no penis.

Iguanas have two penises, Water said.

Thank you, Sunil said. Have either of you had any trouble with your mental health before?

No, Fire said.

Water shook his head.

Have either of you seen a psychiatrist or been admitted to a psychiatric facility before?

No, Doc.

Sunil nodded at Fire, then looked pointedly at Water.

Charlie Chaplin once won third place in a Charlie Chaplin look-alike contest, Water said.

Sunil shook his head, irritated. Do you have any problems with your physical health, he asked.

No, Fire said.

Water shook his head.

In the past?

Yes, Fire said. I get burned regularly in my work. I'm a fire wizard.

A fire wizard?

A very good fire wizard, Water said.

Just to clarify, Sunil asked, is this part of your act?

Yes.

So outside of your act you don't think you are an actual wizard?

Like in *Lord of the Rings*?

Yes.

No, no, I don't, Doc, 'cause I'm not suffering from dementia.

That's the wrong term for what you would be suffering from if you thought you were a wizard, Sunil said. And you, Water, are you a fire wizard too?

Wrong element, Fire said.

Sunil ignored him. Water, he pressed.

A cockroach can live for nine days with its head cut off, Water said.

Good to know, Sunil said to him. Is either of you currently on any medication?

No, Fire said.

Water shook his head.

Have you taken medication regularly in the past for any condition?

No, Fire said.

Water shook his head.

As far as you know, has anyone in your family ever had any problems with mental health?

The twins shook their heads. One head was where it should be, at eye level; the other, hanging halfway off Water's side, made the otherwise banal action disconcerting.

Do either of you suffer from any hallucinations—visual or otherwise?

No, Fire said.

Water shook his head.

Would you tell me if you did?

Neither brother spoke.

Were you trying to commit suicide at the lake and, if so, have there been any previous attempts at suicide, Sunil asked.

No, Fire said. No, he repeated emphatically.

If you weren't trying to commit suicide, what were you doing in the lake?

Swimming, Fire said.

Did you tell the police that you were swimming?

No.

Why?

Neither twin spoke.

Would you say either of you is impulsive, Sunil asked.

Hard to be impulsive when you are chained to someone's side, Fire said.

Right, Sunil said. What about you, Water?

Water shook his head.

Can you explain the blood the police found?

No, Fire said.

You're being completely honest?

Fire shrugged. He looked like a shuddering rat.

You know, Sunil said, in my experience it never pays to play with the police.

I thought you were evaluating our minds, Fire said. Now you just sound like you're trying to solve the case for the police. We plead the fifth, Fire said.

In a medical exam, Sunil asked.

Fire drew his fingers across his lips, mimicking a zipping motion. Water copied him.

Sunil changed tack.

If I let you go now, would you try to harm yourself or anyone else?

Who can say, Fire said.

You can, Sunil said.

Fire looked away. Water was examining his nails.

Even if you didn't kill anyone, attempted suicide is an extreme measure, Sunil said, voice softening. I am not convinced that it is in your best interest to release you. I think that a combination of medication and counseling could really help you. It is important that you are well enough to help the police resolve this matter.

So you think we are crazy, Fire asked.

Crazy is not a useful term. Now, at least for tonight, I'm going to recommend that you be put on a forty-minute-interval suicide watch. This is a county hospital; I am afraid that their facilities are limited, so I am having you transferred tonight to the institution where I work. The police, I am sure, will find that acceptable.

Anything has to be better than county jail, Fire said. I knew you weren't a state employee, he added.

I work for the Desert Palms Institute. It's a very nice facility with the best doctors. We'll take care of you. Sunil hesitated for a moment. I can't imagine how hard your life has been, but I do think that we can help you.

Neither twin spoke.

I am going to set up your transfer. The next time I see you will be at the institute, he said.

Tonight, Fire asked.

No, tomorrow morning, Sunil said. I'll check you in tonight, but I won't be there until tomorrow.

He stepped out of the cubicle, then went looking for Salazar to make transfer arrangements and to tell him to check out the motel. The curtain fell behind Sunil and the irregularly shaped stain that Fire had noticed before seemed to suddenly fill the green field of it.

I wonder if it is dried blood, Fire said, pointing at it. County, he scoffed.

A dark tree, Water said.

It was well after ten that night before Sunil finally left County Hospital.

Thirteen

Birds on a wire, a drunk leaning up against a Dumpster, a homeless man sprawled on a stained mattress in the corner between the drunk, the Dumpster, and the wall. Salazar slammed the car door and the birds took off. The wire dropped water in benediction. Fucked neighborhood, Salazar said under his breath, crossing the street to the run-down motel. THE PINK FLAMINGO, the sign said. A lone flamingo grew out of the roof of the office building. These kinds of motels had once been so important to the city. Now they were reduced to being long-term residences for those on welfare or otherwise down on their luck. A sign outside the office window offered free lunch with a room. He shuddered to think what the lunch was made of. It was already past ten at night and he hadn't had anything to eat, but he wouldn't touch it.

The clerk behind the desk didn't look so much old as resigned, his expression giving him the appearance of the archaic.

Hey, Salazar said, and put his shield down in front of the clerk's face.

Hey, the clerk said, taking in the shield, expression unchanging.

Are there Siamese twins staying here?

The freaks? Yeah. Room 12, the clerk said. He took a key down from behind him and handed it to Salazar, in anticipation. That way, he pointed, losing interest. As Salazar turned to leave, the clerk looked up with what seemed like extreme effort. They checked out two weeks ago, though, he added.

Salazar stopped. Then why did you give me the key?

The clerk shrugged. Nobody's been in there since, except the maid. I thought you police types like to do your forensics shit.

Salazar shook his head and handed the key back. The room would yield nothing and the CSI team would not come out for this. If there had been anything unusual, like a decomposing body or stuff like that, the clerk would already know. He walked back to his car. An old black man leaned against it, smoking. Salazar ignored him, got in and gunned the engine, and the old man moved off reluctantly. As Salazar drove away he reached for his cell and called Dr. Singh.

Have the twins talked yet, he asked.

Sunil struggled to keep the irritation out of his voice: Nothing you will find useful. How are your investigations going?

We haven't turned up a body yet. But I am at the address you gave me.

Did you find anything interesting?

No, it's just an old motel.

Did you find anything in the old motel?

No, they checked out of here two weeks ago. Fuck, Salazar said. Do me a favor, Doctor. Get them to explain what the fuck is going on.

All in good time. Good night, Detective.

Good night, Salazar said. Then under his breath, Fuck you very much.

He decided to head back to the station. Maybe he had overlooked something. He just needed to go over everything repeatedly until he found it.

Fourteen

It was cold when Sunil got home. Desert cold was the worst. Hot all day, with the temperature dropping by so many degrees at night that he went from sweat to shivers. The fact that the central air was on all the time probably didn't help. He crossed the room and flicked a switch to turn on the fire.

This was his routine: set keys into the valet on the sideboard in the hall, briefcase down next to it, sift mail collected from doorman before putting it down next to the briefcase. The only variations today: a piece of candy from the bowl laid out for trick-or-treat, popped into his mouth; and tucked under his arm, the envelope containing a research file on twins from the institute, also handed over by the doorman. He meant to read it that night. Tomorrow was Saturday but he intended on interviewing the twins in the morning. No one worked a five-day week at the institute.

Sunil lived in a soft loft in one of Vegas's modern, hip buildings. He argued to others that the incredible architecture of the place was the draw, but its location just five minutes off the Strip probably had more to do with its appeal for him. He could be near all that noise and energy, and just distant enough to remain a voyeur—all of the excitement, yet no risk.

The soft loft was one of those real estate terms for condominiums with high ceilings and an elevated but open sleeping area. Since the '80s nobody had bought or wanted to buy a condo, so real estate brokers got creative. It was nice on the inside, noise- and weather-insulated blue glass walls on the far side. Cut stone floors, an immaculate kitchen, a den hidden behind sliding wood doors, and a second bedroom just off the front hall.

He put the file down on the marble-topped island in the middle of the kitchen and opened the Sub-Zero refrigerator, careful to leave no fingerprint smudges on the polished silver door. He took out a beer, a piece of tuna, and a cantaloupe.

On a plastic cutting board, he cut the cantaloupe neatly in half with one smooth movement. He placed one half face-down on a plate and returned it to a shelf in the fridge, then cleaned and cubed the other, enjoying the sound of the cutting.

Next he set the tuna on a wooden cutting board, noting the time on the microwave clock—11:00. He hesitated for a moment, then picked up a balanced ceramic knife that had cost too much and sliced perfect slivers of fish. The shape of the pieces, and the sound of the knife scraping the wood, reminded him of slicing plantains in Johannesburg for Dorothy to fry. Pausing in his slicing, he inspected his work, mentally checking for precision. He couldn't remember the last time he had been this concerned about order. Perhaps it was a reaction to the memory of Jan. He put a piece of cantaloupe into his mouth and thought about her.

Their first date, Sunil came to realize later, hadn't been a date at all, just coffee that Sunil brought with him from home and his lunch of fried fish and hard-dough bread. Even with this new experiment in integration, the black students weren't allowed to eat in the cafeteria, so they all brought lunch from home. Once, early on, Sunil had tried to eat in the cafeteria, but one of the blacks cleaning the floors had come over to him, and barely able to make eye contact for shame, pointed to the sign on the wall above Sunil: VIR GEBRUIK DEUR BLANKES—FOR USE BY WHITE PERSONS.

He left and never returned, opting to eat under the umbrella tree outside the science building, on the only stretch of lawn where the black students were allowed to be. Every day, they spread out like a flock of blackbirds at lunch, pretending not to see one another.

That day, on a whim, Sunil asked Jan if she would like to have lunch with him.

Yes, she said, her easy assent taking him by surprise.

She followed him to the patch of grass under the tree as though it were the most natural thing in the world. He turned his jacket inside out and spread it for her to sit on. He remembered every detail fondly for days afterward: that they shared coffee out of the cap of his thermos because he hadn't brought any cups; that she ate the hard bread and oily fish with a relish that he could still summon like a taste to his mouth; that he had no napkins so she sucked on her fingers and he felt himself swell with desire. Finally he remembered his handkerchief and handed it to her. It was pretty threadbare, but clean, and if she noticed its condition, she said nothing. She dabbed delicately around her lips with it and handed it back.

Later, he walked her back to class, and then after, naturally, easily, to her car. They stood in the gloom of the car-park lights, lingering, neither wanting to go home, it seemed.

Yet the next day, in class, it was as if none of it had happened. She was still very polite to him, but nothing more, until a week later, when they happened upon each other in Gogo's, which was the only neutral space in the city, where all races could interact without fear or concern.

Returning to the present moment, he placed the fruit and raw fish on a stoneware plate garnished with ginger and then cleaned up.

He took the food to the living room, crossed to the sectional, and flopped in front of the fire, over which hung a large print of a William Kentridge painting, *Felix in Exile*.

Reaching for the remote control on the coffee table, he turned down the fire and turned on some music—Chopin's Nocturnes in E Minor. He ate quickly, barely taking in the view that spread fourteen floors below. When he was finished, he fetched the rather thick file from the sideboard, adjusted his glasses, and began to read.

There were two theories about how conjoined twins are formed—fission and fusion. Fission theory postulated that conjoined twins occur when a fertilized egg begins to split into identical twins, but is somehow interrupted during the process and develops into two partially formed individuals who are stuck together. Fusion theory argued that conjoining happens after an egg has split into two distinct but identical embryos and that the joining is a result of early cellular development in embryos in close proximity.

A human embryo in its early stages consists of three layers of cells that seek out cells of the same type and use these stem cells to build organs and the rest of the body. When identical embryos lie in close proximity, such as in the case of identical twins, these cells can have mixed signals, which cause them to attach to the cells of the same type but that are already part of the twin embryo.

Sunil rubbed his eyes and skimmed the rest, letting only the major classifications jump out at him. Craniopagus twins are joined at the head. Thoracopagus twins are joined at the upper chest, usually from clavicle to sternum. Omphalopagus twins are joined at the abdomen from their groin to their sternum, resulting in a shared liver and even parts of the digestive tract. Xiphopagus twins are joined at the sternum but only by cartilage, like the famous Chang and Eng, and only rarely share organs. Ischiopagus twins are joined at the front of the pelvis and at the lower spine, with their spines twisted at a 180-degree angle from each other. These twins can have three or four legs between them; the third leg in these tripus cases is a fusion of two legs that didn't separate. Ischio-omphalopagus twins have spines joined in a *Y* shape, three legs, and a single set of genitalia; and on and on, in a seemingly unending list.

Sunil thought that it all read like a bizarre biblical genealogy, or the taxonomy of dinosaurs. He understood only too well this need to classify; that had been the backbone of apartheid.

At the back of the file he found a reference to Edward Mordake, a nineteenth-century Englishman with no recorded birth or death dates. He was unusually handsome and gifted as a scholar and musician. He had a second face growing out of the back of his head. This other face, rumored to have been female, wasn't fully functional and couldn't speak or eat. But it could laugh and cry and its eyes would follow people around a room. Edward claimed that this devil twin, as he called it, whispered awful things to him at night while he tried to sleep. He begged to have it removed, but no doctor would agree to the risky operation. Finally he secluded himself until he succumbed to suicide at twenty-three. This was clearly a case of parasitic twinning and Sunil wondered if Fire and Water were parasitic twins. But which was the parasite?

In spite of himself, Sunil yawned. It was late, or early, and he nodded off, sprawled on the sectional with papers and photos strewn around him.

Fifteen

The moon was high and fat. Pregnant moon, Water said under his breath, the way Selah used to, the boys in her lap, rocking in the porch swing on those late nights when they couldn't sleep. A full moon always rises at sunset, he said to himself. Selah used to say that. Water was fifteen when he realized her death would always be inside him. Selah is tree, he whispered.

The swath of light falling through the window, however, was not from the moon but from the violet streetlamp on the hospital grounds. He swung his legs to the floor and got up slowly. Fire was snoring slightly, the sound muffled by the caul. Drawn tight, it would grow warm and then hot against Water's side, as though he were carrying a hot water bottle.

It was light enough to make it across the room and as Water crossed to the window, Fire stirred, yawned, and then went back to sleep. Water searched the sky as if for some truth. Auguring; that had been Selah's skill. Reading the future from the sky, by watching birds or clouds. Tracking to see if they were flying together or alone, the truth revealed in their formations. Water couldn't sleep and lay awake for a long time gazing up at the moon, humming a lullaby, one that Selah had sung to them.

Sixteen

Sunil woke with a start. He peeled a sheet of paper from his cheek and crossed to the window. Below, the Strip was awake, like a sentient being made of neon, all pulse and wink, but it wasn't dawn yet, probably nearer five in the morning. Sunil closed his eyes, shook his head rapidly, and opened them again. Dizzy, he watched the lights make a new pattern, like a kaleidoscope. He closed his eyes again. This time when he opened them and looked, he was so dizzy he had to put his hand on the cold metal of the window frame to keep from falling over. This was a game he'd played as a child, only the lights had been the stars, and back then he could get dizzy without feeling nauseated.

Dorothy taught him that game, said it was how the old soothsayers read the future. Izikhombi, she'd called it, bones used to divine the way, except she said they used the bones of the stars.

She was a good storyteller. Some people call that being a good liar. But that was just frivolous gossip, as Reverend Bhekithemba would say. Remove the log from your own eye first, he would add. The reverend had a soft spot for Sunil and Dorothy, which of course only made people gossip about the reverend and Dorothy. There has always been in African communities a deep suspicion of the Catholic priest's professed celibacy. Father Bhekithemba was the priest of St. Francis, the Catholic church on the corner of Sunil's street. But none of this, of course, changed the fact that Dorothy was a good storyteller.

She came to Soweto in 1960 to study nursing. She meant to return to her small town in the KwaZulu homeland, but no one ever leaves Soweto alive, as the saying goes.

She worked at Chris Hani Baragwanath Hospital on Old Potchefstroom Road. Baragwanath was more of a city than a hospital, serving about a million people every day. Much of what she saw there—the misery, the pain, the loss, the despair, but also the incredible strength of the people of Soweto—shaped her. She was a good woman who did what she could. Brought home medicines for the local mothers to give to their children. Nothing serious, just the basics—vitamins, cough medicine, painkillers, fever reducers, disinfectants, and iodine for scrapes and cuts. She cut quite the figure striding through the neighborhood at dusk, dressed in her nurse's uniform—crisp, starched white dress and bonnet, palm flat on her belly, resting on the big buckle of the purple belt that marked her rank, a black handbag draped from the crook. Sunil followed her discreetly, pretending in his mind to be her bodyguard, and if Dorothy was aware she didn't show it. Meanwhile, Johnny Ten-Ten, sitting on the low wall of the church smoking with other teenagers in the shadow of the statue of Saint Francis, called him Mommy's Shadow.

Between St. Francis and Sunil's house was an open lot of land that ran down to a ditch at the back of the township. Over the years, Dorothy put the local children to work turning it into a communal garden. They grew everything there—potatoes, tomatoes, spinach, carrots, peas, and even some onions—and gave it all away to those needier than them.

It seemed like the only things Dorothy kept for herself were the truth of Sunil's father and the three tangerine trees she planted and replanted by the side fence of their house, a fence made of rippling and rusting corrugated iron sheets.

The trees never really grew much larger than shrubs, but they wore their size well, with all the gravitas of trees. Three trees Dorothy planted and replanted every year. Three trees were all they had room for, crowded as they were by the tomatoes and curry and potatoes and onions overflowing from the communal garden just over the fence. Three trees that seemed so superfluous they could as well have been chocolate trees instead of tangerines.

They always grew to about three feet high, branches thick and low like a shrub, and heavy with the small citrus. As soon as they bore their yellow fruit, and Sunil and his mother harvested buckets of them for themselves and their neighbors, they would begin to die and Dorothy would gather seeds and cuttings that still had green signs of life in them, and replant the tangerines in the cluster of three by the fence, where the off-flow from the kitchen sink kept the dusty Soweto soil moist and fragrant with decay and rebirth.

Always three, a mystical number not intended. Planting and replanting every year until it seemed she, like the tangerines, would die of happiness. Sunil love to peel the zesty fruit and bite into the soft sweet flesh. What a freedom.

But these were still the days of terror, of tear gas in the streets. Of armored Casspirs rolling through Soweto like hyenas on the prowl. These were still the days of beatings, and of the lynching of suspected informers by locals. When police enforced pass law. When they drank from illegal shebeens and then burned them down. When they kicked in the doors of frightened Soweto families and dragged the men out to be shot in the street in the middle of the night. When the police drove by emptying rounds of ammo into the houses of the ANC leadership who crouched behind the cast-iron stoves with their children in the kitchen, the safest place in the house. When rape was a state-sanctioned form of policing. When children playing in empty lots came upon dead bodies decomposing in the heat, or half-dissolved from chemicals. When the ANC and Inkatha Freedom Party recruited young men and women and trained them to be warriors.

If Dorothy had any misgivings about any of it, about Sunil training to be a freedom fighter, she didn't show it. Maybe she suspected his heart wasn't really in the fighting but more in becoming an impi, like the one in the story she told of his mythical father, as though he were trying somehow to make a connection with the absence that his father had become.

Maybe that was why she told stories, stories to counter, or perhaps balance, the ones the political movements were telling the children—stories of a different path, and maybe a different future. It was hard to tell, because she kept so much to herself.

She was a good storyteller and Sunil and the others gathered by the communal garden to hear her.

Have you heard about the Sorrow Tree, she asked them.

No, Nurse Dorothy, they chorused.

Deep in a mythical forest lost to time is the Sorrow Tree. Its existence was known only to the wisest of the sangomas, who kept it a close secret. Once, a very long time ago, the people who would become our ancestors went to the chief sangoma, a man so old no one could remember a time when he hadn't been there, and asked him to remove the suffering and misery from the world. He told them that he couldn't do it but that there was a tree called the Sorrow Tree that could bear everyone's pain for a short while. He took them on a pilgrimage deep into the forest until finally, after nearly a moon of traveling, they came upon a clearing. There stood the most beautiful tree anyone had seen. It was as wide as many townships and as tall as Mount Kilimanjaro, and yet its limbs were thin and wispy as though made of smoke. And though the tree was so big and tall, it took only a few minutes to walk around it and even the shortest person could reach the tallest limbs.

The sangoma told the people to make a bundle of their suffering and sorrow and hang it from a limb of the tree. And although many thousands of people hung their sorrows from those delicate limbs, they barely swayed from the weight of it. At once the people felt a deep happiness come over them and they danced and sang for days. As they prepared to leave, the sangoma told them that there was a condition that he hadn't mentioned before. They could leave none of the bundles of sorrow on the tree; otherwise the others to come would have nowhere to hang theirs. They must leave with a bundle, but not necessarily the bundle they came with. Everyone walked around the tree examining the bundles, but in the end they each settled for the bundles they had come with. It seemed that no matter how bad their lot was, they did not prefer anyone else's to theirs. As the people left with their sorrows on their heads, their happiness faded, but they found instead a deep joy.

FAIRY
TALE

What possible harm can a story do, you ask yourself as you fetch the small photo of your father from the mantelpiece. You don't have a fireplace, so it really isn't a mantelpiece, just a rickety shelf on a wall. There in the small cramped living room with the bare cement floor painted red by your mother because, as she says, poverty is no excuse for uncleanliness. No harm at all, you tell yourself as you nearly knock over the small plastic vase that holds the plastic flowers your father gave your mother on their first date. You have seen her dust around it carefully, every Sunday, wiping each petal with a soft cloth while she sings softly under her breath. You right the vase and dash into the kitchen, although even to you that word seems too big for this space.

Here, you say, showing the woman the picture. She is stirring a pot of beans on the stove in the small kitchen-cum-pantry. This is my real father, you say. I know that for a fact, you insist, although no one is arguing. The one in the fairy tale you are about to tell is your father too, but you don't say that. I mean, he can't be your real father if he is in a fairy tale, can he? It is just a story, like Red Riding Hood, and that isn't real, and telling it never hurt anybody, did it? Although if the truth be told, Red's big mouth did alert the wolf to Grandma and though everything worked out really well in the end, there can be no joy in being eaten by a wolf, swallowed whole.

Even if you are old, even if it is temporary. Like the nine-year-old boy in the homelands that *Drum* magazine says was swallowed whole by a python, but bit his way to freedom, right through the snake's belly, from the inside out.

Tell me more, the woman says. Each time you have lunch, since you first told her the story, she presses you to tell it again. And you want to because she comes to you while your mother is still at work and feeds you, and you want to because she is your mother's special friend. It's the same every time; you always begin with the photo that is your real father, not the father in the story. Because what harm can it do? What a rarity; a grown-up who wants to hear the stories of a child. Not just any grown-up, but a white woman too, although that is not immediately obvious when you look at her—she looks more colored than white, but this is South Africa in the '70s and who can tell for sure. This you can understand, because your mother is Zulu and your father is Indian but there is nothing clear about that when people look at you, especially in this land where you are what your father is. But only women surround you, and so there is no clear proof that you are who you want to be. Especially since everyone thinks you are just another Zulu brat with a father lost to the mines, the war, the struggle, the bottle, or all of them, and this story your mother tells is a lie that makes her not the slut she really is, and this photo of a Sikh man in a turban, this photo could not be real. Who would admit to a marriage, a relationship, that clearly broke the anti-miscegenation laws? And you know children are just being cruel when they say this; you know it's not true because your mother told you it isn't, but it hurts nonetheless. And then your mother adopts this strange woman who claims she is white, and brings her home and says, Here is your auntie Alice, even though everyone else calls her White Alice.

So what harm, telling her this story?

And like always, like a game she plays with you, this lonely only child half-starved for attention, she asks, Have you ever seen your father? And you say, No, but he is a hero, just like the father in the story. And then White Alice says, Tell me the story, then, Sunil, tell it to me, you know I love it.

And she listens, rapt, moving only to keep the beans from burning and sticking to the pan. And then you begin.

Long ago and far away, but today and so forever, there lived a brave. Then one day, a big ogre invaded his land. He was a strong, evil ogre from a land far in the north where the sun hid its face. At first the people said to the ogre, There is plenty of land to share, why not share? But the ogre began to kill everyone, so the warrior fought the ogre, but it was too powerful, so the warrior fled, escaped to the land of the Shona, a powerful but kind people to the north. And there the warrior made his home, training other men who also escaped to the land of the Shona, driven off by the ogre, how to be warriors.

And where does he live in the land of Shona, White Alice asked.

He lives by a big baobab tree, you say, on an island that looks like a mudfish in a big sea called Kariba. There he and the other impis trained and grew strong to become better warriors and they would return soon to defeat the ogre.

It is a short story, but with each telling, you add detail: the dusty road that leads through the mystical forest of Chete Safan, which is the name of a powerful witch who protects all who dwell there; the strange Sibalians who roam free and are powerful medicine men who can fly to the top of Mount Kilimanjaro; the reeds by the water's edge that hide the magical fish-shaped island from view like the ones that hid Moses as a baby.

And then while you stuff your face with beans and bread, sipping delicately on the Coca-Cola that you aren't allowed but which is part of your secret, White Alice spreads a map out and asks you to tell her the story again, pen poised over the map to mark something, and with each telling, the map gets more and more marks.

Today, like all the other days, she draws lines across the map that has Rhodesia printed on it in big letters. She draws lines connecting the Chete Safan area with the small town of Sibalia on the shores of Lake Kariba, looking, searching for an island shaped like a mudfish or a whale.

But it is only a story, and what harm can it do? And if your mother trusts this white woman who looks colored and if she wants to hear your fairy tale, then what of it?

And then a few days later you come home from playing to find your mother crying on the floor, kneeling as if in prayer, shoulders heaving, a telegraph lying like a dead moth beside her. You know someone has died. That's the only time telegrams come to Soweto. You know better than to ask any questions, better than to approach her. So you sneak to your room and you listen to her prowling and muttering to herself as she deduces the mystery, and you hear the terrible words that confirm a fear that until now has sat in the pit of your stomach, gnawing away.

How did White Alice know the truth, she asks herself. Was it Sunil? Was it Sunil's story about his father, about where he was hiding, that led Alice to the truth?

And you know she has put it all together. And you realize that this was no fairy tale, even though she had said it was, said the word in Zulu, *ignanekwane*. This was no mere tale. Your father was the father in the story and he is real. He was the head of an armed ANC faction launching guerilla attacks on shopping malls to bring down apartheid. He fled to Rhodesia to escape and he was hiding in an ANC training camp on an island. The fairy tale contained the directions and White Alice finally figured it out on a map while you ate beans and bread and drank Coca-Cola and told your story. And although you tell yourself you could not have known the truth, you know it is a lie, because you were four when your mother first told it to you, because your father left when she was still pregnant with you, and you needed it. But now you are twelve and if what the Bible says about Jesus is true, then old enough to debate your elders in a temple; and certainly in Soweto, in the '70s, to be twelve is like being twenty, but there is still a four-year-old who missed the father he had never seen and who needed someone to hear his story. This is what you tell yourself.

But you hear the terrible whispered truth as your mother prowls the house like a hungry ghost. And White Alice, who was once white but turned colored because of a sickness; White Alice, who lost it all—her husband, her kids, her nice home in a white suburb, her white pass card, her privilege—and had to live in Soweto like a kaffir; White Alice, whom Dorothy had taken in, taken to, a fellow lost soul, Alice had betrayed her. Stolen Sunil's story and day by day reconstructed the truth. A truth she sold to the secret police in the hopes of getting her life back, her kids, her husband, her home, her whiteness. And who wouldn't, Dorothy muttered, and who wouldn't. But still, but still. And now her husband and many other men dead, and Sunil without his father, not even a mythical one. And all because of a story, a story and a mouth that told it. She was good at stories.

The last sound you hear that night draws you into the kitchen. And you see your mother sitting there, shoulders shaking with sobs. Terrified, you approach, terrified because you have never seen her this way, this woman whom everyone deferentially calls Nurse Dorothy.

And then she looks up when you call to her, and you scream.

You don't scream because of the mascara running down her face in black witch tendrils, or the rouge of her cheeks smeared with tears and sweat. It is her mouth that terrifies you. She has sewn it shut, the needle still dangling from a piece of black surgical thread. Not a mouth at all but flesh, meat, raw and bleeding.

And so you run. Run to White Alice's house.

And then the men come in an old ambulance and take your mother, and though there is a murderous rage in her eyes when she sees White Alice, there is also an understanding, gratitude for this gift of the men dressed in white uniforms.

And Dorothy looks from you to White Alice and because her mouth is still sewn shut, the women can only exchange looks.

Yes, White Alice says, yes, I will take care of Sunil.

Again that murderous rage and gratitude, then Dorothy is gone.

You are twelve.

You never tell your story again.

Johnny Ten-Ten, who lives down the street at Ten-Ten, says: You know why your mother sewed her mouth shut and then got taken to the crazy house?

You know better than to answer, you know that children can be cruel.

SATURDAY

Seventeen

It was early, and a mist thrown by the heat and the sprinklers covered the grounds of the Desert Palms Institute. Invisible in the whiteness, peacocks shrieked like god-awful creatures. Water, unable to sleep all night, was wide-awake when the nurse came round on the forty-minute-interval suicide watch. Although Sunil didn't actually believe the twins would kill themselves, he wanted to be sure.

The nurse brought coffee. Is it how you like it, he asked Water, passing a Styrofoam cup of hot liquid.

Four hundred billion cups of coffee are consumed across the world every year, Water said, sipping gingerly.

You didn't sleep much, did you?

The record for the longest time without sleep is eighteen days, twenty-one hours, and forty minutes, Water said.

Is your brother still asleep, the nurse asked, pointing to the caul-covered Fire.

Water's stomach growled loudly in response. The rumbling made the nurse smile.

I'll bring you something to eat in a minute, he said, closing the door gently.

Water walked across the room and stood by the window. The mist was dissipating, revealing well-manicured Japanese-style gardens rolling down to a fence. Even with the landscaping, the place still looked like a corporate park. The room, decorated as it was like a high-end but impersonal hotel room, added to the effect. The nurse returned.

The kitchen isn't open yet, but I did find these in the vending machine, he said, holding out a bag of M&M's and a packet of Red Vines.

The main flavor of licorice candy is anise but for red licorice it's cherry, Water said, putting a Red Vine in his mouth.

I'll be back in forty minutes, the nurse said, turning to leave just as the caul covering Fire snapped back like a venetian blind.

Fire blinked, adjusting to the light. Sniffing theatrically, he said: Red Vines.

Water passed one. Fire chewed-on it for a minute, eyes closed, then spat the chewed-up red candy into his cupped hand. The nurse watched from the half-closed door, mesmerized.

Fire looked up. Hello, he said to the nurse.

Hi, the nurse said.

Disgusting habit, I know, Fire said, but I'm not good at digesting anything that isn't liquid. I get most of my nutrition from Water.

Like a baby, Water said. That's why I eat for two.

You eat for three, Fire said.

Water laughed so hard, Fire looked like he was riding a mechanical bull.

That's quite all right, the nurse said, retreating.

Did you sleep, Fire asked Water.

No, Water said.

Is the coffee any good?

No, Water said.

What's that horrible screeching?

Peacocks, Water said.

What's with the curt answers, Fire asked. Are you in a bad mood?

Water shrugged. The peacocks screeched again.

Jesus, Fire muttered, how many of those fuckers are there?

An ostentation, Water said.

A what?

A group of peacocks is an ostentation, Water said. Like a bouquet of pheasants, a kettle of hawks, a deceit of lapwings, a descent of woodpeckers, an exaltation of larks, a murmuration of starlings, a siege of herons, an unkindness of ravens—

Fuck, Fire said, you really are in a bad mood. He passed the handful of spat-out Red Vines to Water and retreated under the caul. I'm going back to sleep, he said, voice muffled. Maybe you should try and get some.

The caul snapped shut.

Closed for business, Water said, and finished his coffee.

Eighteen

Eskia crossed his room to look out the window at the still-rising sun. He hadn't slept much. He never did, really. He had resigned himself to this a long time ago. His insomnia held the full weight of his guilt; the heft of his father's sniper rifle.

He'd already spent three days at this hotel and would have to check out today. Routine made it easier to be found. To be marked. It made intelligence operatives careless. From following him, he knew the Venetian was Sunil's favorite, so he decided on there.

Eskia cupped a mug of coffee in his hands. The room service delivery had not woken the sleeping Asia. He studied her sleeping form, sheets half off her. She had impossibly long legs; so long they made her torso seem short. And her hair was thick and worn in a crowning Afro. Flawless amber skin betrayed her biracial identity. Something a South African would spot easier than anyone else. He was somewhat surprised at the abandon with which she slept. He was irrationally angered by it. What right did she have to be so carefree?

Glancing over at the breakfast for two on the cart, Eskia wondered why he had bothered. He wasn't that hungry, and while he didn't typically frequent prostitutes, he was sure they didn't expect breakfast the morning after. But this wasn't just any hooker. This was Sunil's special hooker.

He knew Sunil from college, and while he was the closest

thing Eskia had to a friend then, their relationship had always been fraught.

Eskia came from Soweto royalty, an upper-middle-class family of Anglican ministers, doctors, and lawyers. People who lived in Orlando, the part of Soweto the locals sometimes called Beverly Hills; people who sat in the front pews at church on Sundays and sent their kids to private schools abroad; people who made up the cream of the ANC leadership.

Eskia's parents were paying his way but Sunil was on scholarship, one rumored to be bestowed by the apartheid government. Because of that, ordinarily Eskia would never have befriended Sunil, but they were the only two blacks in their cohort and so an uneasy friendship developed between them, an alliance that affirmed each other's humanity in the face of the crushing shame of apartheid. But Eskia perceived his need for affirmation as a weakness on his part and so he came to resent Sunil for it.

A resentment that festered into a deep hate when they both fell for Jan. But she chose Sunil, and Eskia's ego couldn't take the blow. That someone like Sunil, a township rat with no pedigree, could have taken Jan from him was too much, was unimaginable to him. Over time, Eskia realized that it wasn't just his pride that was wounded. He came to love Jan and he burned with the fire of unrequited love.

When Sunil left for Europe on an internship, Jan fell apart. Eskia consoled her and a firm friendship and then a romantic relationship grew between them. Eskia struggled though. As a member of the ANC it was seen as a betrayal to date a white woman, not to mention that it was illegal under the apartheid government. But all through their relationship, all five years of it, what was hardest was the knowledge, though unspoken, that Jan still loved Sunil. And not even hurting Sunil's mother made Eskia feel better. Then Jan disappeared in a raid and just like that, Eskia lost her.

He turned his gaze back on Asia and watched her breathe. He smiled cruelly. The nicer you treat a person, the more it hurts when you turn on them. That was a pleasure he knew well. Asia was stretching and he admired the tattoo on her arm as she flexed. It read: *Trae Dhah.*

Breakfast, she said with a smile, spotting the room service cart and the two place settings. She helped herself and dug in. Eskia watched the unbridled pleasure with which she ate and found himself lost in her delight.

Not hungry, she asked, pausing briefly.

He shook his head.

She smiled, shoved the last of her eggs into her mouth, and stood up, crossed to her clothes, and began to dress.

You can use the shower, he said.

Thank you, she said. Maybe next time.

As the door closed behind her, Eskia returned to the window. Sitting in this kind of meditation was a discipline he knew well. When he was a boy, his father, a former sharpshooter from the British Army, had been very active in the ANC's armed wing. Many a Boer policeman had fallen to his skill.

He sometimes took Eskia with him. Together they would cross the vast desert of stubby grass and garbage that marked the divide between Soweto and Johannesburg. Keeping to sewers, culverts, and other places only the blacks knew about, they would travel for miles in the night, Eskia bearing the weight of his father's Lee-Enfield rifle. By all expectations, a Lee-Enfield wouldn't make a very good sniper's weapon with its limited range, but the caliber was solid, and in the right hands even a boomerang was a deadly weapon. A relic of the First and Second World Wars, it should not have fired evenly. But Eskia's father kept the rust away with oil and a leather rag and a high-caliber bullet. In his expert hand, that projectile could travel nearly a quarter of a mile to bury itself into the resolve of his chosen target.

At first light they would arrive on the edge of a leafy, tree-shaded suburb and, climbing a select tree, they would sit the whole day, unmoving, until at dusk, just before the abrupt curtain of night, Eskia's father would take the rifle from his son, hold it steady, and, with the tender caress of a whisper, pull the ratchet back. He would wait for a long moment and breathe slow, then he would squeeze the trigger, and before the crack could echo and reveal their location, they would be down the tree, melting back into the depth of night. Eskia, carrying the heavy rifle, always struggled to keep up. But this one time he tarried and saw the target fall. A plump man in his forties with a shiny bald spot. He saw a child running down a garden path to meet him. And then he saw the spurt of blood obliterating the bald spot and darkening the face of the child. And then Eskia turned away and ran after his father in the dark, the weight of the rifle heavier than usual.

He turned back from the view of Vegas, put his coffee mug down with exaggerated care, and walked into the bathroom to shower. He had much to do.

Nineteen

Salazar tipped the last of his coffee onto a white shell, staining it brown, flecks of coffee grounds standing out like black growths. He kicked sand at the shell, then watched the sun come up over Lake Mead. He was always amazed that something man-made here in the middle of the desert could look so natural and blue. The tire marks from the night before were still visible.

Unable to sleep after signing the twins over to Dr. Singh, he had returned to the station, typed up his report, and then driven to Jake's, an all-night diner off Fremont Street. His other favorite diner, right next door to the Gutenberg Museum on South Main, had gone out of business. Now it was a Chinese fast-food joint that closed at ten. When the Library Gentlemen's Club and the Gun Store, on the other side of the museum, went out of business as well, he figured he should move on and so he'd migrated to this diner ten years ago.

He liked the old parts of Vegas, ever since he moved here as a teenager. Parts that were now seedy and decrepit. Things seemed more honest here, less beguiling than the Strip or the new developments spreading into the desert. Jake's had been in the same place for more than forty years, and it seemed that the staff hadn't changed in that time either. It was the only place in Vegas that didn't have any slot machines or gambling of any kind. Just a simple menu and a loyal clientele of people often down on their luck. He watched an old homeless man carry his bulldog past the diner, pause, then come in.

Spare some change, he asked Salazar.

Why the fuck are you carrying your dog, Salazar asked.

He's tired, the homeless man said.

Who carries you when you're tired?

Jesus, the man said. Spare me a dollar?

Get the fuck out of here, the cook yelled from the kitchen.

The old man shuffled out before Salazar could give him the dollar. He melted into the night with his dog, leaving Salazar with his thoughts, his guilt, and his desire. He really wanted to solve this case. Not just for his career, or because he had been working on it for so long, but because there was the matter of the dead teenage girl who had been found in the second batch of dead homeless men two years ago. Her discovery was a shock for everyone working that day. As they pulled the pile of bodies apart, there she was, like the dramatic reveal of a magic trick gone wrong. Salazar could still see it clearly in his mind's eye. The near emerald-green dress in the midst of all that dirt and gray; an orange high-heeled pump on one foot, the other bare. A shock of red hair and a face twisted in agony. Everything about her was incongruous, not in keeping with the scene. There was no ID on her and even now, no one had come forward to claim her. Putting her to rest was what really drove him. The department therapist told him that his desire had nothing to do with putting her to rest. That it was really all about him.

Fuck you, he'd said then. Fuck you, he thought now. Even if she was right, there was still the fact of the dead girl. Buying a coffee to go, the size of a Big Gulp, he'd driven out to the lake.

All night he sat in the dark trying to figure it out, to get into the killer's head as he liked to call it. Was it the twins? Why would they do it? How did they do it? The truth was, gruff and tactless as he was, Salazar was no criminal. He couldn't really understand why people did the things they did, much less how. It was a severe limitation for a detective and he compensated for it by obsessively working his cases, going over the same ground again and again until something broke open for him.

So he sat in his car in the soft light waiting for that break, that crack in time.

Twenty

In the kitchen Sunil filled the kettle and set it on the range. The burner was the only illumination as he opened the cupboards and reached for a teapot, which he then filled with loose-leaf Black Dragon tea. He liked this tactile relationship with the world and had consciously cultivated it—if he could find everything in the dark then there was still order in his world.

He thought about the body dumps from two years earlier. About the testing of his serum that had led to them. All those homeless men recruited from the streets of Vegas with offers of money and sometimes drugs were housed in seclusion in the basement of the institute.

And then when they had enough viable and anonymous subjects, they'd put them into rooms in batches of ten, administered doses of the serum and a placebo to the control group, and then waited for the results. The drug and its antidote were delivered via an implant in the men's heads that could be controlled from a distance.

Every test had proved disastrous. Not from the perspective of inducing psychotic breaks. That was easy enough. In fact, 50 percent of the placebo group was able to match the ferocity of the medicated. What proved abortive was the ability to control the behavior. The antidote hadn't worked, and neither had electric collars, subdermal shock implants, or even tear gas. The rage just couldn't be harnessed. And in the end, in every test, no matter what variations they made to the serum and antidote, all the subjects died. They simply beat one another to death. In any other clinical trial of a drug, adverse events were expected—side effects, some more drastic than others, escalating from a skin rash to a clinical trial subject dying. But the numbers here were beyond belief.

The body dumps that followed had been Brewster's idea. Sunil hadn't known any of the details. Brewster had simply drafted him to help the investigation as forensic expert with the intent to steer any possible connection away from the institute. Not that the institute's possible involvement ever came up. There just wasn't any reason for the police to suspect them. Sunil surmised that Brewster knew that all along. His motives remained unclear to Sunil. Maybe he should be studying Brewster.

The kettle shrieked. He emptied the water into the teapot and let it brew. From the fridge he took out the other half of the cantaloupe from the night before, laid it on a wooden chopping block, reached for the ceramic knife, and, still in the dark, cubed it perfectly. From the corner of his eye, through the kitchen window, he could make out the spotlight from the Luxor.

He poured some tea, stirred in some sugar, and drank it in the dark, watching the dramatic sunrise through the blue-tinted kitchen windows. He couldn't make up his mind which he loved best: Vegas at night with all the neon and flashing lights, or Vegas in the morning, when the neon was replaced by a fresh light—an innocence.

It was a Saturday and he wished he weren't going in to work. It would be nice to hike today. Somewhere hot but shaded, like the many arroyos that hid the scars of an older Vegas, of a past that was now held only in unreliable narratives; a confounding mix of hoaxes and urban legends. Sunil was drawn to those stories because he believed that there was real history embedded in their occluded forms and he loved nothing more than collecting them, sifting through them, and decoding the deeper truths he was sure were hidden in them—as if he could read the mind of the landscape, uncover its intentions and motives, and recalibrate its secret histories.

In the meantime, he'd settle for being able to uncover the secrets the twins were concealing. The real secrets, not the ones they had half buried for him to stumble on. He knew they were playing some strange game, but he couldn't tell what it was. The thing about half-truths littered in among outright lies is that they distract from the deeper secrets, the ones you really want to find. But Sunil was good at finding secrets. That's what he'd done at Vlakplaas all those years ago. Found secrets and used them against their owners.

Twenty-one

Sheila, Sunil said as Sheila stepped into his office.

Sunil, she said, and it sounded like a seduction. I was kind of hoping you'd made some of that amazing coffee you have, she said, and pointed to the machine on the sideboard.

Sunil smiled. Of course, he said.

This had become a little game they played. Every morning Sheila came in and pretended she was only asking for coffee. He didn't know where it could lead, if anywhere, but he liked it just the same. Watching her cross the room he couldn't help but notice how attractive she was: slim, fit, and tight, with perfect black skin. She stirred something in him. But in that same moment, while Sheila was a rational impulse in his mind, Asia was an ache that made him cross his legs.

As she stirred her coffee, Sheila turned to him. Sleep well, she asked, licking the wooden stirrer before throwing it into the trash.

Not really, Sunil said.

Oh, why?

You mean you haven't heard about the conjoined twins, he asked. You must have, there aren't any secrets inside this building.

Sheila gave him a look. What the hell are you babbling about, she asked.

Yesterday while I was meeting with Brewster I got a call from Salazar, he said.

Don't know him, she said.

The detective from the homeless killing case I consulted on two years ago, Sunil said.

She shrugged: Okay. And someone killed some conjoined twins?

No, he arrested conjoined twins as suspects in the homeless murders.

Sheila looked bewildered. No fucking way, she said. The twins are the killers? How is that even possible? How are they joined?

Sunil opened the folder on his desk and passed her the Polaroid.

Oh my God, she said, holding it away. They're undifferentiated. I've never seen a case like that.

I know. It's crazy. I mean this one—he pointed at Fire—is barely a foot long and yet he talks incessantly. It's crazy, the way they are joined. Fire, the small one, looks like a sea slug growing out of his brother's side. And this one, the normal-looking one, only talks in factoids.

Factoids?

Yes, like, oh, I don't know, giraffes have no vocal cords. Stuff like that.

Is it true, Sheila asked.

Is what true?

That giraffes have no vocal cords?

Yes, it's true.

It's weird that you know that, she said.

Whatever, he said. Anyway, the detective asked me to conduct a psych eval on them last night. I wanted to say no, but Brewster insisted that I do it.

Wow, you certainly had an adventurous evening, Sheila said, taking a sip of coffee. It was really good, as always.

So now I have the twins here, Sunil said. And we'll keep them for at least seventy-two hours. I think Brewster wants to keep them indefinitely, but we'll see.

You have them here at the institute?

Yes.

But if you don't want Brewster to have them indefinitely, why would you bring them here, she asked.

Salazar can't hold them legally so—

He's asking you to keep them here. But why?

Well, when he arrested them, they were near a blood dump, but there were no bodies and so no evidence to tie them to the blood dump except proximity.

But if they are the killers—

I know, I know, Sunil interrupted. He filled her in quickly and she sat on the edge of the couch the whole time. When he was done, she sat back.

Jesus, she said. Why does stuff like this always find you?

I don't know. Another troubling thing is that I think Brewster is running tests behind my back using my research, and I think these two things are connected.

That's creepy, she said.

I'm not worried about the creepy factor. More important is the blood.

How so?

Well, Sunil said, if the blood dump is connected to my research it can mean only one thing.

Brewster is testing the drug you developed to trigger psychopathic behavior?

Yeah, Sunil said. Human trials of a psychopathic pathogen.

So what will you do, Sheila asked.

I don't know.

Do you feel conflicted about holding them?

Yes.

That means you haven't completely sold your soul to Brewster, she said, smiling.

In that moment he felt like he could fall for her, that he could make a life with her. He knew she liked him, was attracted to him. So what was holding him back? Was it because she was unabashedly black?

Sheila, he said, before he could stop himself.

What, she asked with a smile.

And he wanted to say, I like you, we should explore that. Instead he said: They have odd names, the twins.

Really, she said, and he could tell by the tone of her voice that she was disappointed. That she clearly thought he would say something different.

Yes, he said. His speech was quick, awkward, filling the space between them. One is called Fire and the other Water, and the one called Fire is a fire wizard. A sideshow thing, their act is called King Kongo, African Witchdoctor. Anyway, I noticed something really curious. Even though Fire is the wizard, there were burn marks only on Water.

Realizing she'd lost him to his work, she clenched her jaw. I have to go, she said, getting up abruptly. I have something to do. She hesitated in the doorway.

I'll be brewing fresh coffee all day, Sunil offered.

She nodded and closed the door behind her. He stared at the smudge of lipstick on her coffee cup for a long time.

Twenty-two

So what is your diagnosis, Brewster asked as soon as Sunil picked up the phone.

Fuck, Sunil swore quietly. He wanted to say, Who doesn't say hello when they call someone? Instead he said: You know how I feel about making hasty diagnoses.

Would you present them as psychopathic, Brewster pressed.

Always this shit with Brewster. Look, Sunil said, nearly every person in the world, at some point and under some condition, presents as psychopathic, from road rage to actual murder, but I don't want to waste time researching twins who present nothing more unusual than their physicality.

Their twinning is everything, Brewster countered. We haven't had an opportunity to study monsters before. We need to run an MRI on them. Judging from the photo on file, we may need to ask the zoo to assist, because the twins clearly won't fit our own machines.

The zoo, Sunil echoed.

Consider their width, Brewster said. We can't fit them in a regular MRI.

But the zoo?

What do you suggest, Sunil?

I don't know. Aren't there facilities that might have bigger MRIs that aren't zoos? Shouldn't we check with an obesity specialist first?

Yes, Brewster said, we could. But the zoo is a safe bet.

You don't think taking a pair of conjoined black twins to a zoo for a medical procedure presents a problem, Sunil asked.

No, Brewster said. Whatever your sentiments, which are duly noted, make the arrangements for the MRI. We should probably try for tomorrow, as it will be less busy there on Sunday and cheaper for us. I'll send them with a senior intern if that makes you feel better.

Sunil was silent at first.

Fine, I'll have the intern handle all of it, Brewster said. That way you can keep your moral high ground. Brewster sighed impatiently. Listen, maybe the twins can provide the breakthrough we need for your X7 serum to work.

If they turn out to be psychopaths, Sunil said.

Well, we can only hope, Brewster said.

Twenty-three

Sunil was pacing when Sheila knocked and walked in.

Back for more coffee, she said sheepishly.

Sunil kept pacing.

Sunil, Sheila said. Sunil, stop.

That man, Sunil said.

Brewster?

Sunil nodded.

I know, Sheila said. He is such a dick.

Sunil smiled tightly. This isn't your problem, Sheila, he said.

I know, but still, you know? So what happened exactly?

He wanted me to take the twins to the zoo to get an MRI tomorrow.

The zoo!

My point exactly.

So what's going to happen?

An intern is taking them, Sunil said.

Well, that's not the I-told-him-to-fuck-off I was expecting, but at least you don't have to do it, she said.

Before Sunil could answer, there was a knock at the door. A nurse stood there with a DVD in his hand.

Good morning, Dr. Singh, he said. This is the recording of the twins' room from last night.

Thank you, Sunil said, taking the DVD.

You recorded them, Sheila asked as the nurse left.

Yes, they were on suicide watch. Of course I recorded them.

Did they consent?

Sunil crossed to his desk, ignoring Sheila's question.

Maybe a little of Brewster is rubbing off on you, she said.

Sunil put the disk into his computer and pulled out his chair to sit. As the screen lit up, he became aware of Sheila's breath on the back of his neck as she leaned over to watch. Goose bumps rose on his skin, but he pretended not to notice. The first twenty minutes of the DVD were uneventful, the twins moved about restlessly, trying to settle down. But then Fire slipped his caul over himself and retreated, to sleep no doubt. Water lay around for a while and then got up to cross to the window.

Sunil moved to fast-forward the video, but Sheila's hand stayed his, and he felt her breasts brush his back. In the six years they had worked together, this was the closest they had come physically. He had a moment of guilt, like he was cheating on Asia, which was stupid. Asia was a prostitute. But he loved her.

What is he doing, Sheila asked.

They watched Water as he leaned up against the window. He was hugging himself and his lips were moving but the audio was really bad and they couldn't make out the words. It sounded like a melodic hum.

I think he is singing, Sunil said.

I think you're right. How odd, Sheila said.

Yeah, that is odd, Sunil agreed.

They watched Water, occasionally forwarding through the footage. Sometimes he was by the window, other times he was in the corner, and then sometimes on the bed. But wherever he was in the room he seemed to be singing the same inaudible song. Finally he fell asleep and then woke with a start less than an hour later when the duty nurse checked in on them.

This is exciting, Sheila said.

About that, Sunil began.

Don't send me away. I can help, Sheila said. Besides, I'll be gone on Tuesday. So let me help. Please.

Sunil looked at her from behind his steepled fingers.

I'll even make the coffee, Sheila volunteered.

Actually, I'll let you stay only if you promise not to make the coffee, Sunil said.

She smiled. I like this. We should hang out more often. What do you think the singing means?

Sunil was sitting back, legs crossed, crease pinched, chewing thoughtfully on a wooden stirrer. More important than what it means, he said, is the question of his manner.

How do you mean?

When the police and I interviewed the twins yesterday, Water exhibited traits of autism. He spoke mostly in factoids that were only tenuously connected to the conversation, and only when pushed.

So?

Some experts say twins can swap consciousness. What if Fire is the one singing, and Water is the one sleeping?

That's creepy, Sheila said.

Sunil smiled. Are you going to attempt a diagnosis?

I work on robots, Sunil, not psychopaths.

Some could argue that's the same thing, he said.

She laughed. I have to get back to work, she said.

Okay.

I won't wait forever, Sunil, she said.

I know, he said.

Twenty-four

It's Dr. SS, Fire said as Sunil knocked and entered their room. The twins were sitting in the chair in the corner. Water was surfing through channels on the television, a bored look on his face. He barely glanced at Sunil, who was flicking through their chart, a nurse hovering by his elbow.

I told you not to call me that, Sunil said.

What should I call you?

Why don't you just call me Doctor?

There are eighteen doctors in the U.S. called Dr. Doctor and one called Dr. Surgeon, Water said.

It is important that we establish some boundaries in our communication, Sunil continued. When you call me Doc, you sound like Bugs Bunny.

Mel Blanc, the original voice for Bugs Bunny, was allergic to carrots, Water said.

How are you feeling today, Sunil asked Fire, changing the subject.

I'm good. We are good.

Could you maybe expand a little on that, Sunil asked.

We had eggs for breakfast, after an early snack of Red Vines and M&M's. I'm not sure what level of detail you're looking for.

I see you're being difficult again. Water, how are you?

Sharks lay the largest eggs in the world, Water said.

Really, Water? You're going to keep this up?

Tone, Dr. Singh, tone, Fire said with a smirk.

Sunil took a deep breath. Your chart looks good, he said, your vitals are holding strong. How did you sleep?

I slept like a baby, Fire said. But then I always do. Water, on the other hand, he doesn't sleep much.

And your appetite?

Pretty good, Fire said.

Water?

Selah is a tree, Water said.

I'm sorry?

Selah is a tree and that's why I can't sleep, Water said.

Selah was our mother's name, Fire said, his stubby hand rubbing Water's face gently. His head, however, never looked in Water's direction. And even his hand movements seemed forced and clumsy: unnatural. Sunil made a note in the chart.

And why is she a tree, Sunil asked.

Trees are the oldest living organisms, Water said. He still hadn't looked at Sunil.

Sunil was leaning against the bed. Why is she a tree, Water, he asked again.

Water was silent.

Can you tell me why he thinks your mother is a tree, Sunil asked Fire.

Fire looked away.

What can *you* tell me about your mother, Sunil asked.

She is dead, Fire said. She passed on when we were twelve.

I see, Sunil said. And your father?

We never knew our father. For all we know he was God.

And that would make you what, Jesus?

The Bible is the Word of God, Water said.

Look, I'm trying to conduct a basic evaluation here of your mental health. If you keep up with these kinds of answers I'm going to have to assume that you actually believe them.

The mustard seed was a parable by Jesus, Water said.

Fire was silent.

Understand that if I take your answers seriously, Sunil said, then I have to conclude that you suffer from delusions.

Delusions of biblical proportions, Fire said, smirking.

Fifty Bibles are sold every minute across the world, Water said.

What does that mean to you, Sunil asked Water.

Water shrugged. Shakespeare was forty-six when the King James Version of the Bible was compiled. In Psalms 46, the forty-sixth word from the first word is "shake" and the forty-sixth word from the last word is "spear," he said.

Do you both realize the severity of your situation? You will either go to prison or be remanded to a secure wing of a mental hospital. Is that what you want?

What will be will be, I can't worry about that, Fire said.

I think you should, if not for your sake, then your brother's.

I've been taking care of my brother for years, since Selah died, so don't tell me how, thank you very much.

Fire and Water are always together because we are born of steam, Water said.

Sunil sighed. This was going to be hard.

Look, Doc, this whole thing is loaded against us, Fire said. We can't win in a rigged game.

How do you mean exactly, Sunil asked.

I just don't think the justice system works for people like me, Fire said.

Are you saying you're above the law?

This is exactly my point, Doc. When I admit that I don't believe in this country's justice system, you think I'm saying I am above the law, which you might call a grandiose sense of self-worth. If I keep making jokes you will say I am exhibiting glibness and superficial charm. If you decide that I am not answering your questions or at least not answering them honestly, you will think I am a pathological liar and that I am cunning and manipulative. If I complain about any of this, you will say I am not accepting responsibility for my own actions. If I admit to being bored, which I am by the way, you could read that as a need for stimulation and proneness to thrill seeking. I am living off the side of my brother, so I do qualify for parasitic lifestyle and I think you will agree that I'm pretty high on the aggressive narcissism scale, which makes me think you are going for an evaluation of us that fits with something you've already decided.

Such as?

If we're supposed to be serial killers, Fire said, then my guess is we are supposed to be psychopaths.

An American study found that one in twenty men was a psychopath, Water said.

Well, Doc, am I right so far?

No, Sunil said. I'm here with an open mind. Are you?

If you are, then what am I, Fire said, and cackled.

Interesting how you keep switching between the pronouns we, us, and I.

Is it? I don't think so. Fire paused, then, taking a shuddering breath, began again. About Selah, she killed herself—hanged herself, to be precise, from the branch of a bristlecone pine that grew on the edge of our property.

I'm sorry, Sunil said. That couldn't have been easy for you at twelve.

It wasn't.

Do you know why she did it?

We were downwinders, you know, downwind from the nuclear tests. She had leukemia, she was dying, so she gave us away and hanged herself.

Gave you away?

She gave us to Fred's dad, Reverend Jacobs, and his freak show, the Lord's Marvels.

Is that how you grew up? With a circus?

A sideshow, Doc, a sideshow. Not a circus. Yes, we grew up as freaks and hardcore downwinder nationalists. Sideshow or die, Fire said.

Why do you call yourselves freaks, Sunil asked.

It's a badge of honor, Fire said. That's what Reverend Jacobs gave us. Pride. You see, freaks are made, not born. Birth defects, unusual genetic formations, they make you less capable in this able-biased society, but they don't make you a freak. Freakery you learn, you cultivate, you earn.

And what's a downwinder nationalist, Sunil pressed.

Oh for fuck's sake, Doc, Fire snapped. Look into it, do your own fucking work.

Your attitude is not very constructive right now, Sunil said.

Yeah, whatever, Dr. Phil, Fire said. We want a phone call. Don't we get a phone call?

The telephone was invented to talk to the dead, Water said.

Sunil noted that Water's tongue seemed to protrude a little from his mouth when Fire was speaking, but not when they were both silent. It was a small thing but one he'd noticed the day before at County. He didn't know what it meant, or if it meant anything at all.

When you say the telephone was invented to speak to the dead, what do you mean, he asked Water.

Just that, Doc, Fire replied. That's what Edison invented the telephone for.

When Thomas Edison died in 1941, Henry Ford captured his last breath in a bottle, Water said.

If you could have a phone call, who would you call, Sunil asked.

Fred, Water said.

Fred, Fire agreed.

What is Fred's last name, Sunil asked.

Fred Jacobs, Fire said. So do we get our call, Doc?

The word "doctor" comes from the Latin *doctori,* meaning to teach, Water said.

Thank you, Water, Sunil said. Is there any way you can get your brother to speak to me, he asked Fire.

He is speaking to you, Fire said.

I see, Sunil said. Giving the chart to the nurse, he said, I've modified their medication, be careful with the dosage. And with that, he headed out the door.

What about our fucking phone call, Fire yelled.

Twenty-five

I miss my mother terribly, Sunil thought as the gondola sailed under the fake bridge. In truth, Dorothy had died many years—when her mind folded in on itself and opened along the crease—before her body gave up the struggle. It had been a lonely and difficult time for Sunil and he would most certainly not have made it without White Alice.

A drizzle of crumbs from a bag of chips that a fat Midwestern family were stuffing into their faces on the concrete arch above brought him back to the gondola and the chlorine smell of water and the blue sky that was so blue it couldn't be real. He watched the family with a mixture of envy and disgust. To be part of a group so oblivious seemed attractive. The gondola turned a bend and his thoughts returned to his mother.

I miss my mother, he said aloud to the gondolier. Is that a childish thing to admit?

The gondolier shrugged.

Sunil was twenty-three when Dorothy died. He was far away in Europe, in Venice, that city she had loved but had never visited. Dorothy was locked up in the Soweto mental hospital for blacks. It was housed in the barracks of an abandoned mine workers' camp. The barracks consisted of one long bungalow built to house five hundred men and sat in the middle of half an acre of dirt and bush scrub, with broken windows and walls that had not seen paint since it was built. The air of abandonment around it was real.

In Dorothy's room, pictures of Venice cut out of magazines were pasted across the walls. Other than those colorful walls, the room was bare except for a bed and an altar. On the altar were a single candle, a small statue of the Jesus of the Sacred Heart, and a statue of Mary with a half-melted face, probably from being too close to the candle flame. The altar also held, in a glass jar, a coiled piece of string stained dirt-brown from dried blood. It took all of Sunil's willpower not to look at the string—it represented everything that had driven his mother here.

On one visit to see Dorothy, Sunil brought a large detailed map of Venice stolen from the library. They spread it out on the floor and she touched each of the sites she loved: the Basilica di Santa Maria Gloriosa dei Frari, which held Titan's *Assumption of the Virgin*, a painting she loved because the model for the Virgin was a famous courtesan; the Piazza San Marco, with the dual columns crested by Saint Mark's winged lion and Saint Theodore standing on a crocodile, tiles laid out like a flat labyrinth; the Doge's Palace; the path of the Grand Canal; the Rialto Bridge; and even the brown patch that was the beach at the Lido. Omar Sharif used to holiday there, Dorothy said. Even then Sunil knew she would die in those barracks.

As soon as he left South Africa to study in Europe, Sunil went to Venice and crisscrossed the canals, touching walls, gazing at paintings in churches and galleries and museums, even approaching the statutes that terrified him but held such grace and awe for her. That was when the telegram had arrived announcing her death. He took a ferry to Isola di San Michele and wandered around the graves, watching a bulldozer push the headstones of funeral-plot debtors into a pile for trash against a far wall. Picking a spot by a tree, far away from the giant statue of the angel in the middle of the cemetery, he laid a single rose under it and said the Lord's Prayer.

On the ride back, he tore the telegram into many pieces and watched them flutter into the oily water. Then, and for a long time, he felt nothing more than an overwhelming sense of relief. Years went by before the grief arrived, the way it often does, unannounced, as quiet as the morning when you break down into your cup of coffee, crying.

After Dorothy died, Sunil couldn't bring himself to return to Venice, the real one, but when he came to Las Vegas and discovered the Strip, he began to come to the Venetian. And there he would ride a gondola for hours lost in this private rosary, this ritual of faith and grief.

The ride has ended, sir, the gondolier said, interrupting Sunil's thoughts. Do you want to go again?

Sunil had been around twelve times already in two hours.

No, thank you, he said, getting out.

He tipped the gondolier and walked into the hotel lobby. After checking in, he went up to the room to wait for Asia. She'd finally called back and agreed to meet him there. While Sunil waited, nursing a scotch from the minibar, he became aware how sad it was for a forty-four-year-old to have had only two serious relationships, both plagued by gulfs of impossibility. Asia's arrival brought him back to the present, and with it an animal hunger.

Later, Sunil traced the tattoo on her shoulder. *Trae Dah* it said in cursive made from the winding stem of a rose. It took him back to the first night they'd spent together. He'd found her online, on Craigslist, and she came over in less than thirty minutes, like her ad promised. That night she'd worn a tank top and he'd noticed the tattoo on her shoulder.

She'd stood at the door for a long time before saying, Aren't you going to ask me in? Of course, he said, stepping back to let her through. He peered out of the door, down the corridor. It's okay, she said, I'm alone. Of course, he said, and shut the door. She sat on the couch and looked around. Nice place you have, she said. How old are you, he asked, thinking she didn't look a day over sixteen. Twenty-two, she said. Then: But I can be younger if you are into that. No, he said, not sure exactly what he was into. What does your tattoo mean, he asked. An ex-boyfriend, she said, and her voice was sad. You can have it removed, he said. I don't want to, she said. Silence. So, can I get you a drink, he asked. No, thank you, she said, but you are welcome to have one if it helps you relax. She got up and walked over to the floor-to-ceiling window and looked out at the city. It looks so beautiful from up here, she said, a wistful tone in her voice. Is your name really Asia, he asked. She turned and smiled. Yes, she said, taking off her tank top. She had a pretty bra on. Do you want to do it here or in the bedroom, she asked. Here, he said, not sure why. She came over to the couch and, sitting down, she took a Bible out of her bag and placed it on the coffee table. The donation. Please put it inside the Bible, she said. There is a bookmark, she added. He opened it at the bookmark, to the book of John, and his eye was drawn to an underlined passage. He slipped the crisp dollar bills between the onionskin and shut the book. He never asked her about this ritual. Not then and not since.

She rubbed her hand over the cushion next to her and patted it. Lie down, she said. He lay. Take your clothes off, she said. As he struggled with his pants, she said, Have you never done this before? What, he asked. This. No, he said, no. What made you call? I was lonely, he said, almost defensively. I know, she said, me too, and there was a sincerity in her voice. Lie back, she said, and he did. You can touch my breasts, she said. Thank you, he said, touching them tentatively. She smiled and bent to wrap him in her mouth, but then winced. What is it, he asked. Do I smell? No, no, she said hurriedly. I just had an abortion, she said. Oh, he said, suddenly uncomfortable, but not wanting to talk about her abortion. He no longer wanted to ask her anything, didn't want her to speak. He only wanted sex. And she obliged. Later she held him and the move surprised him. Can I stay tonight, she asked. Please. Just tonight. Sure, he said, holding her firmly but gently. When he woke up she was gone. That had been three years ago and he had seen her regularly at least once a week since then.

Why do you keep this thing, he asked, still tracing the tattoo. Do you still love him?

No, she said, eyebrows arching at his tone. I keep it to remind me never to be so stupid again.

Love isn't stupid, Sunil said, surprising himself.

Of course not, she said. She got up and crossed the room to the minibar. Want something?

No, he said, and headed into the bathroom. When he got back she was draped in a chair sipping on a glass of scotch. Why did we meet here, she asked.

I was at work. It was convenient.

You live closer to your work than this, she said. Is something going on?

It's not like we're dating, he said, a little sharper than he'd meant to.

You're right, she said with a hurt tone.

Look, he said, I've been seeing these twins and—

Twins?

I mean at work. They are my patients. Anyway, they are conjoined twins and treating them is stirring up stuff for me.

You've never talked about work before, she said. Should you be telling me about your patients?

I'm sorry I brought it up.

She smiled and took a sip of scotch. It's fine. I just don't want to talk about work. I mean, imagine if I talked to you about my work.

Point taken, he said, and crossed the room to pull on his pants.

We can talk about other things, she said in a conciliatory tone. Like why you love this hotel so much.

How do you know I love it so much?

Well, I know you come here a lot. You said as much in the past and I've seen you here several times.

On dates with other men?

Not talking about work, remember, she said sweetly. So why do you love it so much?

It reminds me of my mother, he said, buttoning his shirt.

That's a little weird, if you don't mind me saying. Is that why you wanted to do it here?

I have to go, he said, stepping into his shoes. The room is paid up until tomorrow, you're welcome to stay as long as you like.

She crossed the room and wrapped her arms around him, her head soft on his chest. I'm sorry, she said, I didn't say that to hurt you. I was just surprised.

He held her for a moment, nosing her hair. It smelled of sandalwood as always. He pulled away. This was a mistake, he said. I shouldn't have called you.

Don't say that, she said, her voice small.

I don't know what I expected.

I do, she said, knowing full well that he was in love with her. But you know what I do, I can't, she said. I just can't. As she spoke she rubbed her tattoo reflexively.

He stopped at the door. It's in the Bible in the bedside drawer, he said.

She didn't look at him. Thank you, she said.

He closed the door behind him and immediately wanted to walk back in. He leaned against it for a moment to steady himself, wishing he had showered. Now he would have to stop at home on the way back to work. Just as well, he thought, pushing away from the door and heading down the corridor. He didn't want to carry the smell of her around with him all day. Unknown to him, she had been leaning on the other side of the door and as she heard him walk away, she rubbed the hard wood of it.

Twenty-six

I have a complaint, Fire said as soon as he got in the door.

Sit down, please, Sunil said, pointing to the couch.

The twins sat.

Some coffee first, and then we can get to your complaint?

Turkish bridegrooms promised their wives on their wedding day to always provide them with coffee, Water said.

We will both have coffee, Doc, Fire said.

Sunil poured two Styrofoam cups of coffee and passed them to the twins. Pouring his into a real cup, he leaned back.

Coffee was discovered in the Kingdom of Kaffa in Ethiopia, Water said. Even though there the bean was called bunna, coffee took its name from Kaffa.

Do you realize that the police think you are killers? That you are connected to a series of deaths from two years ago?

Serial killers? We are the witchdoctor, Doc, not killers. You know this deep down.

I have to keep you here until you tell me what you were doing by that lake with the blood.

We never saw the blood until the police pointed it out. We were there to sightsee.

I find that hard to believe, Sunil said.

I think you're keeping us here because you are chasing old ghosts, Fire said. Something about us reminds you of them.

Is that so, Sunil asked. But he knew better than anyone that psychiatry *was* all about chasing ghosts. There was no precision to its science, no technology that allowed a doctor into a patient's head. It was a game of deep insights, good instincts, and luck—the same as for any good priest. Eugene had told him as much.

We are songomas, you and I, he'd said to Sunil. We throw bones and read them for meaning, for hope, for direction. Your bones are more ethereal than mine. I mean, I usually throw people's actual bones, but in the end it's the same, we are both chasing spirits. We are hunting the demons that haunt others. We get a smell and off we go. And you know why, Sunil? You know why we are so good at hunting the demons of others? Because we are so good, gifted even, at stalking and evading our own. But all demon hunters think that they are really heroes, and you know what all heroes need? They need a myth. For me it is the ideal of order, of understanding that the world would spin off its axis without the order I bring. For you . . . for you it might be the illusion of doing good, of saving others.

The illusion, Sunil asked. What are you talking about?

Eugene smiled, a cruel peeling back of the lips from the teeth. Your myth, Sunil. I mean that you have yet to find your myth. When you do, you'll be free like me. You will be a pure angel of purpose.

As much as he hated it, Sunil realized that Eugene was right. He hadn't found his myth. What he didn't know was what kept him from it.

He looked at Fire and shivered when he saw his lips peel back in a smile not unlike Eugene's. Were the twins the gatekeepers to his myth? Was that why he was chasing them in a pointless game of bait? Something an intern could handle for him? The twins weren't the killers from two years ago, but he didn't know what they were. Two years ago he'd been clear about why he was helping, or pretending to help, Salazar. Now he had lost track of what the charade was about. Was he stalking himself, or Brewster? Or was Brewster stalking him? He remembered something Eugene had said. If a hunter ever loses track of his prey, he becomes prey.

You okay, Doc?

Yes, Fire, I'm fine, Sunil said.

Are you sure? Because you don't look so good. You look like you're suppressing something, something unpleasant, like, say, a sad truth?

The truth shall set you free, Water said.

Perhaps you're projecting something onto me? Something you'd like to share, Sunil said.

Classic evasion, Doc. Very good, Fire said.

Why don't you leave the psychiatry to me, Sunil said. You may be a little out of your depth there.

You know I'm right, Doc, you know you're holding us because somewhere deep down you think we can help you with this truth that's burning a hole in you.

Did you make your call to Fred, Sunil asked.

No, we didn't and we want to, Fire said.

Fred will come for us, Water said.

And where is Fred right now?

Fred is in the desert, Water said. I love Fred. Fred is whom I love.

Can you tell me where to find Fred, Sunil asked.

Water was drinking his coffee, but Fire was just twirling the cup in his hands, not drinking. Sunil made a note about this, wondering if Fire could actually ingest anything. In spite of his earlier protestations to the contrary, he was looking forward to the results of the MRI that Brewster would be performing.

Why do we have Styrofoam cups and you have a real one, Fire asked.

Institute policy, Sunil said. Patients can't use breakable crockery.

It's not like we are terrorists, Doc. That's apartheid, Fire said.

You never answered the question. Where can I find Fred.

Does it matter? Like Water said, Fred will come for us.

But what if I wanted to see your circus act, Sunil said. Where would I go?

Sideshow, Fire said.

I'm sorry, I don't understand, Sunil said. What's the difference?

Circuses are about entertainment and juggling and animals and all that shit. Sideshows are about freaks, about people and the limits of acceptability. We push those limits. If a circus is an escape, Fire said, a sideshow is a confrontation.

I see, Sunil said, writing. And you feel empowered by this difference?

Damn fucking right we do, Fire said.

"Circus" comes from the Latin for "ring" or "circle," Water said.

What does a fire wizard do, exactly, Sunil asked.

I can show you, Fire said.

You're not going to burn the building down, are you, Sunil asked.

Fire just glared at him. Watch, he said.

But it was Water who moved, not him, reaching for a piece of paper. With quick but graceful movements, he shaped it into a white origami moth with an eight-inch wingspan. Water held it up to Sunil and cupped his hand around the paper moth.

Fire began a mesmerizing incantation, and as Sunil watched, Water opened his hands and the paper moth fluttered into flight for thirty seconds. It hovered over his palms for another ten seconds and then burst into flames, the ash falling into Water's cupped palms. He rubbed them together and once again held up the white origami moth.

Smiling, he passed the paper moth to Sunil.

How did you do that, Sunil asked, turning the fragile paper moth gingerly over in his hands.

We are the witchdoctor, Fire said.

Impressive, Sunil said.

Water got up and walked toward the wall of photos. What are these, he asked.

They are photos of cows, Sunil said.

A cow stands up and sits down fourteen times a day, Water said.

I would like to meet Fred, Sunil said.

Well, we all like what we like, Fire said. Did you take these photos?

Yes, a very long time ago, with a dinky old Kodak camera. I was seven or eight. They are Nguni cows. They remind me of home.

Ah, home. More nostalgia than memory, Fire said.

The Nguni name all their cattle, you know? This one here, Sunil said, pointing to one of the cows, is called Inhlakuva, sugar bean, because its markings resemble a sugar bean; and this one is Imfezi, the spitting cobra; and this creamy speckled one is called Amaqandakacilo, egg of the lark, Sunil said.

For real, Doc, Fire asked.

Sunil explained that each beast in a Nguni herd was an individual that carried its uniqueness in its color patterns, horn shapes, and gender, which bestowed on it a status and even a history. With the respect accorded to family, the cows were classified according to what symbols or landscapes the color patterns of their hides resembled. And while the monikers were used primarily for identification, this system of naming was part of a highly sophisticated philosophical worldview.

This one, Sunil continued, is Insingizisuka, the ground

hornbill takes to flight. These ones here probably have a compound name, Sunil added, pointing to a group of cows under a thornbush tree. Izinkonwazi Ezikhula Zemithi, I would guess. It means the cows which are the gaps between the branches of the trees silhouetted against the sky. And this one is Inkomo Ebafazibewela Umfula, the women crossing the river.

You're making that last one up, Fire said, laughing.

No, I'm not. See here? It's because the cow has white legs and belly and a colored body with this wavy line here separating them. The wavy line looks like water lapping the legs, see?

And all the cows are named, Fire asked. Strange, don't you think, that the Zulus were so good at classification, and then the Boers came along and used it against them.

Sunil shook his head. It was too much to consider. All empire is about classification, he said. For the Zulu it was cattle, for the Boers, it was blacks. The Boers perverted everything.

They had help, Fire said.

Sunil turned his attention back to the photographs. With his index finger he traced the horns of one of the cattle.

There is a whole other nomenclature associated with horn shapes, he said.

Yeah, Fire asked.

There is a beautiful saying that refers to the first light of dawn that makes me think about cattle horns silhouetted against the byre sky. Kusempondozankomo, I think it is, which means the time of the horns of the cattle, Sunil said.

What's that one called, Fire asked.

That one is called Umndlovu, the elephant, because its horns are curved down straight like the trunk of an elephant. I can't really release you if I don't think there is someone who I trust to vouch for you. I need you to tell me how to find Fred.

You're not going to release us anyway, Doc, Fire said. Why would you when you can keep us here and study us? Now, tell me more about the cows.

I think that's enough for now, he said.

Are we ever going to get that phone call, Fire asked.

I'll call a nurse and I will come by later this evening to check on you.

Twenty-seven

Salazar pulled across the wood, the sharp wood plane shaving a slight curl that fluttered to the ground. He ran his finger over the grain and, satisfied, put the wood plane down. Light balsa wood showed through, contrasted by the walnut stain around it. Salazar had been building boats for almost twenty years, and this one, a replica of a seventeenth-century Spanish war galleon, for about two years.

He'd built them since his first kill on the job: Jim, a junkie kid.

Jim had been something of an institution in the Fremont section of town, and cops were always called out to handle him. He was basically harmless, Sergeant Vines, Salazar's partner and ten-year veteran of the force, always told him. But then they'd been called out because Jim was wielding a knife and threatening a homeless woman.

Following procedure, Salazar trained his gun on the kid, while Vines, a Vietnam vet who loved to chew on cheroots and was plainspoken, tried to talk Jim down.

Now, son, put down the knife.

Stay back! Jim shouted. I'm warning you.

What's happening, son? You know you don't want to hurt anyone, Vines said.

Stay back!

See that man over there with a gun, Vines said. That's my partner, fresh out of the academy. I don't want him to shoot you, but right now he's more scared than you are.

Jim lowered the weapon, then suddenly lurched forward. It was unclear if he meant to lunge or if he had merely felt his legs giving way, but Salazar panicked and squeezed off a shot. The 9mm slug slammed Jim against the wall behind him before he dropped. People seldom die in real life the way they do on TV, and Salazar watched Jim writhe for a long time, bleeding out. When the paramedics arrived, it was too late.

Hell of a fighter, Vines said. As messed up as he was you'd think he would've died sooner.

Yeah, Salazar mumbled.

Sorry, rookie, hell of a first week. Listen, there'll be a board of inquiry to determine if it was a good shooting. Don't worry, you'll be fine, just don't say anything without a union rep present.

Okay.

Good. They'll also want you to see the department shrink, who'll try and get you to talk about your feelings.

A shrink?

Don't worry. It's procedure. Just do it.

Okay.

That won't help you much, you know?

How do you know?

Stop asking questions, rookie, and listen.

Sure, yeah.

More than likely, you'll start drinking a lot to calm yourself, and then you'll get the shakes every time you draw your weapon, so you'll drink some more to control those shakes, and then your hands will shake some more and you'll either kill someone else or you'll get killed. Either way, it's no good.

Jesus, Salazar said. Internal Affairs hadn't even arrived on the scene yet to determine if it was a clean shoot. Everything was moving too fast.

Vines said: The thing that will save you is finding something that you used to love as a kid, something that involves your hands and labor and time. You understand? And I don't mean masturbation. Find the thing. I don't care what some newfangled shrink theory says; building things has saved generations of American male souls.

A few months after the shooting, waking up drunk, Salazar decided to take Vines's advice. He dug deep for the redemption Vines promised would be there and a memory of sailing toy ships in the park with his dad, Elian, came to him. Elian Salazar had been a fisherman in Cuba, but in Miami he worked twelve-hour days stacking boxes. When he could, he would escape to the park with young Joey Salazar, sail toy boats, and regale him with stories about storms off the coast of Cuba that washed up sea serpents and mermaids. His father drank too, and when he did, he was liberal with his fists. Those moments by the small pond in the park, their boats competing with the ducks, were some of the happiest for Salazar.

His first attempt was a lucky accident. As he felt the sharp edge of the wood plane catch and shave the first sliver off, he surrendered to his rage and shaved and shaved, feeling all the fear and self-loathing fall away in soft wooden curls that littered the floor of the garage like the locks of a blond Pinocchio. What he was left with was barely big enough to make a two-inch rowboat out of. But he worked hard and finished it with an exactness that slowly brought peace. A few days later he presented it to Sergeant Vines, who looked at it with something approaching awe as he moved the one-inch oar about.

I see you found your therapy, he said.

Salazar followed that first dinghy with a fleet of craft—slopes, canoes, sailboats, and yachts. Most of them were arranged in display cases around the garage. A few he gave away to friends and to kids at the local hospital at Christmas. Only rarely did he ever put any of his boats or ships into actual water.

The first time had been to honor the junkie he'd shot: a kind of warrior's send-off. For that, Salazar had driven out to Lake Henderson, where he'd placed the second boat he built on the water, drenched it in lighter fluid, and set it on fire. He watched it sail away until it burned to nothing twenty feet from the shore. Since then he'd built only five craft that had touched water, five for the five people he'd shot over his twenty-year career. It was an unusually high number, but over time Salazar had come to wear his kills with an odd kind of honor.

This new ship, the Spanish galleon, had been ongoing for two years, the longest it had taken him to build a ship. Destined for the water—not in honor of any of his victims, but rather for the girl whose murder he'd been unable to solve—it was growing more ornate. It measured four feet from stern to bow and it had eight sails, twelve cannons, three decks, and real stained glass for the windows of the captain's quarters. It was essentially finished, but since he hadn't solved the case, he couldn't let it go. Then yesterday he began what he realized was the final touch, a masthead, nearly a foot long: a siren with the face of the dead girl. It was a cool evening and Salazar was sanding down the siren, wondering what colors he would paint her.

Vines had dropped by earlier. Long retired, he spent his days playing golf and his nights gambling in the casinos off the Strip where the locals went.

Vines took in the muddy black shoes in the corner. Been fishing, he asked.

Salazar followed Vines's gaze and shook his head. I've been out by Lake Mead searching for shallow graves. Fucking muddy and shitty work.

Still fucking around with that case?

The killings started again, Salazar said, catching Vines up, telling him about the twins, Sunil, and his frustration.

Aha, well, at least you've got the divers, Vines said. They find anything yet?

No, and they left this afternoon.

Shit, so you have no help?

Not even a partner, Salazar said.

No partner? That's just what the department does as you get close to retiring.

It's not that, Salazar said.

Shit, I was just trying to be nice. You know, maybe no one can put up with you since I left.

Fuck you, Salazar said, laughing. I do have some help though.

The shrink.

Yeah, the shrink.

That's all well and good, but don't get lost in all that profiling shit, Vines said. Good police work is about following the small details diligently. Don't forget who taught you that.

In your fucking dreams.

Any good leads?

No.

Vines walked around the workbench in the middle of the garage. Ever notice how a ship kind of looks like a coffin, he asked. Square at one end, tapered at the other. This one's about the size of a child's coffin, he said.

A fly alighted on the ship. Salazar flicked at it. Aren't you late for senior discount at the casinos, he asked.

Fuck yeah, Vines said, glancing at his watch. At the door he paused and, looking back, he said: Burn this one quick, rookie, and move on.

The moon was full and yellow as Salazar walked Vines to his car. Harvest moon.

Twenty-eight

You look like shit, Sunil said to Salazar.

Salazar, unshowered, unchanged, unshaven, sporting blood-shot eyes and nursing a cup of coffee, stared at himself in the reflective glass of the casino door. Yeah, he said. Well, you're no fucking beauty queen yourself.

When his cell phone rang thirty minutes before, Sunil had just walked into his apartment and was quite looking forward to some downtime with a beer and basketball on TV. Salazar wanted Sunil to meet him at Fremont Street in front of the Golden Nugget. Immediately. Salazar sounded so like a B-movie gangster, Sunil was tempted to laugh. But there he was, meeting a surly Salazar and wondering to himself how much neon there was in this city. Now, that was a question he was sure Water had an answer for.

See those kids over there, Salazar asked, pointing to a group of kids lounging in the middle of the covered pedestrian walkway that sheltered this part of Fremont. They were sprawled across a white bench reflecting the crazy video projections on the roof of the walkway, eating hamburgers and sipping noisily on drinks. You remember that text you sent me about Fred, Salazar said.

Yeah, did you find anything on her?

No, no record, nothing in the system, not even a social security number.

Then why am I here?

Well, I figured if you were looking for a freak lover with a sideshow, where better to start than with the freaks themselves.

And you need me for what?

Freaks are your thing. Besides, I don't have a partner so you're it.

Who are these kids?

Street kids. I try to watch out for them and they in turn keep me informed on things I want to know. They're kind of like CIs.

Hey guys, Salazar said to the kids. This is Dr. Singh. Dr. Singh, meet the gang. This is Horny Nick, he said, pointing to a teenager with star-shaped horns implanted in his forehead.

Coral probably, Sunil thought. With time it would fuse to look like real bone. They were disturbing but beautiful. When Nick smiled, Sunil could see that his teeth had been filed to points and he was sporting two-inch-long fingernails painted black.

And this, Salazar said, pointing, is Annie.

Annie took off her sunglasses and tucked them over her hair, revealing pointed ears, like an elf or a Vulcan. She ran her tongue over her lips and Sunil saw it had been split down the middle, but it was her eyes that transfixed him. Her sclera were a deep purple and her pupils a royal blue. There were two other teenagers with Annie and Horny Nick, a boy and another girl, and although their entire bodies, faces included, were covered with tattoos and piercings, they looked normal in comparison.

These two delinquents here are Peggy and Petrol, Salazar said.

Sunil nodded. Salazar thinks you might know someone we're looking for, he said. He reached into his back pocket and took out a photo of Fire and Water. The kids studied the photo for a while before passing it around. Sunil watched their eyes, noticing shifts in expression, but it was only Annie who said: a real freak! She sounded envious.

We haven't seen them, Petrol said, passing the photo back almost reluctantly.

Who else might have seen them? Where would they go, Salazar asked.

You should ask Fred, Annie said. Fred knows everything.

The others glared at her and Sunil caught the look.

I'm not a policeman, he said. I'm a doctor. I don't want to harm Fred. I just want to talk to her. In fact, Sunil said, pointing to Water in the photo, this one says he is in love with Fred.

The kids laughed.

Everyone is in love with Fred, they said, almost in unison.

Where can we find this fucking Fred person, Salazar asked.

The kids looked away.

Please, Sunil said.

She lives out in Troubadour, Horny Nick said.

The ghost town, Sunil asked.

Fred doesn't like uninvited guests, Petrol said.

Here, Sunil said, digging into his pocket and passing a twenty-dollar bill over to Peggy.

As she took it she leaned into him. Be careful, she whispered. Someone is following you.

Why would anyone follow me, he asked.

How the fuck should I know, she said. But I'm never wrong.

As they walked away, Salazar turned to Sunil. What was all that about, he asked.

She thinks I'm being followed, Sunil said.

Do you think you're being followed?

No. Why would anyone follow me?

Salazar looked Sunil over for a minute, then said: Listen, is the ghost town far from here?

Yes, a couple of hours.

When do we leave?

Why don't we go tomorrow morning? Come by my place about nine a.m. You're driving, by the way.

What's your address?

Like you don't know, Detective.

As Sunil drove home, he kept glancing in his rearview mirror. Two cars behind him, Eskia smiled.

Twenty-nine

In this dream, Selah is an angel oak and all her leaves are yellow, a bright yellow like the soft down on a chick and irradiated by sunlight so the very air, the sky, is all yellow.

The tree is in a field of yellow shrubs: a yellow sky, a yellow field, and a yellow tree. The only things that are not yellow are the black limbs of the tree.

Water stands in the soft down of the shrubs and looks up at the tree. Selah, he says, crying, Selah.

The yellow tree shakes in a sudden wind until it is stripped of leaves, of everything. Now Water is standing in a brown field next to a small cabin leaning drunkenly.

Selah, he calls again, Selah.

Where is your brother, the tree asks.

Water looks down to his side and Fire is gone. He runs his hands down his sides and he is healed, his skin unmarked.

I don't know, he says, his voice heavy with awe. What does this mean, Mother?

The tree turns white. A rude tree in a field of green and white and in the distance the white shrubs. Water looks around, confused.

Where am I, he asks no one, because there is no one to ask.

And the sky grows dark and brooding like a storm was coming, but there is a purity to the tree, to it all.

Selah, he calls one last time to the tree.

There is nothing but the searing whiteness everywhere.

Wake up, Water.

When he opened his eyes, a nurse was standing over him in the glare of the fluorescent overhead lights.

Time for your medication, the nurse said.

Water took the pill and swallowed it, then lay back, his breath shallow and ragged. Beside him, wrapped in the smoothness of his caul, Fire snored.

BUTTER-
FLIES

The sign outside painted in uneven lettering on a piece of plywood read: GOGO'S CURIO AND BOOKSHOP. Run by Gogo, a shriveled old woman who could have been colored or Indian or even a sunburned Boer, it was a place where people from different races overlapped without worrying about the authorities. Perhaps it was Gogo's racial ambiguity, or her reputation as a fierce witch with so much muthi that even the police were unwilling to come up against her; whatever the reason, Gogo's curio shop was probably the most liminal place in all of Jozi, sitting as it did in a dead zone between the Wits University campus and the Fort. The wall facing the street was covered in a colorful mural, and a ditch and a fence hid the entrance, which was down an alley.

Her customers included university students, interracial lovers hiding from anti-miscegenation laws, sangomas, curio hunters, rare-book collectors, and more. It seemed sometimes to Sunil that all the misfits in Jozi met up there.

He had been coming to Gogo's since he stumbled on the store as a sixteen-year-old and Gogo had given him a torn paperback copy of *Tropic of Cancer*. He came because he imagined his parents must have met in a place like this. Gogo's always smelled of frankincense, which she kept burning on coals in a small black cauldron behind the counter.

Keeps the customers honest, she said to Sunil once with a wink. Besides, it smells like church, holy and mysterious.

He had to agree. Seen through the thin haze of smoke, everything looked mysterious. The mummified animals; the mummified human hand and head; the strangely formed rocks; animal pelts and skins; freshly killed owls; bones; dried herbs; the books—stacked everywhere; and strange jewelry from Tibet (malas and turquoise rings)—amber with insect fossils, and rings and necklaces with butterfly wing fragments encased in resin.

It was the last place Sunil expected to meet Jan. He'd never seen her at the bookstore. She looked up at him when they both reached for the same book. They each knew the risk of it, in those days, but that only made it more exciting; and during a conversation on the amazing hummingbird moth, held over the book neither would let go of, she touched his hand and asked if he would like to go back to her place. Her forwardness both attracted and frightened him.

Her small flat was made smaller by the glass cases and frames that covered every surface: walls, tabletops, couch, the dining chairs, and the floor.

Come in, she said, walking in and dropping her handbag in the middle of the rubble. He followed somewhat timidly, fighting a strong urge to tidy up. Jan grabbed mugs from the draining board in the kitchen, poured wine from a half-empty bottle, and handed him a mug.

Cheers, she said, clinking. Well, it's not much, but it's all mine.

Quite, yes, Sunil said, thinking the untidy mess of her apartment didn't match the somewhat severe Jan of the classroom. But then, that wasn't uncommon among white South Africans. It was common knowledge that most led a double life. What was shown in public was a repressed, conformist, and exaggerated morality. But the home life was completely different, revealing everything from messiness to deviant sexual behavior. A double life, however, was a privilege no blacks had because while whites were safe from scrutiny behind their front doors, blacks were always under scrutiny.

Come see this, Jan said, and sat at her kitchen table, bent over a butterfly she placed carefully under a microscope. Come see, she said. He shook his head and sipped the cheap wine. Watching her, he'd loved that she could get lost so easily in her study. He thought it a wonderful thing to sort and label whole species, to mount them behind glass as proof of certainty. She smiled up at him and he smiled back, wondering in that moment if what Lacan said was true: that loving someone else is impossible. That all we love is the space between our own desires—to be seen and to be wanted. It wasn't unusual, he supposed, that as a psychiatrist-in-training he would think of Lacan when he thought of love, but he did find it irksome the way his mind seemed to get between him and his body, between him and the world. He imagined it was different for Jan. She seemed to have a more visceral engagement with things when she was in her own world.

And he knew her power, her raw power, when she got up from the table and came to him covered in the tinsel from the butterfly's wings—iridescent and multicolored. Knew from the way she moaned when they made love later that night, from the way she got out of bed and ran into the cold kitchen to get something to eat because sex made her hungry. Knew from the way she bit into a pear and closed her eyes for a second as though tasting it for the first time. For him it was secondhand always, the facsimile of the experience.

That night passed in a blur of sex and sleep, and he woke to a proliferation of color and wings, and in that cold morning light irradiated with butterflies, he felt an ache unlike anything else before or after. He knew then as he watched her sleep that he would leave and never come back. If he stayed, his life would never be the same. The mystery of it, the danger of its change, also carried with it the terror of healing. He wasn't ready for that. The ache he felt could never be filled, not by her, not by anybody. He knew enough to know that if he stayed, she would become the scab over a deeper wound that he would pick and pick until there was nothing. Before she woke, he left.

That day he went to Gogo's and bought a beautiful men's signet ring in silver with a Blue Mormon wing fragment in a clear mount. Beautiful, it was more than he could afford. When Gogo found out it was for a girl, she slipped it onto a silver chain.

For her neck, she said. Strange gift for a girl, but she will never forget it. Bound to make an impression, she added.

The next day in class, he sat next to her. She ignored him at first, but then he placed the unusual gift on top of her red Bible, blue on red, and she blushed and smiled, her hand coming to rest on it.

For me?

Yes.

Thank you, she said.

But before class was over, he left, and a week later he was on a plane to Holland on a government educational exchange program. While he was away, he found out through an old acquaintance that Jan and Eskia became an item, that they even dropped out of school to be together. He would not see Jan again until Vlakplaas.

SUNDAY

Thirty

The sunlight was filtered to a muted blue by the stained glass of the kitchen window. It was the only room in the house that had only one window—high up and small, like the opening in a monk's cell.

Asia paused in front of the fridge, her reflection catching her by surprise. Long black hair, full lips still stained a little red from last night's lipstick, a long lean neck, and a body taut from dancing. The pristine steel of the fridge door bothered her, and before she opened it to take out the eggs she made sure to smudge it a bit with her fingertips.

Normally Asia would be turning in after a long night. The only other time she was up this early was when she'd slept over with a client who'd paid for the whole night. Then she would wake and sneak off, unless of course there was breakfast. But everything was different when it came to Sunil. Even the money he still left in the Bible for her was now a mere formality for her. She took it and paid it into a bank account that she never touched. She only took it because it allowed her to maintain a certain distance to protect her heart. He'd called her late and asked her over, and even though he was a client she'd spent the night with, she was up making him breakfast. She never made breakfast for herself.

But there was something so ordinary and everyday about cooking for a loved one that left her breathless with anticipation. Coffee percolating in the pot, made from fresh, rough-ground beans and distilled water; toast burning slowly, held down twice·in the toaster because he loved to scrape the burned crumbs off with a knife, the sound like metal on wood; and scrambled egg whites; and for her, a quartered grapefruit and green tea with honey.

It was like a curtain being pulled back on a magic show. The quotidian nature of other people's lives was fascinating to her. She had grown up in the cold, crowded squash of Chicago and had loved nothing more than riding the train, staring into the lit windows of other people's lives trying to read something about them from those brief glimpses. She came to believe that those lives were better than hers, the tease of those windows proof of the fact. Breakfast was just one of the ways she pursued the lives hidden from her.

And what might make a person desire another's life so much? Someone perhaps whose real name was Adele Kaczynski, a biracial woman born on the east side who turned out darker than her white mother could live with, and was left on the steps of the Northwestern Teaching Hospital. Someone who had grown up on the South Side moving from foster home to foster home. Someone who fell in love with her last foster father and who began dancing in strip clubs at sixteen to pay for his drug habit and who finally left him and fled to Las Vegas to pursue her dream of becoming a real dancer. Someone who changed her name first to Egypt, then Nile, before deciding they were too common, finally settling on Asia; maybe that kind of person.

She had a couple of dance auditions in the afternoon for some new shows that would open in the New Year that she was excited about. It was tough competition, though, and with each year it got tougher as she got older and her competition grew younger, a ridiculous thing for a twenty-six-year-old to be worried about, but this was Vegas.

Landing a role in a show like *Zumanity* would mean she could give up prostitution. It was possible to make fifty, sometimes sixty thousand a year in a show like that, minus tips. Perhaps then she could give in to Sunil, give in to her own feelings. But until then, there was breakfast.

When she'd first shared her dream with Sunil, about dancing in a big show, he'd asked: Why not just dance in one of the strip clubs until then? That way you can give up prostitution. She'd never told him about her past, but that didn't make it hurt any less. Sunil's impression of her was the only one she cared about, and the fact that he thought she was a prostitute through some thoughtless action on her part felt unbearable. She wanted to tell him all of this. Instead she'd said: What would we have if I weren't a prostitute? And although she'd been happy to see the look of shame cross his face, she regretted saying it.

Today there would be no real fight, just the pretense of one, the kind that added to her fantasy of domestic ordinariness. Things like—I wish you'd take your head out of your paper and look at me once in a while. Or—Why do you always leave burned toast crumbs in the butter? Or—That's way too much milk. You should watch your cholesterol. And he would reply in safe, predictable ways. That kind of fight turned her on and she would make sure she got one this morning.

Hey, he said, kissing her on the cheek before reaching for a cup and pouring some coffee—black, two Equals. The casual manner of that peck on her cheek turned her on, made her sticky and breathless. He sat at the table and turned on his Kindle to read the *New York Times*.

Sleep well, she asked, pouring the whipped egg whites into the melted butter in the pan.

Not really, he said, sipping loudly on the hot coffee. You?

I always sleep well when you hold me, she said. But the muttered words seemed stirred into the sizzling contents of the pan, drowned by the scraping of the plastic spatula on the Teflon.

He looked up briefly and then returned to the *Times*. The little electronic pad wasn't the same as actual paper, but it was just as good in different ways.

Eat while it's hot, she said. She put the eggs onto a plate, laid the toast next to it, and gave it to him.

Thank you, he said, scraping the toast slowly. The black granules of burned bread gathered in a small pile in the corner of his plate. A few black crumbs missed the pile and flecked his eggs like pepper.

She had her back to him, cutting the grapefruit, releasing a zest of citrus into the kitchen. The sun was higher now and the earlier deep-blue light was now much lighter. He studied her. Every movement she made seemed calculated—no, not calculated, deliberate. As though she was in total control of every muscle in her body.

What, she asked, blushing as she turned into his gaze. She placed the bowl of grapefruit on the table opposite him and sat. There was something in your look, she said.

There was, he asked, looking up from his toast.

Yes, she insisted, spoon poised like a snake ready to strike. He thought he'd never seen her look so beautiful. The whistle of the kettle reprieved him.

Well, she asked, and dunked a bag of green tea in the hot water. The mist reached in a thin column for her face as though in caress. He watched intently, and while part of him wanted to smile, the other felt lost. He had never felt less certain about anything than he did now. The last few days had proved unsettling. In the early years of his internship in Europe he'd had a stint as a family counselor and he always asked his clients what kind of animal their relationship would be, if it were an animal. Now he found himself thinking the same thing about him and Asia. A startled colt came to mind, a colt trying to find its way out of a paddock on a cold winter day. At once terrified and thrilled by the moment and all that it had to offer.

I don't know what you mean, he said, and his voice trailed off as he shoved some toast into his mouth.

In any other context she would have left the comment where he had, dangling. But this was breakfast and she had made it and it was, well, it was different. This was what couples did, she thought. Fought over nothing.

It sounds like there's something, she said.

He shoveled the last of the eggs into his mouth, swallowed some coffee. Asia always made him feel this way. Like he had done something wrong, like if he wasn't careful, he would break this thing between them. He wanted to tell her he loved her. But she knew that. He wanted to have a different life, but he couldn't articulate what that would be. So he said nothing, gazing into his coffee with resolve. The cup was almost empty, but he didn't think it was a good time to push back from the table and get some more.

You say you love me, but you keep things from me, she said.

This was getting ridiculous. Might as well get more coffee, he thought, standing.

This was such a nice breakfast, she said. Her grapefruit sat untouched, the cooling green tea clutched in her fist.

I love breakfast with you, he said, pouring coffee into his cup. He returned to the table, where he stirred the fine white powder from the Equal packets into the dark cup. Some of the sweetener spilled around the cup. He thought it looked too much like top-grade heroin and wondered if that was what they used in the movies—all those scenes where actors heaped fingers of uncut heroin into their mouths to test the drug.

That much uncut heroin would probably kill a person, he'd said to Asia as they sat watching *The French Connection* one rainy Saturday. Shh, she'd said. It's just make-believe.

You're not eating, he said.

Not much of an appetite, she said, and stood up. At the sink she emptied the fruit down the garbage disposal and ran the tap. He wanted to tell her that the rinds would gum up the works, but the noisy whirring made it impossible and he thought it was probably just as well. He wasn't sure why they were fighting, not sure if it was just what he'd said or if there was something else, something he would never guess at. Psychiatry wasn't much use in a relationship.

She turned the garbage disposal off but left the tap running, playing her fingers through the water. With her back to him, Sunil couldn't see the small smile forming on her lips. She was ridiculously, unaccountably happy. She loved him, that was true, but she loved these moments more, where she got to play at being normal, fights and all. The way it felt in her body. Like an itch that released deliciously under a slow scratch.

Asia, he said. I'm sorry.

She was so happy, she thought she would cry. Don't be, she said. I'm just being foolish.

And then his cell phone rang. He looked at the display. It was Salazar calling to tell him he'd be late.

May I ask why, Sunil said.

Another batch of dead homeless men turned up at the city dump. I would ask you to come out, but it's just the same as all the other times.

Identical to two years ago, Sunil asked.

Sunil remembered the bodies. No particular order. No particular ritual. Just tipped out in an untidy pile. He hadn't been bothered by the fact of the bodies, by the putrefying smell of it all, everything turning to decay so quickly in the

Vegas heat. What had bothered him was deliberately misleading Salazar. He was there when Salazar found the girl, and for the briefest moment he felt bad. But he had lost so much himself that the deception was easy to live with.

Identical, Salazar said. I'll fetch you closer to ten or eleven. I'll bring road-trip food.

Sure, why not. If you're chewing, you can't be talking, Sunil said.

Charming, see you soon.

Sunil hung up.

Asia, watching intently over the brim of her teacup, was smiling.

What is it, he asked.

I was just thinking, she said.

Listen, I've got to go get ready. Stay as long as you like.

Do you have a photo album, she asked.

He paused at the door, surprised.

What?

A photo album, she repeated.

No, he said.

So you have no photos of your family?

Where is this coming from, he asked. I thought we weren't allowed to discuss family, your rules.

My family, she said, not yours. And a lady always reserves the right to change her mind. *Lady,* she repeated as he opened his mouth to say something.

No, he said. I don't have any photos of my family. I'm not really the family type.

Let's change that, she said.

What's gotten into you, he asked.

Come here, she said.

He came over and she hugged him. She lifted her phone and took a picture of them.

See?

It was cute, cheesy almost, like something a teenager would do. It surprised him to find that he liked it.

You're in a silly mood, he said, and walked to the bathroom.

The shower was already hot and the room steamy when she joined him.

I don't have a condom, he said.

Shh, she said.

Later as the water drummed over them, she said: Let's change the past. Let's do that.

Yes, he wanted to say, with something akin to abandon. Instead he soaped her back.

Thirty-one

Telephone poles lined the road like a girder of wood and wire. It seemed like they were all that kept the road in a near-straight line, desert falling away on each side. Salazar drove so fast the poles blurred alternately into one, then back into a row like a serial crucifixion, becoming more presence than fact, more blur than thing, lurking always at the edge of consciousness, but then quickly and conveniently forgotten. With each slight turn or sway in the black thread of road, the sun shifted, alternately blinding, alternately bathing everything in a halo. Rocks and hills rose out of the brown scrubland like ancestors birthed from myth. Sunil could see why deserts inspired both the belief in God and the call to seek Him here. Wasn't Jesus tempted in a desert such as this, forty days into a fast? And didn't the jinn inhabit the dark caverns of caves and sand dunes? And who wouldn't believe—especially lost or camped out here, in the time before this road and electric and telephone wires everywhere and cell phones and the noise of it all—that things were supernatural? He knew it made no rational sense, but he did believe in ghosts. Who wouldn't after what he had seen in the death camp at Vlakplaas?

All the nuclear explosions held in underground aquifers here pointed to how hollow the desert really was. Even before the bombs, there had been the endless mining expeditions during the gold rush. It was easy to see the traces on the surface—ghost towns littered the desert—but it seemed that subterranean Nevada was left to legend. These legends, of an earth populated by spirits, were so rampant that even Herbert Hoover, thirty-ninth U.S. president, himself a onetime Nevada hard-rock miner, had written about them.

Did you know that this place is rife with myth and history, Sunil said to Salazar, who was stuffing a handful of orange Cheetos into his mouth.

Nope, he said, spitting crumbs everywhere.

Dusting the shower of orange crumbs from his arm, Sunil continued. The moon landing is believed to have been faked somewhere here, he said.

Bullshit.

Well, you know it won't be the first hoax involving science and the moon, Sunil said. In 1835, Sir John Herschel, on the front page of the *New York Sun,* claimed to have found intelligent life on the moon. He described vast forests, seas, and lilac-colored pyramids, even herds of bison and blue unicorns.

Sounds like he could have a job out here designing hotels and themed attractions, Salazar said.

You see these telephone poles? They are only here because of lynching, Sunil said.

That's fucked up.

People usually are. When they were first introduced into neighborhoods, Americans hated the poles so much they chopped them down. Made the landscape ugly, they said. But when someone discovered they could lynch blacks in the middle of town using the poles, they really caught on. Doesn't hurt that they are shaped like crosses.

Do you think anyone was lynched on one of these poles?

Hard to say, although I doubt it. These haven't been here long enough. There is only one recorded lynching in Vegas history, which means there were probably less than a hundred actual ones. That's racist math for you. Still, the thought of driving under them is disturbing.

Yeah, fucked up. There was awe in Salazar's voice. Why do you like history so much if it always tells you that we're a race doomed and full of shit?

I keep hoping to find out that we aren't, Sunil said.

And are you guys in South Africa as fucked up as us?

At least, if not more, Sunil said.

Shit.

Yes, sir, shit.

The landscape alternated between sand and rocks, ghost buildings and dead-end exits and a barrenness that defied that particularly American notion of manifest destiny. They drove in silence for a while, each lost in thought. Sunil's mind turned to the myths of the Nevada desert and the twins.

Everything old and telling about the human past is always buried, always submerged, in earth, in water, in language, in culture, one overlapping the other. It seemed sometimes to Sunil that humans couldn't wait to escape the past, to escape from things no longer desired. Forgotten. Until a new genera-tion, their wounds sufficiently blunted by time, arrives on the scene to begin excavations.

He wondered what some future generation or even an alien culture of anthropologists and archaeologists would make of the current city of Las Vegas if it became lost under the desert long enough. Would it be read as the perfect Earth culture, its acme? With representatives from all over the world building what could only be described as embassies? Each casino no longer the bizarre facade it was but rather coming together as the true United Nations? Or would it be seen as the home of world religion, each casino a representation of one group or the other? The temples were already here—pyramids, sphinxes, lions, Roman ruins, statues of liberty, all sainted icons, and the famous searchlight on the Luxor some beacon to an indifferent god? It was not without precedence—many a bizarre and crazed cult of holy people had journeyed here to flower and then die in the anonymity of the desert, only the strong surviving, like the Mormons.

With the push westward, the link to the civilizing European force grew weaker, and it wasn't long before Las Vegas and her inhabitants developed a serious self-esteem problem. Nevada governors, businessmen, and newspapermen were all in search of a truth and an ancient mythology that would validate them, make them the cultural equal of the eastern United States, prove that this land and its recent arrivals weren't so raw, that there was an antiquity here to rival Europe.

And soon, submerged and subterranean cultures began to play a flirtatious hide-and-seek with the fevered men who so desperately wanted these myths to be true. Before Lake Mead flooded towns and even cities in the 1930s, drowning out the Mormons still lingering on the fringes of Mammon, ancient civilizations were found that would be lost again to the waters of that blue fractal—but not before they fueled the lunacy of the Cascadian theory of human evolution.

Captain Alan LeBaron, amateur archaeologist, who explored much of Nevada and Utah from 1912 to 1930, claimed that the human race began here. The evidence piled up. In 1912, LeBaron claimed to have found Egyptian hieroglyphs on a rock in Nevada that dated back to before the Egyptian civilization. In 1924, LeBaron discovered the hill of a thousand tombs, each tomb exactly two square feet and concealed under stones fitted without the use of mortar. Then Babylonian and Mesoamerican heliographs, ideographs, and glyphs were discovered. Then caves covered in Chinese script and the skull of a man believed to be seven feet tall and whose cheekbones clearly identified him as Chinese but whose hair proved he was of Caucasian origin.

And on and on it went, one discovery after the next; proof that human life and culture, of all races in fact, began here in

Cascadia and then spread to the rest of the globe. LeBaron contended that the colonization of America by whites was simply a result of the biological imperative to return to the land of their origins and reclaim it.

Sunil jerked back from his ruminations when Salazar pulled off the road into a gas station.

Are you all right? You looked lost there for a while, Salazar said, killing the engine.

I'm fine, Sunil said, yawning and stretching.

Salazar got out and headed for the convenience store. He returned with a new bag of junk food.

What have we got here, Sunil asked, opening the bag of food. There were more Cheetos, some Snickers, a bottle of water, a browning banana, a small Coke, and a fistful of Twinkies.

Wasn't sure what you wanted, so I got a bunch of stuff, Salazar said, backing out of the gas station and merging back onto the main road at seventy without a glance at his mirrors.

You drive like an Egyptian taxi driver, Sunil said.

I'm the police, Salazar said.

What's with all the junk food anyway, Sunil asked.

Great American road-trip tradition, Salazar said. You have to eat enough junk to gain a pound a mile.

But Twinkies?

What are you talking about? That's bona fide American grade-A cuisine. Guaranteed to survive a nuclear holocaust. Shit, have you even had one?

Yes, I have, and I must say it was one of the most disappointing moments of my grown life.

What the fuck? Come on, you're joking, right?

When I was a kid in Soweto, every comic book I read, from *Batman* to the *Silver Surfer,* all had amazing ads for Twinkies. It was sold literally as the food of superheroes. I could almost taste the creamy vanilla sinfulness of one of them. Oh my God, how I wanted one. I don't think I've ever wanted something as bad as that, except perhaps sea monkeys. I waited thirty years, until I got here. First thing I bought when I got off the plane was a Hostess Twinkie. I couldn't believe how awful they tasted! Like sugary petroleum jelly. I was so mad, so fucking mad.

Salazar laughed. If it's any consolation, they took us all in, he said.

Agh, man, you have no idea how disappointing it is to want something since you were a child so much you begin to develop a nostalgia for it, even when you've never had it. And then to finally eat it, and it's like a mouthful of rancid grease.

Easy there, Doctor. It's just a cake.

But it wasn't just a cake. Not to me.

What about the sea monkeys? Fare any better there?

Fuck no! Magical families of smiling creatures with nice faces and crowns that would perform underwater stunts for you and keep you entertained? A child's best friend, instant pets, all that shit. I sent off for them but all I got was a tank of dead brine shrimp.

Salazar was laughing so hard his eyes were watering.

Well, at least mine were alive, he said. But I can see how disappointing it might have been if you were expecting literal miniature underwater monkeys. You know what, Doctor? I'm going to buy you real live sea monkeys when we get back to town. Hand me a Twinkie, will you?

Thirty-two

Still daydreaming, Salazar asked Sunil.

They'd been driving for at least an hour in silence, punctuated only by the radio, which was on an easy rock station. It seemed to Sunil that he'd heard Boy George perform "Karma Chameleon" at least five times before Salazar shut the radio off to talk.

A little bit, Sunil said, sipping on some water.

We'll be coming up to another town soon, Methuselah, I think. We can stop there for lunch and gas up again for the return trip. Apparently this town is farther out than you thought. Ghost towns, Salazar said, his tone dismissive. Can't imagine why anyone would want to visit one, much less live out here in one.

It's the desert, I think, Sunil said. You have to admit there's something supernatural about it. For some people it's like falling down the rabbit hole. Besides, ghost towns are perfect places to be invisible in America, drop off the grid, so to speak. You can squat in a ghost town for a very long time if it's set back far enough from the road. You would have easy access to water, electricity, and good shade from the sun, and disguise from any overhead searches by plane or helicopter. I mean, there are roads, so you wouldn't have to build any new infrastructure. Hell, there are even enough farms within a day's hike to poach from.

A billboard flashed by announcing JESUS IS COMING. It wasn't that there was a billboard in the middle of the desert announcing Jesus's return that caught Sunil's attention as much as the fact that someone had spray painted LOOK BUSY under it.

Strange name for a town, Salazar said, pointing to a sign by an exit.

Sunil read it: KING OF PRUSSIA. Again, it wasn't the unusual name that surprised him as much as the fact that the exit looked blocked off with a sign that said NOT AN EXIT, and yet from where they were, it looked like a normal town spread out in desert-style adobe and wood-framed buildings. There was even an airstrip to one side of them.

I've always wondered what it would be like to live out here in a town like that, Salazar said.

This town, and many more like it, is part of something called the Nevada Test Site, Sunil said.

Where they exploded nuclear bombs back in the day?

Yes, but not just back in the day.

I'm forty and I have never seen the mushroom cloud from a nuclear explosion, so I would say yes, back in the day.

Of the fifteen hundred or so nuclear test explosions in Nevada, only three hundred were aboveground, so just because you've never seen one doesn't mean there haven't been any.

That's some Mulder and Scully shit you got going on. I never pegged you for a conspiracy nut.

I won't even dignify that with an answer.

In a couple of minutes the sign for Methuselah flashed by.

Well, here we are, Salazar said.

I for one would love to have a burger. Best thing about America is burgers and ketchup-soaked French fries and a cold drink, Sunil said.

Finally, something we can agree on.

They pulled into the lone gas station, one pump under an unsteady lean-to, and filled the tank. If there was an attendant, he was nowhere around.

Just off the road to their left was a paddock and couple of hungry horses standing listlessly around a trough full of rank water. One of the supports of the paddock was a bristlecone pine, all gnarled and twisted into a shape that belonged more in a nightmare than in the bright desert sun.

Odd tree, Salazar said, spitting.

Sunil wondered if that was some superstition or just bad manners.

It's a bristlecone, he said. Oldest living organisms on the planet, I think. In fact, there is a bristlecone pine somewhere in Nevada that is perhaps the world's oldest tree. It's over five thousand years old.

No shit.

The tree was named Methuselah. I wonder if that's what this town is named after. The location of the tree is a well-kept secret by the parks service, but maybe it's around here somewhere.

What's a Methuselah?

I figured you would know, being a Republican and quite possibly a hardline Christian.

Just tell me what the fuck it is, Salazar snapped.

It's the name of the oldest man to have lived, at least according to the Bible, Sunil said.

Bible's never wrong, Salazar said, walking over to the tree and peeing on it.

Is that some animal territory-marking ritual, Sunil asked.

Never seen a man pee on a tree before?

Sunil opened the door of the car and slid back in. There's a bar-cum-diner over there called Cupid's, he said. Let's see if we can find a burger to fall in love with.

Salazar shook himself at the tree, inspected his work, and, satisfied, zipped up and returned to the car.

Thirty-three

Eskia had been waiting two hours and was already irritated when Asia arrived at his hotel, a little breathless, at ten thirty.

Sorry, she said as he let her in. I had to be somewhere. As always she laid out the Bible. He hurriedly stuffed some bills into it and barely let her undress before taking her roughly, bending her over the edge of the bed. He came quickly and as she straightened her clothes, he said, I'm not done yet.

Multiple pops count as multiple visits, she said, pointing to the Bible and walking into the bathroom to freshen up.

He walked over to his wallet and grabbed some more bills, which he stuffed into the Bible. The first time he found the ritual cute, but now it angered him. He guessed that part of Sunil's attraction to this woman had to do with that Bible. That Asia was, in a way, a surrogate Jan. Even the Bible, that little detail, Sunil hadn't overlooked. It wasn't red, but one can't have everything, Eskia mused.

While she was gone, he thought about Jan. How brave, single-minded, and so stubbornly sure of her convictions she had been—enough to risk everything. Jan had turned away from her upbringing as a racist Afrikaner, from her training and job as a spy for the South African Security Services in deep cover in a liberal South African university, to become an informer for the ANC. Although Eskia wanted to believe it was Jan's love for him that turned her, he knew it wasn't. The tipping point came the day she opened her father's Bible. Eskia was there, saw her turn pale and let the book fall to the ground. He bent to pick it up and saw that her father had crossed out the handwritten dedication from President Botha, scrawling in red capital letters across it, the word "LIAR." He saw the look that crossed her face, as if her entire universe was folding in on itself. There was a long moment when neither of them moved or spoke. They barely breathed. And then he let her kiss him. And make love to him.

Of course he fell, who can resist that kind of love, a love where you are needed desperately? Jan loved Eskia with a zeal he knew was driven by her fear of falling back into the old hate she'd been raised in. But in those dark times you took what comfort you could because in the end it was all grace.

Jan's ring, which Eskia now wore on his thumb, was now the shape of his heart, hot and weighty with despair. It was all he had left of her. He lost track of Jan when she got arrested. She was gone long enough to accept, even beyond his verbal denials, that she was dead. In a way, his search, when it began, was not to find her, but rather to let her go properly. Working in the new government's security services was a great help. That's how he found out about the bodies turning up around the farm at Vlakplaas, and some in the river, too.

He had a hard time finding Vlakplaas. Trauma messes with recollection; things that never existed become part of your memory of a place, and the very things that are absolutely vital to remembering are erased. He got lost several times, stopping always to ask for directions, careful to choose only blacks or coloreds or Indians because it seemed like whites would never tell him how to get there. But everyone pretended they had never heard of it. The most feared place in South Africa, and people who were mere miles from it couldn't remember where it was, or how to get there.

When Eskia finally found the farm, there was a white Afrikaans family, with very young children, living there. How was it possible? Everyone knew what had happened there. The bars on the windows, bloodstains on the guardhouse, faded but still visible. All of it still there and these people bought it to grow food on? Brought children to live there?

He saw them, a couple of slight girls, blond and sprightly, swimming in that river that had held so many rotting bodies. It was unnatural, and perhaps that was worse even than what had really gone on there.

Farther back from the edges of the farm, up in the hills, a small group was digging for bodies, like people prospecting for treasure. They moved across the stubby grass of the hills, in bright red or black, prodding the ground with converted ski poles or sharpened sticks, feeling always for a looseness, a hollowness in the red earth, for a hint. The figures would straighten up, heads cocked into the wind, listening as though hearing their names. A couple would stop while the others moved on. Engaged in some beautiful ballet only they understood. Moving forward, slowly, but always forward. Leaving a legacy of holes behind them.

Eskia approached and greeted them softly in Zulu, Sawbona. They paused and looked up and that was when he realized they were mostly women. They smiled and returned to their digging, stopping only when they unearthed a body, or bones, or whatever fragment of a person they found. Then they lifted the remains reverentially out of the ground and laid them on a white plastic sheet, awaiting identification. There was a tenderness in this scene, the sheer sorrow that stills anger into a river of serenity, into a clarity so cold its brittleness is more threatening, quivering before shattering into a rage that can obliterate.

He sat on an outcrop of stone and took deep breaths, noticing for the first time the small crowd of people walking between the excavators, pausing by each set of remains, looking for something to identify a loved one, something as small as a tuft of hair or a birthmark. When someone was identified, there was a silence as the remains were gathered and carried back down the hill, past the farm to the road where cars were parked, as though any sound—a cry, a wail—would desecrate the delicate balance the excavators worked with.

Eskia came regularly for six years, joining the silent search, until he found, among a pile of bones, Jan's ring, with the shimmering butterfly wing. Unlike the others, he took no remains, just the ring. There would be no mourning for him, no grieving. Just a vain hate, one that had no target, no focus, until he found, on a list of names of Vlakplaas personnel, Dr. Sunil Singh.

Asia came back into the room, startling him. With the practiced ease of a croupier, she counted the money in the Bible without seeming to look. She crossed to the middle of the room, stripped, and said: I'm ready.

He tied her to the bedposts with the belts from the hotel robes, and he fucked her until she cried out from an orgasm, then he dozed off beside her, only to awaken half an hour later with a scream.

Shh, she said, holding him with one arm, the other still tied.

Absently he wondered how she'd freed herself.

Are you okay, she asked.

Eskia gasped, coughing, the taste of rust on his tongue as he woke from the dream. It felt like he was back in it all.

Asia hugged Eskia from behind. Hush, she whispered, hush now.

Eskia leaned back into her, felt her full breasts pressed into his back. God, he thought, she smells so good.

Will it help to talk about it?

No, he said simply, no.

There was something in his voice that chilled Asia, made her want to recoil from him.

He reached behind him and ran his hand down her thigh, feeling her shiver. Are you cold, he asked.

Why?

He wanted to say, Because you're shivering. Instead he looked at her, noting the orgasm-softened face, her eyes tender in spite of herself, and said: What do you think Sunil would say if he knew his friend made you come?

She scuttled back from him abruptly; face shocked as though he'd slapped her, one wrist still bound. What the fuck, she said.

Precisely, he said.

Fuck you, Asia said. Fuck you!

You just did. Multiple pops, remember? Although since you also popped you should refund some of that money.

She spat at him and struggled to untie her other wrist.

Eskia wiped his face and looked at her for a moment. He opened his mouth as though to speak, but instead he punched her full in the face and her neck snapped back, her head hitting the headboard. He swung at her again, but she recovered quickly and moved so he only caught her a glancing blow to her eye. Still it puffed up shut.

She knocked the phone from the beside table, hit the concierge button, and screamed as loud as she could. Eskia stopped midpunch. He could hear the concierge's voice: Mr. Kent, is everything okay? Asia screamed again and passed out.

Eskia jumped up and dressed hurriedly. He had about three to five minutes before hotel security got to his room. Las Vegas casinos didn't fuck around with the security of their guests. Safety was imperative for business.

He grabbed his small bag stuffed with cash and passports and walked out leisurely, heading for the elevators. In his thick glasses, he was invisible, and he only had to step aside as security guards barreled past him in the hallway headed for his room. As he stepped into the elevator he wondered why all casino security guards wore red jackets.

Outside the casino, Eskia walked a sweat-fueled pilgrimage down the Strip. Down heat-melted sidewalks, gum-stained, dirty, littered with fliers for escorts and shows, through the crowd of overweight sunburned tourists, past the drunks and homeless, past the partly inebriated gambling veterans, ever south.

Thirty-four

Outsider art guarded the exterior of the bar—horses, dinosaurs, and aliens shaped in everything from scrap metal and wood to plastic, concrete, and plaster. Inside, bras in every color and every size—dirty, tattered, stained, and gray from age and wear—drooped down from the ceiling like tired flags. Even though they were higher than head level, Sunil kept ducking, afraid to find himself trailing through the years of sad, pathetic drunken moments the bras represented. A disproportioned Buddha, an odd creature neither frog nor toad, and rabbits with cold maniacal plaster eyes guarded the edges of the bar.

The walls inside were made of wood and every surface was covered with old coasters sporting beer logos. The floor was a mix of cork, sawdust, bare concrete, and fraying rugs. Where the roof sloped at the back into what looked like an anteroom, two decrepit and rickety pool tables sat, their racked balls gathering dust in the gloom. Behind the bar, bottles of liquor struggled for ascendancy. There were two taps—Budweiser and Heineken. A small pug-faced dog squatted on the bar top drinking milk from a saucer.

It seemed like everything inside, even the air, was coated with grime, determined dirt that nothing would ever clean. Sunil instinctively reached into his pocket for his handkerchief.

Put that away, Salazar said, settling onto one of the barstools. You're embarrassing me.

Sunil ignored him, dusting the barstool before sitting down.

The bar was far from full, but nowhere near empty. There were a few men and women littered around, drinking by themselves or with one another. Sunil guessed they were regulars.

Heineken for me, and whatever my friend is having, Salazar said to the barman.

Same, Sunil said.

We'll also take two burgers with fries, Salazar added.

The barman, a sour-faced man about fifty with long, stringy, greasy blond hair balding at the crown, a faded denim shirt, and jeans stiff with dirt, dipped some glasses in water, shook them out, and pulled a draft for each man without saying a word.

Listen, Salazar, Sunil said. I want to ask you something personal.

What?

Have you ever been married? Any kids? Do you have a girlfriend?

No to all three, Salazar said.

May I ask why?

We've known each other two years and we never had this conversation before. Odd. I don't do well with women. What about you?

No. I've never been married, but I do have a girlfriend of sorts, Sunil said.

A man, drinking by himself at a table in the corner, got up and walked over to them. He had the heavily muscled look of a recent ex-con and all the black spidery tattoos of prison.

We don't get many new faces around here, he said.

You trying to violate your parole, Salazar asked. Fuckers like you are always on parole.

The barman came back with two burgers and fries. Salazar

put a fry in his mouth, got up, and walked across the room to the jukebox. Selecting a Charley Pride record, he shoved some change in and came back to the bar. The music transported Sunil back to the shebeens of Soweto as he ate. Packed full of sweaty, desperate men and women drowning unspeakable sorrows in the homebrew so strong it could take your voice with one shot.

After White Alice left, Sunil picked up a job at a shebeen. It was owned by Johnny Ten-Ten's uncle Ben, and Ten-Ten arranged it for Sunil out of sympathy, and for Nurse Dorothy's sake, he said. Sunil went to school and came straight to work at the shebeen every day until about eight p.m., and then after a dinner of Bunny Chow with Uncle Ben, he went home to do his homework. The money from the bar helped him pay the rent and keep the house Dorothy had worked so hard for. He imagined she would get better and come home to live there with him. He was fourteen.

Three years passed like that. Sunil worked washing glasses, sweeping floors, and running errands. And then dinner with Uncle Ben, always Bunny Chow; he ate it so much he came to love it too—the way the lamb stew soaked its way through the hollow chamber of the loaf of bread. Bunny Chow and Cokes; he could have as many Cokes as he wanted, but no alcohol. Uncle Ben was strict about that.

Never drink this shit, Sunil, he would say, spitting through the holes where several teeth used to be. It will rot your liver, your brains, and your soul.

But you drink it, Sunil said.

So now you have proof of what I'm saying, Uncle Ben said, laughing.

Every day they played this game, and yet somehow Sunil never got tired of it.

One day, Ben asked Sunil to stay late and help him close up. Ben had never asked before, so Sunil stayed. He had never seen the bar this late. It looked different, felt empty, everything sounding hollow. The music was off, and what little sound there was, in the harsh lighting, was amplified: the swish of Sunil's broom across the floor, the grating of metal chairs being pulled across concrete and then stacked, the insistent buzzing of flies around pools of spilled beer and bits of food, the tap running as the metal cups were washed by Ben's wife, a dog in the distance barking to the ghosts of night, a Casspir rumbling by on patrol a few streets away.

But it was the two or three drunks who wouldn't leave who fascinated Sunil. They sat, heads hung over the dregs of their drinks, holding on to the metal mugs as though drowning. Several times Ben came out and asked them to leave. Still they sat as though afraid of the night and the silence beyond it.

It's like this every night, Ben said with a sigh. Usually Ten-Ten is here to get them out.

I'll get them out, Sunil said.

Ben nodded.

Two of the drunks left easily enough when Sunil pried them up and gently shoved them out into the dark street. The third, a regular he knew only as Red, was harder to get out. Sunil could barely pry his fingers off the metal mug, and his butt seemed glued to the chair. Red was a small man and Sunil couldn't figure out where he got the strength.

Please, Red begged. Please, it's too damn lonely out there, bruh. You can't send me out there.

Go home, please, we have to close, Sunil said.

No, no, you don't understand, Red begged. They come every night, every night they come and I can't, man, I can't. I know you're young, but surely you understand.

Go home, Red, Ben said from across the room. It's the same every night. Go home.

Who comes every night, Sunil asked. The police?

My wife, Red sobbed. My wife and my boy, they come every night.

Go home, Red, Ben said. The boy doesn't need your stories.

But he should hear them, Ben, then maybe he'll understand.

Go home, sir, Sunil said.

I only informed on a couple of undesirables, Red babbled. Only a couple of times on criminals we all hated. Then I tried to stop, I did. I told the police I was no longer informing for them. So they told the ANC boys about me and they took my wife and my son to teach me a lesson. They just took them. I wasn't there. I was here. I was here.

Go home, Red, Ben said again, this time crossing the room and pushing him gently to the door.

Where, Sunil asked. Where did they take them?

Red stood at the door of the shack, a bent shade of a man, bent even lower by the alcohol. He lifted a trembling finger and just pointed. Into the dark, man, into the night, he said.

Ben stepped up and gave him one last gentle but firm shove and shut the door. Finish up, he said to Sunil, and went back to the bar.

Finish up, Salazar said, nudging Sunil. We have to get back on the road.

Yeah, sorry, I was lost there for a moment, Sunil said.

Thirty-five

There was a quality to dusk that Sunil liked. There was something frenetic about it—a grouse disturbed from the brambles, or even a chicken with its brood struck by the shadow of a circling hawk. As though day, like Wile E. Coyote, had just run off the edge of a cliff and was winding his legs in space, desperately trying to keep moving before falling into night. But there was something else too, something besides the surprise. Something that had the quality of a dimly lit stage set just before the curtains rise on opening night. There was a rhythm to it, a beckoning, and a bittersweet tear in time.

Ruins too held that tear in time, that melancholic yearning, when detritus clings obstinately to a past that can no longer be and yet is unable to fall into the disintegration of a new thing. A lonely feeling.

They drove through the desert, lost and turned around, for a couple of hours. Finally they pulled up to the outskirts of Troubadour. Sunil and Salazar were tense from the many unspoken things that haunted them both.

They edged past houses blown apart by time and neglect, and others held together by the obstinate will of a rusting hinge dangling a window, or a door leaning drunkenly against a lintel, while in places roofs collapsed politely like deflated soufflés. Past weeds that grew tall from floors, past rusted and stripped cars that still hugged driveways and street corners with the dogged belief of a Jehovah's Witness awaiting the Rapture. They were both silent.

As the road they were on wound even farther away from the freeway, they rolled past a graveyard of signs—giant high-heeled pumps with CASINO printed on the side in pinks and garish purples, studded with holes where neon bulbs used to live; a blue-suited fat man with pince-nez glasses, ruddy cheeks, and a leering smile lying prone as though the giant doughnut in his hand had pulled him over; a rusting fair-ground ride with cracked teacups; a sign in chipped green glass with the legend CARLOS O'KELLY, AUTHENTIC IRISH MEXICAN FOOD under a shamrock from which a taco shell sprouted; a seven-foot-tall duckling mouth open in mid-squawk, wings spread wide, in a yellow so bright it hurt to look at, standing among a litter of dead trucks, like a bath toy thrown from a kraken's bathtub; MOTEL, HOTEL, GOLDEN, LAS VEGAS, EMPIRE, fragments of signs lost in the glossolalia; and the creepiest thing either man had seen, a twenty-foot-tall corpulent king who seemed a cross between Santa Claus and Henry VIII, beckoning with one hand, maniacal eyes wide open and crazed, lips curled back to reveal large white enameled and rusting teeth.

What the fuck, Salazar said as they drove by.

It's as if Vegas came here to die, Sunil said.

Well, I guess we are in the right place, Salazar said. Even the fucking art is about freaks.

The road veered right around a large rock, and when it opened up again, there was the town, spread out before them like a lingering death.

Fuck me, Salazar said.

Extending backward from Main Street was a town with a well-laid-out network of small streets, all lined by houses, or the remains of houses. A few tenacious trees hung around, but for the most part it was just desert chaparral. Some houses looked well maintained, even lived in, and several sprouted satellite dishes. Even from where they were, they could see an airstrip with a crashed plane covered in graffiti to one side. The faint sound of music came from the town, a solemn guitar strum and a plaintive voice. Salazar pulled to the side of the road under the WELCOME TO TROUBADOUR sign.

Do you hear that too, or is it just me?

I hear it, Sunil said. Why are we stopping?

I need a minute here. I mean, aren't you creeped out by this? Plus, it's getting dark.

All the more reason to press on and get out of here as soon as possible, Sunil said.

Okay, Salazar said, but he checked that his gun was loaded first.

Sunil smiled. It was always the loudmouths who were the cowards.

As they headed into town, the sky was an indescribable palette of colors that brought a lyrical tint to the reality below, so that the poverty appeared romantic, artistic, and chosen. It was an alchemy that made denial easy, an alchemy that Sunil was practiced in. How else could people live the way they did in South Africa when they were surrounded by the chaotic set designs of the townships and shanty towns that circled the hearts of cities like Johannesburg.

He was reminded for a moment of Eugene and his love for Dante and the circles of hell. He hated to admit it, but Eugene had been right in his choice of *Inferno,* except their interpretations differed. Where Eugene saw only the internal battle of the privileged soul, Sunil saw the entire architecture and structures of racism and apartheid: three concentric circles of life and economics. Color-coded circles for easy understanding, whites at the heart, coloreds at the next remove, and finally, the blacks at the outermost circle; the closest to hell—the strange inverse sense of apartheid.

All the banks, businesses, and shops of any merit were at

the heart of the circle. At one remove, the colored towns, a perfect ring of defense around the white heart. The coloreds were not white but overwhelmingly wanted to be, and even if it was not exactly white they wanted to be, they did want their privilege; and at least they were one up on the blacks. As in any free market, the coloreds were the middle classes, as it were—those who would give their lives to maintain the status quo, a life they knew they could never improve but which had meaning only because there were those who suffered worse; that in fact, a larger population suffered worse. Sunil knew of course that not all coloreds were middle class, but they could at least all dream and aspire to it. In the outer ring of hell, yet closer to the flames, in an orbit so cut off from the benevolence of the heart of apartheid, mired in a poverty they could never gain enough purchase to dream an escape from, were the blacks. And they had to bus into the heart every day to work for the whites, following only one or two access points, where they were policed and harassed to make sure they had the right passes and work papers. They spent 60 percent of their daily income on transportation alone, and since there were no legal supermarkets or shops in the third ring, they had to spend 20 to 30 of the remaining 40 percent on food in the white heart, or sometimes, and only sometimes, in the colored towns, where the prices were even higher but where there were more shops willing to take their money. Then they had to try to make it home from the heart, through the second ring that loved nothing more than to harass and degrade them, so that if they were lucky, they made it home with one-tenth of their income. Those who were more daring walked ten miles or more one way from Soweto to the outer rings of the second level and then rode buses in—a long column of ants carrying their misery on their heads wrapped with the workloads, trailing the side of the road, inhaling the dirt of the passing cars and the inclemency of the weather; all this to keep a tenth of the money they worked so hard for. And as they tried to make ends meet, the white heart grew wealthier and wealthier because almost none of the money ever left it; what spilled over, the second ring mopped up very quickly, long before it could even trickle out to the third.

While there were some rich and middle-class blacks in Soweto, they accounted for fewer than 3 percent of the township's entire population, a population larger than the neighboring country of Zimbabwe.

The crazy thing was, the blacks made up 90 percent of South Africa's population, which, as it turns out, the whites thought worked for them, because such a large population, kept so far removed from power and divided by hunger and fear, could never fully rise up in opposition. Turns out the whites were wrong. Sunil often thought about America and how the lie of the equality of material conditions would lead to big and violent rifts in the country. Time was the only variable in every equation of power and oppression—how long before the pot boiled over.

This variable of time is something those with power know well and learn to exploit with great measure. Sunil found from experience that the easiest way to do this was to corrupt slaves into tyrants, regardless of their race or imagined position. It worked well in South Africa, on the whites as well as on the blacks, because even though the whites thought they were free, they weren't. In America, too, the improvement of material circumstances, and the gentle padding of minimal power, could seduce even the most cynical citizen. For the blacks the reward was even less: more work than their contemporaries. But work that affords only the essentials, no matter how much better than your neighbors it makes you, can never lead to freedom.

Why are you so fucking quiet, Salazar asked. You're freaking me out.

They were at this point rolling down Main Street, speed cut to a crawl, looking out for signs of life. Even though most of the buildings were boarded up, some light came from the bar, the general store, and the pink building with the neon ANGEL'S LADIES sign. And then there was that music, the guitar and voice that seemed to be everywhere at once.

At least they've got the right businesses open, Sunil said. Food, liquor, and sex.

So?

So they can't be all that weird, Sunil said.

Amen to that, Salazar said, relaxing for the first time since they'd turned off the freeway.

They parked just a few doors away from the bar, by an abandoned diner. Sunil peered through the window. Eerily there were still place settings and coffee in the pot on the counter. It looked open, except for the film of dust over everything and the big rat on the counter next to the coffee-pot cleaning its paws.

Next door was the pink-painted bordello with the hissing neon sign, and Sunil wondered who Angel was, and why there was a bright-blue neon sign in a ghost town, five miles off a freeway. It wasn't like anyone new would wander by and see it, and everyone who knew about it didn't need the sign.

The bar was a low-slung building probably unchanged from when it was first built around the beginning of the last century. ROSE WALTER'S, a sign above it said. Sunil pulled the white door open and walked in, Salazar behind him. The place was empty, aside from the barman, who was older, with long unwashed hair and a tie-dyed rainbow shirt.

Welcome, name is Bob, he said. What can I fetch you gentlemen?

Sunil and Salazar settled at the bar.

Bob, you're shitting me, Salazar said.

You wouldn't happen to have any single-malt whiskey, would you, Sunil asked.

Sure do, Bob said, reaching under the counter and pulling out a bottle. He placed it before Sunil, fetched a rag, and wiped it clean of dust.

Sunil inspected it; good color, good odor. Fine sample, he said.

Bob laughed happily and poured generous amounts into three shot glasses. He toasted them and downed the whiskey, eyes watering. Sunil and Salazar drank it down too.

Really good, Sunil said, feeling the familiar warmth spread through him.

First one's on the house, gentlemen, Bob said.

Where the fuck is everyone, Salazar asked.

They'll be here. Some fly in from Vegas every night, land in the old airstrip where the crash is. Others come by bus and this place usually has about three thousand people by midnight, when the carnival starts. It's been good for us, that carnival.

What's the carnival called, Sunil asked.

Carnival of Lost Souls, Bob said.

Where can we find it, Salazar asked.

Just turn right by the whorehouse and follow the yellow brick road.

You're shitting me, Salazar said.

Ain't shitting you.

Fuck, Salazar said, getting up.

Sunil settled the tab.

The yellow brick road had no bricks, and it wasn't particularly yellow, either. It was just a cracked and pitted tar road with orange paint splattered carelessly over it in a thin film, as if someone had driven up and down holding a paint can from an open window, splashing the road. Perhaps that was what made it extraordinary, because there was no denying that it was. That, and also, perhaps, the sudden blaze of a patch of California poppies to the side, and the weeds that flung back from the road into the houses, their heads bent from a gentle breeze. At the end of the road was a bristlecone pine laden with decaying shoes, hundreds of them strung up like dark lanterns.

Under the tree stood a woman.

She was at least six-three, with very short hair, almost a buzz cut, and a body that was cut and rippling with muscle. She was holding a clipboard in one hand, and a walkie-talkie in the other.

Salazar pulled up under the tree and got out. Sunil followed.

You can't park here, Fred said, her voice deep and husky. Please follow the signs to the visitors' lot.

You must be Fred, Salazar said.

And you are?

Detective Salazar, and this is Dr. Singh.

Well, all our permits are in order and I don't recall calling the police.

And yet we are here to see you, Salazar said.

Has something happened?

Is there anywhere we can talk privately, Salazar asked.

Has something happened, Fred repeated.

We came a long way, Sunil chimed in.

Everyone who comes here does, Fred said, unimpressed.

We can talk here or back in Las Vegas, Salazar said.

Fred laughed. Does that ever work, Detective? I have to set up tonight's show. You're welcome to stay for it. Box office opens at nine. With that, Fred went back to giving instructions to someone over the walkie-talkie.

Sunil stepped forward. I'm sorry if we got off on the wrong foot, he said. We are here to talk to you about two of my patients. I believe they were performers in your carnival.

Fred shoved the walkie-talkie into her back pocket, where the bulge drew Salazar's eyes. She cut him a dirty look and then brought impatient eyes to bear on Sunil.

He suddenly felt breathless. Fire and Water, he said, more in a croak than anything.

King Kong, Salazar added.

King Kongo, she said to Salazar, then turned to Sunil: You have the twins. Thank God. I was worried about them. I haven't seen or heard from them in over two weeks. Yes, yes, by all means, let's talk.

With that she turned and trudged off across a small patch of grass, headed toward a blue Victorian wood house, alone at the edge of a rise. It was so blue; the color was like a shout in the gathering darkness.

She led them up some steps, through the front door, crossing a living room in a soft yellow, and out onto a back porch that was all red. Four Adirondack chairs sat there looking out over a sheer drop of about fifty feet. Below them, spread out across the floor of what was clearly an abandoned quarry, lit up like a scene from a fairy tale, was a carnival. But instead of the usual carney organ music, a young man sat in a wheelchair in the middle of everything, lit by a giant spotlight, playing a guitar and singing into an old-school microphone.

Welcome to the Carnival of Lost Souls, Fred said.

Thirty-six

Eskia stared at the Kentridge on Sunil's wall for a very long time. As he examined it from different angles, he smoked several cigarettes, taking pleasure in knowing that the smell would drive Sunil crazy. Eskia liked Kentridge, also Pieter Hugo. Their work was not invested in obscuring or blotting out the uncomfortable truths about apartheid.

He'd half expected to find Asia hiding out here, and wondered where she was. Normally he would be tracking her down; he hated to leave loose ends. But this was no normal case. He fully intended to kill Sunil on Monday and by Tuesday evening to be home in Johannesburg. Since he had no intentions of returning to the United States in the foreseeable future, she posed no real threat to him. He wouldn't admit it, not even to himself really, but he was glad not to kill her. Asia had something that got under your skin very quickly, and not just because she was beautiful and could do things sexually he never knew were possible. There was a vulnerability to her that brought out the protective instinct in men. In a way he understood Sunil's fascination with her; too bad it felt like such a fucking cliché.

He wandered into the kitchen to open the fridge and poked around. He popped the top on a beer and drank deeply, then set it down on the counter and checked the freezer and every other inch of the fridge for hiding places, shaking every can, every box, opening the yogurt and running his fingers inside, even pulling the shelving panel away from the door frame. Nothing.

The bedroom was next. Bed frame, mattress, behind every picture, chest of drawers, wardrobe, and light fixtures, ceiling: nothing.

Bathroom: medicine cabinet, toilet tank, sink plinth, bathtub. He banged against the tiled walls checking for hollow spaces, emptied out soap and shampoo containers, squirted toothpaste down the sink, checked the floor for hollow tiles, especially in the shower, then the ceiling, and the laundry basket: nothing.

Back in the kitchen, Eskia imagined all the places he would hide a hard drive. He needed Sunil's research. Killing him was personal, but the South African government would want Sunil's research on psychopaths. Where had that fucker hidden it? He wouldn't have it on him; that was too risky. Eskia had already gone over every inch of Sunil's office at the institute. It seemed Sunil kept only one copy of his work on a portable drive. It had to be in his home somewhere. There was no safe, that much Eskia already knew. By the time he left the kitchen for the living room, the microwave, the coffee machine, toaster, stovetop, oven, cupboards—everything—had been taken apart: still nothing.

There would be no time to put everything back together, to make it look like no one had been here, not even with a team of men. That only happened in the movies. The best thing to do was to leave the place looking like it had been burgled or vandalized. Difficult in a secure building like this, so he would have to hurry up so he could hit a couple more apartments, reduce the suspicion. He didn't want to spook Sunil before tomorrow. Being one of several apartments vandalized in a building was an unfortunate accident. If only his was robbed, it would be clear that it was deliberate. Glancing at his watch, he saw it was about five p.m.; Fred should still have them tied up out there in Troubadour.

From his spot on the couch, he stared at the Kentridge. It was a limited-edition print, numbered and signed. Surely Sunil wouldn't have hid it there. It would be a shame to destroy something as good as that. He lit another cigarette and took a deep drag. He decided to leave the Kentridge for last, and started in on the couch, pulling stuffing out of cushions and cutting into the frame fabric. Another myth was that an experienced person could guess where someone was likely to hide something. People were too different and irrational for that kind of prediction to work more than occasionally. Shit, Eskia muttered. It wasn't in the couch. Where the fuck was it? It had to be somewhere easily accessible since he took it to work and back home every day, but where?

He took a break to finish his beer, sitting amid the debris. Absently he tapped on a book while he smoked. Fuck, Sunil, he said out loud, are you really going to make me rip apart the Kentridge? Then he looked down at the book he'd been tapping: the Bible. Eskia laughed out loud, flipping the cover open. There in a perfect cutout sat the disk, in the one book most people wouldn't touch even if they happened to come upon it.

Really, Sunil, Eskia said to himself. You are depressingly romantic. He stood up and stubbed his cigarette out in the middle of the white coffee table. Now to pretend to rob a couple more apartments. He looked at his watch. It was six.

Thirty-seven

Sheila wondered if she should go over. It wasn't that late, not even seven. She had called Sunil several times already to check up on him, to see how he was taking the fact that the twins had their zoo MRI today. Three times, to be exact, she had called, and each time it went straight to his voice mail. She didn't know if that was too many times, perhaps even excessive enough to qualify as stalking. Sheila was a proud woman and yet with Sunil she found all that pride had eroded as she subtly (she hoped) tried to woo him. She wasn't very good at dating, and she had no girlfriends to call for advice. Working for the institute left little time for any relationships outside of work.

The thing is, she had been thinking of resigning from the institute for some time now. There were job offers across the world from universities who wanted her on faculty and although it would be a significant drop in salary, she didn't care. In fact, her trip to Cape Town was part holiday, part job interview at the University of Cape Town. From what she could tell from the photos of the place, it looked like the south of France. Not a bad place to spend the rest of your days, especially if you had the right person with you.

Fine, then. That was it. She was going over to Sunil's. Better people than her had made fools of themselves for love. If they hadn't, the world wouldn't be full of sad love songs and Fellini movies. Still, she thought, selecting a big pair of glasses and a giant scarf to cover her face and head, no need to be caught on his building's security cameras doing it.

Thirty-eight

Asia pulled out of the Bellagio's parking lot and made a left onto the Strip. In less than ten minutes she would be pulling up at Sunil's apartment complex.

After the attack, she had woken up in an office deep in the bowels of the hotel. She was lying on a massage table with an IV drip attached to her arm.

Hey, a pleasant voice said.

Hey, Asia croaked through cracked lips. Her nose was burning and as she touched her face gingerly, she could feel it was swollen like a melon.

The woman with the pleasant voice came over. She was wearing white scrubs and a name tag that said Kim.

Hello, Adele, Kim said.

Asia flinched at her name, a name she used only for legal reasons. The name on her ID, the name from the past she was trying to escape. From the man who had turned out to be a traitor, a word she had tattooed on her arm when she got to Vegas. But the tattoo shop was less than reputable, and the guy who ran it spoke bad English, and so she had ended up with Trae Dah.

You took quite the beating there.

Asia nodded. It wouldn't be the first time, she wanted to say, but she didn't. Chicago would always remain in the past.

You were unconscious when we found you. Mr. Richie,

head of security, thought it would be best if we dealt with this in-house. You understand?

Asia nodded again. Casinos went to great lengths to keep from getting bad publicity, especially in a depressed economy.

A doctor examined you, and it doesn't look like you have a concussion, but you do need to be careful. He left some pain pills for you. Here, let me disconnect the drip. Can you sit up? Yes? I'll help you. There.

Asia sat up and gasped as the room swam into focus.

Kim handed her the bottle of pain pills. Those are pretty strong. Use them carefully, she said.

Thank you.

Don't thank me. Mr. Richie says he's an old friend of yours. There was a bit of steel in her voice.

Asia nodded.

Do you want me to call someone to come get you?

Who could she call? Who did she want to call? She nodded, and when Kim passed her her bag, she fumbled for her cell, took a deep breath, and dialed Sunil's number.

I'll be back in a little bit, Kim said.

Five times over the course of an hour she called Sunil and each time it went to voice mail, and each time she left a message. Kim returned intermittently, and when Asia shook her head, she would leave. But each time she came, she brought something for Asia: tea, then water, finally a giant soda. The last time she came in, she had a regretful face and a clipboard in one hand.

I'm afraid Mr. Richie says you have to leave now, Kim said.

Asia nodded and stood up. She was a little light-headed and her face still throbbed but otherwise she was fine. The ice packs that Kim had pressed onto her face while she was out, and which she had renewed with every visit, had visibly reduced the swelling.

Mr. Richie also needs you to sign this, Kim said, pressing a pen and the clipboard into Asia's hands. It's a release for the hotel, you understand?

Asia nodded and signed. She hadn't expected them to treat her as nicely as they were, even if she had given Mr. Richie a couple of complimentary dates. Fifteen minutes later, here she was, pulling out of the parking lot and heading for Sunil's. She didn't want to be alone. She wanted him to hold her. There were no other women in his life, she was sure, but still, it was a risk going to him uninvited.

Thirty-nine

Brewster gasped for air, choking silently. He moved quickly, replacing the oxygen tank in his pocket. In a few seconds his breathing returned to normal.

Brewster was sitting at his desk, studying the MRI image of the twins on his computer. He could see that a band of tissue connected the twins, but they didn't share lungs or a heart or any major organs. They could very easily have been separated at birth. It's confusing why they weren't. Maybe their parents couldn't afford the operation. But he knew so many surgeons would have performed the procedure for free, just to get papers out of it. Even more confusing was that on the little one there was no brain activity showing up. He appeared brain dead.

It would be interesting to hear Sunil's take on all this. He was far more qualified on matters pertaining to brain scans. He'd have to make up for the whole zoo thing. Honestly, when were these blacks going to stop being so sensitive? Best to call and get it over. Brewster picked up his cell phone.

Forty

Fred held the cigar in her palm, barely moving her hand, as though gauging its weight. Then she let it roll up and down her palm a few times, watching it critically. Pinching it between forefinger and thumb, she brought it up to her nose and ran it across the ridge of her upper lip, inhaling deeply, eyes closed. Satisfied, she put the tapered end in a guillotine and deftly snicked the end off. She took out an old Zippo with the emblem of the Atomic Testing Commission on it, held the flame away from the rough edge of the tobacco leaves, and inhaled deeply as the cigar caught fire. The smoke ran out of her nostrils as she puffed. Satisfied it would stay lit, she leaned back in the Adirondack.

Gentlemen, help yourselves, Fred said through the smoke, pointing to the humidor.

Both Salazar and Sunil declined.

Best Cubans this side of the Mississippi, she offered.

No, thank you, though, Sunil said.

Well, cheers, Fred said, raising her beer bottle.

The men raised theirs. It was growing chilly on the porch, high up as it was, like a bird's nest. A blue orb on the wall behind them attracted and zapped the whirling insects. Without it, the setting would have been almost bucolic.

So tell me, why do you have Fire and Water, Doctor, Fred asked. Are they hurt?

He's a shrink, Salazar said. We got them undergoing psychological evaluation. We think they are serial killers.

Serial killers, Fred asked, sitting up. You have to be joking.

I should add that I am not sure yet whether they are guilty of a crime, much less whether they are serial killers, Sunil said.

They don't have it in them, Fred said.

That's what the neighbors of every serial killer say when the police come by, Salazar said. He was such a nice guy, blah, blah, blah.

I'm afraid he's right there, Sunil said. Most serial killers are high-functioning people who go by unnoticed for a very long time.

And why are you here, Fred asked. You, Doctor, specifically. What is your interest?

Please call me Sunil.

Fine. So tell me, Sunil, what's your stake in all this?

Freaks and serial killers are his specialty, Salazar said. Best in the country, that's why I had him hold them for seventy-two hours. So I'm in charge here, so you talk to me.

Fred took a long drag from her cigar and blew smoke slowly into Salazar's face. Turning her head, she said: Sunil?

Well, it is a rather delicate matter.

Why is that?

There are several parties interested in their incarceration—in prison or hospital. It would help me to have some background on them, something to help with a diagnosis.

Just so you know, Salazar said, I for one believe they are as guilty as fuck and there's little you can say to prove otherwise. I am here because the doctor thinks you are key to this because one of the freaks is in love with you. He figures if they did this, whatever set them off is connected to you.

Fred smiled. Water?

Yes, Sunil said. Is there any truth to that?

I am just one of those women, Sunil. You know the kind.

No, I don't.

The kind men want to possess but can't, Fred said, and laughed deliciously.

You don't seem that perturbed by all this.

All what, Fred asked. This little show you're both putting on? If you had anything serious on the twins, would you be out here in the middle of nowhere asking for my help?

Sunil drained his beer. Why don't I tell you what I think?

With that he launched into a recap of the twins' arrest by the lake and everything that had transpired up till then. When he was done, he stood up and went to the bathroom while Fred went to freshen their drinks and get some snacks. They had an awkward moment at the door as they both reached it at the same time, but that was replaced by amazement when they stepped back onto the porch to find Salazar peeing over the edge.

Shit, he said. You came back faster than I expected. My bad. Old habit.

He zippered up and sat down. Fred passed him a new beer, careful not to touch him in the process.

What, he asked, picking up on her body language. You can work with freaks no problem, but a little public urination is a big deal.

Fred ignored him and turned to Sunil. First to address the love issue you brought up, she said. Yes, there was a time when Water and I were intimate. We were lovers for about a year until it became unclear to me which twin I was actually sleeping with. I mean, it was always Water's body, but there were times when I thought I saw Fire in his eyes.

I understand, Sunil said.

But then I also began to notice Fire peering out at us from

under his caul when we made love. The whole thing got too weird, so I ended it. Do you really think that somehow triggered a breakdown for them?

I don't know. When did you stop seeing Water?

Eight months ago. But they continued to work here at the carnival all that time, until two weeks ago when they just left for Vegas.

What exactly did they do as King Kong, Salazar asked. I mean, did they wear a monkey costume or what?

Both Fred and Sunil contemplated correcting him, but then chose not to.

They were fire wizards, Sunil said. At least Fire was, as I understand.

That's correct, Fred said, shooting him a grateful smile.

Like I know what the fuck that is, Salazar said.

Well, one of their tricks, Fred said, was to set a very long pole on fire and then throw it in the air. As it dropped they would catch it and it would turn into an albino python. Stuff like that. The audience loved their show, but then Fire grew bored of the magic. They were working on something akin to walking on water. I think that's why they may have been at Lake Mead.

Because Criss Angel walked across Lake Mead, Salazar asked.

So you're not a total waste of space, Fred said.

How long have they been with the carnival, Sunil asked.

Since they were twelve, Fred said.

And they spent the last few weeks just developing their new Jesus act, Salazar asked.

Not exclusively; there are no free rides here. They helped out with the midget boxing matches—

The what now, Salazar interjected.

The midget boxing matches. Ferocious fighters. I wouldn't want to tangle with them. Anyway, that's what they did, but since the show only comes on at midnight, they didn't need to make it back here until ten. For the rest of the time they were just gone.

Gone where, Salazar asked.

Just gone.

You're not very good at giving alibis, are you, Salazar said.

I wasn't aware that's what I was supposed to be doing.

Sunil saw where that line of conversation was going and headed off the argument quickly. What do you know of their early life? Before they joined the carnival. Do you know what caused their mutation?

Everyone in the carnival is mutated in some way, Fred said, and we all come from within one hundred miles of each other.

Ah, Sunil said. Downwinders?

Yes, Fred said.

What the fuck are downwinders, Salazar asked. Some cult of farty mutants?

Downwinders are people adversely affected by the nuclear tests in Nevada because they lived downwind from the test sites, Sunil said. The wind literally blew the radiation through their farms, ranches, and towns, infecting them with radiation poisoning.

Of course, as soon as we began to complain, the government did everything they could to hush it up, Fred said.

I'm still not sure I'm buying this Mulder and Scully crap about the government and nuclear tests that can harm its own people, Salazar said. I mean, this is America, for fuck's sake.

That's partly how it works, Sunil said. The clinical term is cognitive dissonance, and trust me, a whole country can be infected with it.

So you're telling me that radiation sickness from one bomb set off in Nevada in the fifties infected thousands of people, Salazar said. Give me a fucking break.

We aren't talking about one bomb from the fifties. I don't think you fully appreciate how extensive the testing is. Most of the current nuclear tests are conducted at five-thousand-foot depths right by the water aquifers that give this entire area its water—I mean, all the civilian populations, Indian reservations, farms, all of it, except the military base, which has its water brought in, to this day. This is the water most of us grew up drinking, bathing in, and watering our crops and livestock with. So you can imagine, Fred said.

The scale of it is staggering, Sunil said.

I still can't believe the government would knowingly go along with this, Salazar said.

People magazine ran an article on the 1956 classic film *The Conqueror* that was filmed on location near St. George, Utah. Between 1956 and 1980, ninety-one members of the cast and crew came down with cancers, including Susan Hayward and John Wayne, Sunil said.

Which side are you on, Doc, Salazar said to Sunil. To Fred he said: Look, our nuclear power is part of what makes this country great.

As long as you don't have to pay for it, Fred said. I grew up in a town within the danger zone. I remember seeing a mushroom cloud. I was playing in an abandoned mine with some other kids when we felt this wall of hot sand blow through the tunnel. We rushed for the exits. We'd been told not to look at the explosion because the intense light would make you blind. But I had to look, I just had to, and it was beautiful, the colors were unlike anything I'd ever seen before or since.

You shouldn't have been playing in an abandoned mine. Where were your parents?

Fuck you, Detective.

Thank you for being so honest with us, Sunil began.

But?

He wanted to say, But I feel like you aren't telling me the

entire truth. I feel like you are holding something back. Instead he said, But nothing. I was wondering if you ever met Selah.

Yes, when I was twelve. My father used to run this carnival before me. He was deeply religious and he believed it was his divine mission to take care of the deformed, so wherever we traveled we tracked down locals with deformities and offered them a life of dignity with the carnival.

So your father took Fire and Water from Selah, Sunil asked.

Yes. She was in a bad way. She was dying of leukemia. She'd been exposed to radiation from an explosion, seen the cloud from within three miles of its epicenter.

So that's why Water says she's a tree? The mushroom cloud reminds him of a tree.

No, Fred said. The day after my father met Selah, we went to her cabin as agreed to collect the twins and put her in a hospice. We found the boys crying under a bristlecone tree a little up the trail from their house. It seemed Selah had hanged herself early that morning.

Forty-one

It was dark with the exception of one lamp on a table that cast a dim pool of light on the floor. In the gloom it seemed brighter than it really was. Water sat in a chair near the lamp, reading a copy of GQ, wondering if there would ever be a Hugo Boss suit or Dolce & Gabbana sweater designed with conjoined twins in mind. Beside him, under his caul, Fire snored.

The door was flung open and Brewster strode in, flicking the overhead fluorescent light on, bathing the room in harsh radiation.

Am I disturbing, he asked, and sat on the edge of the bed.

A very nervous nurse flitted by his elbow. They are Dr. Singh's patients, he said. We should call him to come in before you ask them any more questions.

Brewster's look shut him up.

Water put down the magazine. Fire shifted about under Water's robe.

Why even bother reading a magazine like that, Brewster asked. Do you think with the right disguise you can fit in?

A completely blind chameleon still takes on the colors of its environment, Water said.

Is that what you are, a chameleon?

Water was silent.

I asked you a question, Brewster said. I'm not as soft as Dr. Singh, so answer me.

A vexillologist is an expert in the history of flags, Water said.

I know this is just an act you're putting on, Brewster snarled.

Pope Pius II wrote an erotic book, *Historia de duobus amantibus,* in 1444, Water said.

I know you're really the one in control here, Brewster said. I've seen your MRIs.

Michael Jackson holds the rights to the South Carolina state anthem, Water said.

Don't play this game with me, Brewster said.

Black bears are not always black. They can be brown, cinnamon, yellow, and even white.

Do you know that I have the power to keep you here indefinitely?

A dog can hear frequencies that a human ear cannot, Water said.

And then before Brewster could speak again, Water began rocking and repeating facts, rapid-fire, leaving no room for Brewster to speak:

The infinity sign is called a lemniscate.

Take your height and divide by eight, that's how tall your head is.

Pittsburgh is the only city where all major sports teams have the same colors: black and gold.

It is illegal to own a red car in Shanghai.

Zipporah was the wife of Moses.

Donald Duck's middle name is Fauntleroy.

A baby eel is called an elver; a baby oyster is called a spot.

Paper bags are outlawed in grocery stores in Afghanistan. They believe paper is sacred.

Thomas Edison was afraid of the dark.

Shut up, shut up! Brewster said.

He was interrupted by the sound of Fire's caul snapping open.

What the fuck is going on, he asked.

George W. Bush is related to every U.S. president from George Washington to Barack Obama, Water said. Barack and W are eleventh cousins.

Enough, Brewster said.

As soon as Dr. Singh comes in, I will be lodging a formal complaint, Fire said.

With that, he retreated under the caul, snapping it closed.

It's just a matter of time, Brewster said, then you're all mine.

Forty-two

From the small street off Fremont, the lights were close enough to touch. The sound of piped music was loud enough to make conversation hard, not that the group of boys, girls, men, and women strolling the short street was interested in talking. Even though prostitution was illegal in Las Vegas, the police never really bothered the workers there. They were pretty good at policing themselves, and at keeping drugs and violence, which was bad for business, out of their area.

Vegas, someone once said, was no different from any small American town, except that everything hidden and denied there was celebrated in Vegas. It was, effectively, America's, and increasingly the world's, darkest and brightest subconscious.

Horny Nick was bored. He polished his horns and lit a cigarette. He'd had no takers yet, but Sundays were quiet and drew a more conventional crowd less likely to go for a rent boy with filed teeth, tattoos, and implanted horns.

Farther down the street, Annie and Petrol worked a corner. Annie was having a great night, and who didn't want to fuck an elf from *Lord of the Rings*? Petrol drew a class of men who wanted to dominate or be dominated. Horny Nick was an acquired taste but one that cost more, so he wasn't worried. With only a few johns he could make what Petrol and Annie took twice as long to earn.

Peggy patrolled nearby, keeping a watchful eye on her

friends, earning her keep as security. She was walking past Petrol and Annie when she saw a silver compact pass by, headed up the street. There was something off about it, she intuited, and for her that was enough. She began to run up the street shouting as Horny Nick leaned into the window.

Peggy was less than ten feet away as Nick opened the passenger door and got in. The car peeled away from the curb and joined the traffic with practiced ease. Too slow to draw attention, fast enough to get away quick.

I'm Horny Nick, Nick said.

The driver smiled and, turning to him, jabbed a Taser to his jugular. Nick was unconscious in three seconds, a wet patch forming on his jeans.

Outside, receding rapidly, Peggy hadn't given up the chase.

She finally stopped in the middle of the street, breathless, where Petrol and Annie joined her.

What is it, Annie asked.

Nick is in trouble, Peggy said, dialing.

Who are you calling, Petrol asked.

Salazar.

Salazar's phone went to voice mail.

Shit! Peggy screamed. She knew it wouldn't help to call the regular police.

Forty-three

In the growing desert cold, the lights of the carnival were like sharp points. The man in the wheelchair still sat in the spotlight, singing, his only concession to the cold a blanket draped over his legs.

Fred, are you involved in any downwinder action groups, Sunil asked.

Salazar sat forward.

Do you think we're eco-terrorists now, Fred asked.

Fire said he was a downwinder nationalist, Sunil said. That's a direct-action group.

Even if that were true, you think I'm involved?

It bears thinking about, Sunil said. Given that you share a similar . . . I'm not accusing you of anything, just trying to understand.

No offense, but that's just dumb. How would getting arrested at Lake Mead next to a blood dump help you commit an act of terrorism?

I don't know, Sunil said.

Let me ask you something, she said.

Fair enough, Sunil said.

Where are you from? There's an accent.

South Africa.

Well, since you share the fucked-up history of South Africa, have you ever killed anyone on either side of the political divide?

Sunil shifted. Killed someone, he said. No.

Fred smiled cruelly. Watched someone die, she asked.

Sunil looked away.

I'm not accusing you, Doctor, I'm just getting to know you.

So you think that Fire and Water are innocent of all charges and they aren't crazy?

Yes, Fred said. Let me come and talk to them, she said. I will get them to open up. Get this whole thing cleared up by tomorrow afternoon.

That would be very helpful, Sunil said. You would do that?

For the twins? Sure, she said.

Hold up here, Salazar said. Now, wait just a fucking minute. They are my twins, my case. You get to help on one condition.

What is your condition?

That you come into the station voluntarily and that we run your prints and take a statement.

Fine. Can I talk to them, she asked Sunil.

Now? On the phone?

Any objections, Sunil asked Salazar.

Now you care what I think.

So?

Let her have her fucking phone call, Salazar said.

Sunil called the institute and asked the duty nurse to put the twins on.

What's up, Doc, Fire said.

Hold for Fred, Sunil said, passing the phone.

Fred took it. Some privacy, she said.

Sunil looked at Salazar, who nodded. Fred left them on the porch and stepped back inside, closing the door behind her. She was on the phone for only a few minutes before she came back out and handed the phone to Sunil and thanked him.

Now you two need to leave, as I have a carnival to run,

Fred said. She herded them to the door, taking their beer bottles.

So you'll come by in the morning, Sunil asked.

Yes, I'll meet you at the institute at ten.

She walked them back to their car. Two men sat in a golf cart beside it.

I see you have your own security, Sunil said.

It's a ghost town. We need to keep it safe, she said.

Crowds were already beginning to mill about. The town suddenly looked alive, like a horror-film town, or a Stephen King novel, where everyone was dead in the daytime but came to life at night.

Where the fuck did all these people come from, Salazar asked.

All lost souls come to commune at the carnival, Fred said, laughing.

Fuck, Salazar said. He got into the car quickly and started the engine.

As Sunil turned to go, Fred touched his arm. Thank you for coming, she said. This is the closest thing the twins have to a home. I would like to bring them back. You understand, right? You lost your home too. Have you ever been back?

Sunil smiled. Good night, he said, and got in beside Salazar.

As they drove down the yellow brick road, Salazar said: You know she's lying, right?

Of course she is, Sunil said. The question is, what is she lying about, and why?

The drive home was faster. Ten miles from the town, both of their cell phones began to beep.

Finally, some service, Salazar said.

Yes, Sunil said, looking at his phone.

Asia had called seven times. Sheila five. Brewster five.

Wow, he thought, busy night. He was curious about Asia's

calls, but Sheila and Brewster could wait. He tried Asia's cell. There was no answer. As they hit the open road and gathered speed, Sunil thought back to Fred's question: Have you ever been back?

He had been once: but not to J'burg, or Soweto, but to Cape Town. Thinking about it now, Sunil was reminded of one of those moments of uneasy grace that he'd found on a beach in Cape Town shortly after his return.

An overweight woman walked across the sand with one arm tucked close to her right side, body bent into a slightly angled sway. Sunil recognized the signs of a small shame, of a person used to an unkind gaze. The young woman sunbathing topless, spread to the glory of the sun with the abandon of the proud. Older women more modest with their bodies, but less with their envy, shot her disapproving glances.

An old white man slept in the sun: fully dressed and looking like an untidy pile of towels in the sand. A woman on her cell phone turned away from him, her muscled and uncovered back had a Ganesh tattoo spread like a rug across it. Kids of all colors and races clustered around an old black man selling ice cream from a blue-and-white cooler.

Returns are never what we expect them to be. The glory of old wins pales in the face of the reality of compromise. The Cape Town beach with whites, blacks, Indians, and coloreds fading into burnt sepia—the color of tolerance, a smudge over the sharp, angled pain that still struggled under the wash of it—was no different. There was no feeling of restitution in this. There should be more than giving back what was free and collective in the first place. He didn't know what, but felt that there should be.

Near where he lay, a rock still held the rusting scar of a sign that used to declare THE DIVISION COUNCIL OF THE CAPE—WHITE AREA: BLANKE GEBIED. He'd stubbed his toe on it coming down to the sand. A Boer somewhere is smiling, he thought. Everyone on the beach seemed to be having a good time and he couldn't understand at first why he was so angry. Then he realized what it was; the air was heavy with it—amnesia.

Restorative, isn't it, a woman next to him said.

What is, he asked, always precise.

The water, she said, the water and the breeze.

They had water and a breeze on Robben Island, he said. I'm not sure how restorative that was.

She took off her sunglasses and looked at him, intrigued by his non sequitur. He returned her look, taking in details: she was of indeterminate race, probably colored, he thought, and young, maybe thirty, and attractive in an unusual way.

I like the way the breeze makes everything seem good, she said, choosing her words carefully, responding not to his statement but to something unsaid, something she sensed.

Like apartheid, he said, unable to help himself. I imagine all the whites lying here during apartheid, the breeze and the water making it possible for everything to seem good, he added.

Yes, she said. I suppose you are right. There was a smile behind her words.

You seemed amused by it, he said, offended.

Not by it, she said, stressing the syllables. I am amused by your tone.

Why?

You just came back, she said.

Yes, he said, wondering how she could tell. His accent?

Gone for a long time?

Ten years, he said.

She nodded. It is a long time, she said.

Yes, he said. Too long.

She bit down on her sunglasses and sighed. It is not just time, is it? That bothers you, I mean.

No, he said.

Lost people to the darkness?

He was simultaneously drawn to and repulsed by her description of that time. It was darkness—of the spirit, the heart—but why that word? Why was it always used in the negative? It had been whiteness, a lightness that made it hard for the perpetrators to see the limits of their souls, not blackness, that destroyed them all. He wanted to say that but was held back by his knowledge that it was only partially true. Mostly, but not completely, and as his mother used to say, quoting a Zulu proverb, You cannot eat meat you mostly caught, only meat you actually caught.

Yes, he said, instead. My mothers.

She nodded, eyes sad for him. If she noticed the plural and thought it odd, she didn't say anything. Perhaps she knew that it took more than one mother to raise a child through those times.

Nobody could stop the sickness, she said. Not even Madiba. It had to run its course. There was no blame in the loss of those times.

It seemed to him that there was plenty of blame and he had a share in that. There is always blame, he said. There has to be. What is life without it?

She smiled and said: Good old South African guilt, shared by all races.

I shouldn't have to feel guilty, he said. I didn't do this.

If she wondered what he meant by "this," she said nothing. Instead she said: I know, but we all do. It doesn't help anything though.

He nodded and looked away, suddenly tearful.

Let the water restore you, the woman said, replacing her glasses and falling back onto her beach towel.

He closed his eyes and listened to the waves, feeling the spray on his face. It did feel good.

Without looking at him, the woman spoke: I know this seems wrong, not like justice, but here we take freedom day by day, moment by moment: What else is there?

She was right. What did he know? He'd been gone ten years. My name is Sunil, he said. It seemed important to state who he was.

She smiled, still not looking at him. Welcome home, Sunil, she said.

Thank you, he said.

What the fuck did you say, Salazar asked him.

Nothing. I was thinking about Cape Town, about the time I went back. I was having a coffee in this café and I saw Robben Island from the window. I said to the old waiter serving me, if the island was visible every day how come they pretended nothing was going on? He smiled and said, It was often quite foggy in those days, sir, the island was rarely visible.

It's a skill, Salazar said. Like witnesses who can't remember anything at a crime scene.

Selective blindness made Sunil think of White Alice.

White Alice got her name from the locals in Soweto when she moved there from Cape Town. Her name wasn't a result of her complexion—she looked somewhere between colored and Indian, no different really from the thousands of biracial South Africans who were caught between apartheid's denial of mixed unions and its fear of miscegenation. It wasn't unusual for people to try to pass as white. Those who couldn't pass settled for delusion: claiming to be white, which is what White Alice had done. She told anyone who would listen that she had been born white but had turned black after an illness. No one believed her, but no one minded either. This was Soweto.

White Alice was Dorothy's best friend. The two women became inseparable, spending at least an hour or two a day over at each other's house, drinking sweetened tea and eating biscuits, complaining about life and the difficulties of loss. White Alice talked about her three children in Cape Town, all white, whom she hadn't seen since her husband took them away from her on account of her sudden and mysterious blackness. When Sunil asked his mother about White Alice's condition, she told him White Alice was probably just a very light-skinned colored who had passed for white for much of her life, but, as Dorothy said, blackness will always exert its revenge, and Alice had just grown into her true shade. It made sense. Sunil found out in medical school that White Alice might have been telling the truth. He discovered a condition called hyperpigmentation, a result of Addison's disease, which had been known to darken the skin of white sufferers enough to alter perception of their racial heritage. But by then, White Alice had betrayed him twice, and his discovery of her condition and the pain it must have caused her wasn't enough to engender his sympathy or his forgiveness. Not even when, on his eighteenth birthday, a strange white man who identified himself as Colonel Bleek visited him with a generous scholarship package for college. What good would it have done to stare such a gift horse in the mouth, so to speak? He'd asked only one question: Why me?

Alice Coetzee spoke highly of you, Bleek said. She recommended you for this.

Oh, was all he said at the time. But Sunil had since lived with the regret of not asking more questions. Like what would the gift cost him? He thought it particularly poignant that while taking German at college to better understand Freud, he found out that the word "gift," in German, meant poison. In many ways, it seemed that the Germans had a real philosophical handle on life.

He wanted to tell Salazar all this. Instead he said: I'm sure you're right.

Forty-four

A blue sky but not night. An eeire dusk, an unearthly light. A blue mist alternately obscures and reveals a field of blue grass in the shadow of a darkening sky. Alone, in the middle of the field, a dark tree spreads its black foliage across the frame.

Water walks toward the tree in the middle of the field, but no matter how fast he moves or how much he tries, he can't reach the tree. It never moves but it is always just out of reach. The blue sky gets bluer and the blue grass waves through the blue mist like blue algae in water. Still, Water can't reach the tree.

And the blue tree morphs, shifting in agony as its trunk twists to form a bristlecone pine, standing in the middle of an empty muddy field.

Twisting slowly from a branch bent so low it seems like it can't hold its terrible burden is a young woman, eyes closed peacefully, something close to a smile on her face.

Selah, Water calls, softly at first, then louder, Selah, until it is a scream.

He wakes abruptly; alone, Fire fast asleep under his caul, sitting in the chair by the window. If anyone heard his scream, they don't respond. Reaching out, Water touches the cold glass of the window.

Selah is a cloud, he says, a star cloud, constellation of the dog.

Forty-five

The moment's awkwardness when Asia answered Sunil's door to find Sheila was compounded by the fact that Asia was wearing lacy underpants, sporting a black eye and a shirt that could only have been Sunil's, two buttons keeping it on.

I'm sorry, Sheila said, not knowing what else to say.

About what, Asia asked.

Is, er, Sunil home, Sheila asked.

No, Asia said, not stepping away from the door but not shutting it either.

Asia was curious about Sheila, but not unduly worried. She knew she was the only one Sunil was sleeping with, and he'd never mentioned this woman. Still, the day had been full of surprises.

I'm Sheila. I work with Sunil. He hasn't been answering his cell. I was worried.

Hello, Sheila, Asia said. I'm Asia.

Hi.

Asia didn't like that Sheila had been calling Sunil on his cell and felt comfortable enough to come over, clearly unannounced. I haven't heard from him either, she said. I thought he was at work.

No, I checked, Sheila said.

He's never mentioned you, Asia said.

This is the first time I've come over. I'm really embarassed. Look, I'll go, just tell him I came round, Sheila said.

You should come in, Asia said, stepping back and holding the door open. That is, if you want to.

Are you sure, Sheila asked.

Asia wanted to say, I don't want to be alone. Not right now, not today. She wanted to say, I'm confused and terrified, because I found out that not only have I been sleeping with my lover's best friend, but he also tried to kill me. And my lover is not really my lover, but my client. And I love him. I do, but now I don't know why because I really don't know enough about him. Instead she said: I'm sure.

Sheila walked in and stopped in the hallway as Asia closed the door. She followed Asia into the living room, where she felt herself stiffen and draw a sharp breath even though she hadn't meant to. Were you robbed, Sheila asked.

Asia took in the ruined living room, feeling good at the implication that Sheila assumed she lived with Sunil. I don't live here, she said.

Oh, I'm sorry, I just assumed, Sheila said.

Assumed what, Asia asked.

I'm sorry, Sheila said.

About what?

I'm not sure, Sheila said, acutely uncomfortable. About coming unannounced.

Yeah, that is kind of forward, Asia said, checking Sheila out. Thinking: late thirties, fashion still caught in the '80s, tight body, cute face. Still, she thought, no competition.

So what happened here?

None of your business, Asia said.

So this has nothing to do with that, Sheila said, pointing at Asia's black eye.

Like I said, none of your business.

Sunil didn't—Sheila began.

Fuck you, Asia said softly. I thought you said you knew him.

Right, Sheila said, I'm sorry.

So do you have a message for Sunil, Asia asked.

What?

A message you'd like to leave for Sunil?

I'm sorry, but I've known Sunil for six years, Sheila siad, and I've never heard about you, Sheila said.

Asia smiled, but her eyes were cold. I've known Sunil for six years too and he's never mentioned you, either.

They stood there, side by side, in the room Eskia had trashed, not looking at each other.

Have you called the police, Sheila asked.

If you have no message for Sunil, I'll just tell him you came around then, Asia said.

Yes, thank you, Sheila said, I should go.

Asia nodded and pushed the door closed firmly, ending the conversation. She walked back into the living room and sat on the floor. For a long time she just sat there, and then she gave in to the release of tears.

Forty-six

It was a full moon. Heavy in the frame of the car window.

Sunil was lost in the memory of Jan, of the last time he saw her alive at Vlakplaas.

There was Eugene, Sunil, Constable Mashile, and Jan. Jan in the light-blue skirt, white blouse with lacy detail, long tanned legs, and her long lean toned arms unadorned except for the ring that sat on her thumb, too big for any other finger. The one Sunil had given her so long ago. He wondered why she'd taken it off the chain.

She seemed out of place here, like a woman on her way to a picnic who had taken a wrong turn, casual in her smile as though the most dangerous thing she faced were whether ants would get into the jam or not. Incongruous in this place, this stark white room with bare cement floors. The paint here always smelled new, because fresh coats were applied frequently.

Eugene loved the pristine whiteness, the way it would show up blood from the more intense interrogations, the patterns on the wall forming a red puzzle. How much pain before that one capitulated. How much before this one informed on everyone—even the innocent. What was most effective on whom—teeth extracted with pliers; good old-fashioned fist work; the cut inner tube of a car tire pulled down over the face to suffocate in controlled measure. But of course, this was an imprecise science, lungs often filled with liquid and sometimes blood, and so on. The point no longer the information, no longer saving the state, but for nothing more than the hunger, the desire to know the body in all its savage beauty.

All of it happened in this room, Eugene's favorite.

The windows opened onto a vista of hills and scrub and low scudding clouds that drew shadows across the stubby rise. Sometimes there were zebus lowing in the heat, driven by a boy trying to find pasture for them to graze before being driven off by gun-toting policemen for trespassing.

Not the usual view from an interrogation room.

Jan sat facing Eugene, a table between them, a slow-moving ceiling fan above them turning the heat over like a blanket drying on a stove, not cooling anyone, just moving the humidity around evenly.

Sunil sat on a stool between the windows trying not to look at Jan or Eugene. Instead he focused on the bowl of fruit that sat between them on the table, noticing the details: three pears, a knife, and an oddly shaped and heavily ornamented silver object, which could have been anything but looked decidedly Victorian.

Constable Mashile was staring intently at Eugene, trying to keep the look of discomfort from his face.

Would you care for a pear, Eugene asked Jan. No? Well then, I'm sure you won't mind if I have one. He reached over and tested each one, finally selecting the one that met his standards. Pears are most delicious at the midpoint of ripeness, between too firm and too soft, he continued.

No one else spoke.

You know, before they get really ripe? The flesh has some bite to it and yet the juices are sweet, Eugene said to no one in particular. He rubbed the pear against his khaki bush shirt and picked up the knife, cutting slowly, deliberately, into the fruit. Everyone watched him pare it into quarters. He let them fall apart and lie there on the table like flower petals. He picked one up, held it to his nose, inhaled, and then with a smile, he placed it in his mouth and bit down on the grainy flesh, his smile widening. He chewed slowly, quietly, and then spoke: Perfect, just perfect. This should really have been the fruit to tempt Adam, don't you think? The apple shows a singular lack of imagination on the part of that particular Bible author, whoever he was. I wonder if Moses was a composite, you know, like Shakespeare? He poked at the three quarters that were left with the tip of the knife, as though testing for the optimal one. He speared one on the tip of the knife and ate it with delight, smacking his lips and looking so lost in his pleasure that everyone else looked away in embarrassment from that particular intimacy. Eugene put the knife down and rubbed his hands together and said: That was good, reminds me of my childhood. My moeder would cut up pears for me, a rare pleasure on that farm so far inland where fruit rarely did well. Memories, eh?

Turning to Sunil, he said: Any luck with your psycho mumbo-jumbo on this suspect? Did the Lady Jan here speak to you?

Sunil glanced at Jan, caught her eye, and, looking away quickly, shook his head. No, he said.

Jan, Jan, Jan, Eugene said. You really should open up to Dr. Singh here. His methods have proven quite effective in turning people such as you. I hate to use violence, particularly on someone who can be reasoned with. It's much better to become an *askari* without the violence.

Jan stared at him intently, with an almost forensic intensity, but she said nothing.

Are you familiar with the Swahili word *askari*? Like Lindiwe over there, these are members of a conquered indigenous people helping their conquerors maintain the status quo. That's not a literal meaning of course, but it's true to the spirit of things. Do you know who came up with it? The British, those fokkers who tried to turn the Boer into *teefs*. Now you conspire with that scum over your people, and to help whom? Kaffirs? You can ask Sunil here, I'm not racist, but there is an order to things, a way the universe runs, and men like me, we are the ones who keep things in place, keep things running the way they should. I take no pleasure in the decisions I have to make, but I make them, I must make them. That is my role. Just as this is the role you've chosen. Mine is destiny, yours is weak-willed. I am here to offer you the chance to be strong.

Why all this performance, Jan asked. Her voice startled Sunil, the venom of it, the hard edge of strength, like a finely tuned wire holding everything in place. This was not the shy Jan he'd known.

Performance, Eugene asked, eyebrows raised, reaching for another lobe of pear.

Why don't you just get on with the torture, with the extermination of the resistance to your white power, she spat.

Eugene chewed thoughtfully, and then with an expression of regret on his face said: I abhor torture. I abhor brutality. These methods, exterminating the native, to borrow your words, are not only barbaric, they are not effective in the long term. The real power lies in securing the cooperation, even the alliance, of the native if we are to hold up this system, and it is not, as you put it, about white power. At least, not for me. I feel more Zulu than white, myself. No, no, it's about law and order. We represent civilization, law, order, and the march of progress, and for better or worse, this must be defended and moved forward at all costs. I more than any am sorry about the cost. And torture makes me sad, it is regrettable when I have to use it.

Jan spat at him, the gob of spittle landing on the last piece of pear.

Eugene regarded it with a strange smile. I am a visionary, he said. That's why I brought Dr. Singh here on board. His job is to use a mix of persuasive chemicals and conversion to bring enemies into the fold, into an understanding of the way.

Gaan naai jou Ma, Jan said, softly, so softly that Eugene had to lean in to hear her properly.

Sunil was shocked at the language; the Jan he knew would never have told anyone to fuck his mother. More than the shock was his fear for her. But if Eugene was upset, his body didn't register it. Instead he leaned forward and picked up the piece of pear with the glistening pearl of spittle on it. He studied it for a moment, then put it in his mouth and, never taking his eyes off Jan, he chewed slowly, thoughtfully.

Talk to Sunil, Eugene said, getting up. Don't make me come back here.

I'll talk to him as much as you want, but nothing will change, Jan said, her eyes glued to Sunil's face, the look in them heavy with pity and disgust.

Eugene paused. He returned to the table and picked up the silver ornamented object.

Remember the Victorians, he asked. They loved to collect the strangest things. This is a working reproduction of a medieval torture device. It belonged to my grandfather, who loved the fact that something so beautiful could inflict so much pain. Do you know what they called this? It's called the Pear because there is this ornamented pearlike extension on the end of this handle, do you see? Do you know how it works? I'll show you.

And he did. Holding the handle in the middle, he turned the knob at the bottom. As he did so, the metal pear opened up into four perfect quarters, spreading like the metal petals of a flower.

You see, it's quite ingenious really. You insert the pear into someone's mouth, and then you twist the bottom here until it begins to open. You keep twisting it and pretty soon it breaks the teeth, dislocates the jaw, even begins to rip the cheeks apart. Of course, the trick is to do it little by little, pausing occasionally to let the victim catch their breath while you wait for the confession you want.

Everyone watched the metal pear as it opened wider and wider.

Of course, Eugene said, if you go at it long enough, you will eventually kill the victim, but only after a very long time and pain that is unimaginable, even for me. Now, the great thing about this, as I found out once, is that it works on any human orifice. Any.

Eugene put the open pear down on the table in front of Jan.

This is a very rare and expensive piece. I don't use it often, but for you, only the best will do. So please, talk to Sunil. Don't make me come back here. I didn't lie when I said I don't enjoy torture, but as you now know, I really enjoy pears.

The door closed behind him and Constable Mashile gently, almost politely.

Jan, Sunil said.

Sunil, Jan said.

Harvest moon, Salazar said, as they drove through the silent desert.

What?

The moon, Salazar said, pointing. It's called a harvest moon.

Ever seen a harvest, Sunil asked.

It's just an expression, Jesus, Salazar said.

Sunil looked out the window. In the dark, the landscape looked like home, like the brush of the grasslands, the heat of the Namibian desert that seemed determined to creep down into South Africa, the hills like those of Cape Town and the gold silts of Jozi.

Why did you become a policeman, Sunil asked.

Always wanted to be a hero, Salazar said.

Everybody does, but was there any one thing that made you want to do that as a policeman?

I don't follow.

Well, you could have been a surgeon or a fireman, but you chose policeman. And don't tell me it's about the gun. In all the time I've been with you, you've never used it, never even pulled it out, or even acted like you have it.

Maybe I'm old-school, Salazar said. Maybe I like to settle a fight with my fists. Maybe I've used my gun too many times already.

Maybe.

All right. My dad was a man who worked hard his whole life in a job he hated. A job that cut him off from his first love, the sea. He gave everything up for me, my sister, Ana, and my mom. He and Ana died in a robbery in a 7-Eleven that went bad. But because he was an immigrant, a Cuban, a brown man, nobody took his death, or Ana's, seriously. The police, it seems, didn't care. The case was closed in a week. Insufficient leads, they said. My mom moved us to Vegas, where she could be as far from that memory as possible. But I never forgot, and I decided to join up when I could and make a difference. I wanted to show that every life is valuable, has meaning, must be honored.

Salazar, I'm fucking impressed. You are some kind of hero, Sunil said.

Yeah, well, twenty years on the force changes you. Teaches you that it's all about compromise, about gray areas, about difficult moral things. Mostly I just want to make it through the day without having to kill anyone. And trust me, I've used my gun plenty. I don't know why the crazies always turn up on my watch.

I know the difficulty of trying to make moral decisions in the face of immoral moments. I know that there is no moral way to take a life, but sometimes life hands you very difficult choices. Still, you always want to do the right thing, he said.

There was a moment of silence.

That's why the dead girl haunts you, she reminds you of Ana, Sunil said.

The worst part of being a cop, Salazar said, is that everyone hates you, and yet as soon as some shit goes down, they call 911 and want you to risk your life to protect them,.

Sunil laughed. You should have been a fireman, he said. Much less complicated.

Damned right. And what about you? Why did you become a shrink and not a surgeon?

Sunil took a deep breath. Fair is fair, he thought. My mother was mentally ill, he said. But she died before I could help her, and that, Detective, is why I became, as you like to say, a shrink.

Salazar was silent for a moment. He took a silver flask from his jacket pocket and, without speaking, passed it to Sunil.

Been holding out on me, I see, Sunil said. He drank deeply, the alcohol burning through him, then passed the flask back to Salazar, who took a swig and returned it to his jacket pocket.

Isn't drinking while driving illegal, Sunil asked.

I'm the fucking police.

Sunil laughed.

Do you think anything ever changes, Salazar asked. That we can make a difference? That we will become a better species?

I don't know, I'm not sure if it even matters. I think all that matters is that we don't shrink away from the truth and that we keep trying, Sunil said.

I like that. Push the stone up the fucking hill because we should.

Yes, Sunil said. There is merit in that, grace even. Maybe

that's what makes us deeply human. Pushing ever against the inevitable. I think the world might just be saved that way.

Fuck, this is some heavy shit. Makes me want to tell a dirty joke as a palate cleanser.

I love dirty jokes, Sunil said.

Okay, here's one. A man wakes up in the emergency room and the doctor says, You've been in an accident. Do you remember anything? The man shakes his head. So the doctor says, Well, we've got good news and bad news for you. All right, says the man, tell me the bad news. The bad news is that your penis was severed in the accident, the doctor said, and it arrived too late to reattach it. So what's the good news, the man asked. The good news is that we can rebuild it, but it will cost a thousand dollars an inch. We found a savings book in your briefcase with nine thousand dollars in it, so you should talk to your wife about this. If you spend three thousand but she's used to six, then it will be dissapointing, but if you spend all nine thousand and she's used to three, well then, that won't be good. So talk to her and I'll check in with you in the morning. The next day the doctor calls the man and asks what he and his wife have decided to get. Well, the man said, she decided we should get the expensive granite countertop for the kitchen that she's always wanted.

The two men drove through the night, their laughter trailing behind them, lighting the way for Eskia's car.

INFERNO

Midway through his life, Dante realized that he had strayed into the dark wood of error. From the look on your face I would say that you have just made the same realization.

Sunil turned to the person who had just spoken. He saw a middle-aged man with a bit of a paunch and large square glasses in thick plastic frames that he kept pushing up his sweaty and blotched nose.

Eugene, the man said, extending his hand.

Sunil.

They shook hands, Sunil trying not to pull away from Eugene's strong but damp clutch.

I know, welcome to Vlakplaas. I am sorry that this was your welcome, Eugene said, waving at the group of men huddled around a barbecue pit on the hillside, drinking beer from bottles, smoking and razzing one another.

Sunil said nothing. He was struggling not to look at the dead man on the ground by the fire pit. The policemen he had ridden up with dragged him from the jeep and took his hood off, throwing it into the fire. Now he stared at Sunil with fish eyes.

Do you read much Dante, Eugene asked.

Sunil shook his head, taking in for the first time the well-read paperback copy of *Inferno* that Eugene clutched in one hand, a beer in the other.

You should, you know. Smart man, Dante; between him

and the *Bhagavad Gita,* I have pretty much found the answers to most of my questions. But Dante holds a special place for me. That tortured descent, all that Catholic imagery of misery and suffering that passes for religiosity. It braces the spirit, enlivens one to the possibilities of life. Are you a philosophical man, Sunil?

Not particularly, Sunil said, taking a swig from the beer he'd been given. He couldn't wrap his head around this bizarre conversation. An hour before he'd arrived at the dusty farm entrance, which was down an unpaved road that led to a dirty, mottled, once-white circular guard hut. Sunil had at first taken the big stain on the side to be a mud splatter, but it soon became evident that it was blood—a big spray of dry and now faded blood. Where had it come from?

The Land Rover he was traveling in also held two white plainclothes officers of C10, and a handcuffed, hooded black prisoner. He had sat next to the hooded figure for the one-hour drive from the police station in Pretoria, where he had been told to wait for pickup. All through the drive, the hooded man sniffled and moaned and cried out: jammer baas, jammer. The two officers in the front drank their beer and turned up the radio, as if no one was in the backseat. Occasionally one would yell over his shoulder, Agh, man, shut up! I don't want any kak from you.

Now, through the gate, the Land Rover rolled into a compound with a paved road lined by trees and well-kept lawns. Several brick buildings with army regulation green doors and trimming sat behind hedgerows and flowerbeds. It was hard to imagine this place was a death camp so famous its name could make a full-grown man piss himself.

The Land Rover pulled up in front of what looked like the main building.

Listen, boy, go get set up there, one of the officers said to Sunil.

Sunil stepped out and shouldered his army regulation duffel bag. As he did a three-sixty and took the place in, flagpole and flag fluttering in the breeze, he wished that White Alice had never come into his life. Because of her he'd met Bleeker, who gave him the army scholarship to college. This he guessed was what they meant by serving the army in return for five years in an area they felt would benefit from his skills. Fuck this, his father had died fighting these people and now here he was working for them. Not for the first time, he was glad his mother was dead. Sunil had been requested especially by the commanding officer of Vlakplaas, a man whose nickname was Optimum Evil, to help reform the death camp. He couldn't see the cells or torture rooms from where he was, but he knew they were there.

Vlakplaas in Afrikaans meant "the flat place"; a farm twenty kilometers from Pretoria, the capital, it served as the headquarters for the South African Police Counterinsurgency Unit, C10—a paramilitary hit squad that killed enemies of the state in neat, efficient operations, as far afield as Angola. Suspected terrorists were captured and brought to Vlakplaas to be tortured for information, and even turned. Those who couldn't be turned were executed, their bodies disposed of somewhere on the beautiful grounds of this farm.

As Sunil came in the door, a pretty blond woman in khaki fatigues rose from behind a desk and approached him.

Dr. Singh, I presume, she said.

Yes, I am.

Come in, come in, we've been expecting you. Did you have a nice ride over? It is a beautiful drive, even though I don't get to do it enough. I just don't like the city, you know, all that violence. She waved him to a chair by her desk. Please sit, sit. Drink?

No, thank you, he said.

Okay, well, here's what we need, she said, putting a pile of papers in front of him. I need you to sign and initial everywhere you see a red mark; no need to read it all, it's standard counterterrorist issue contracts and stuff like that. Life insurance—you know, if you get killed in the line of duty. Your family will get the money. You do have a family? No? What a shame, a nice young man like you should have a family. Oh well, maybe soon. Here's a pen.

It took Sunil ten minutes just to wade through and find all the red marks to sign next to.

All done? Good, good. Leave your bag here and I'll have it sent to your quarters. You will be sharing with the other blacks here; their quarters are at the back. But for now, you are to go to Shed 10, which is over there, she said, pointing, and join the officers you came in with. They will take you to meet Eugene. He runs this place and he is eager to meet you.

Shed 10 was easy to find. He just followed the screams and the subsequent three gunshots. As he got to the front of the shed, which was more like a barn, the two white officers were loading the body of the hooded man onto the front of a jeep, strapping him down like an antelope carcass.

There you are, one of them said. Get in. Eugene wants to meet you.

The Land Rover roared over the rough terrain, heading out behind the farm, across a stretch of hills littered with stubby grass and rocks. The compound fell away behind them, lost in a cloud of dust and debris. Sunil noticed the ribbon of water to his left. Idyllic willows, drooping gracefully over the river, lined the entire length of it.

Vlakplaas River, the driver said. Good, eh?

Yes, Sunil said to be polite.

And now here, over beers, Eugene was asking him if he was philosophical only ten feet away from the body of the hooded man.

You like the more practical things? Maybe love? Do you have a stukkie, Eugene asked.

No, I don't have a girlfriend, Sunil said.

More of a one-night-stander then, eh, love them and leave them, Eugene pressed on. No judgments from me.

None of that, Sunil said, taking a swig of beer.

So what do you believe in then?

I don't know, Sunil said.

The fire in the pit was going strong and the men were roasting kudu steaks on a grill placed at an angle over the fire. The gamey smell was nauseating to Sunil.

I like you; you're an honest man. I can see we are going to get along. When I was a child, I used to believe in God, but as the Bible says, when you become a man you must give up your childish ways, Eugene said.

So what do you believe in now, Sunil asked.

Eugene put his weathered copy of *Inferno* down and scooped up a handful of dirt. As in much of Africa, it was red, like a handful of blood. Even in West Africa where the surface soil was a deep black loam, if you dug a little, the red turned up, underneath everything; like the very continent's blood: everyone was buried in it and everyone came from it. If there was an Africa, this was it. Eugene was crumbling the earth into a fine red drizzle.

I believe in this, this fucked-up land we call Africa, he said. I'm a real Boer like that. Like the Zulu or the Ndebele, I live and die for this earth. I sleep it, I dream it, I taste it, I love it, hell, I even breathe it.

I see, Sunil said.

It was hot, and flies were beginning to buzz around the dead man and the stack of kudu meat, both raw and cooked. The men were eating, drinking, and generally joking around. The mood seemed light, like any picnic Sunil had attended.

Baas, you want some food, one of the men called to Eugene.

He shook his head, never taking his eyes from Sunil's face.

See, I'm nothing like these barbarians, he said. That's why I brought you in. These men care nothing for Africa, even the blacks among them. They care nothing for causes. They only care about having and using brutish power. Without thinkers like me, it will all be taken from them, because that kind of brutish power cannot survive for long. It begins to feed on itself.

That takes no great insight to realize, Sunil said, swatting at a fly. If you brutalize an entire people to have your way then you must always live with the fear of retaliation; it means you can never drop your menacing guard. We can only live like that for so long before we slip up. That's what you do have in common with these men, Dante or the *Bhagavad Gita* notwithstanding.

Eugene let the rest of the earth drizzle from his hands. Sunil became aware suddenly that the men by the barbecue had stopped talking. The only sound was Eugene dusting his hands off and the buzzing of flies. Then there was the unmistakable click of a hammer cocking on a gun. Sunil felt the hair on his neck rise to attention. Although he could not see who had the gun, because his back was to them, he knew it was pointed at him. Eugene looked from Sunil to the men behind him and shook his head. The hammer was released and just like that, the chatting and laughter resumed behind Sunil.

I like you, Sunil. I really need a man who speaks his mind, Eugene said, picking up his book and waving it at Sunil. So what else do you make of a man like me?

Professionally?

It would hardly be personal since you don't know me.

And there won't be a gun to my head?

No, no, of course not, Eugene said, smiling, eyes cold.

Sunil took a swig of beer. He knew this was a test, but he

wasn't sure how to pass it. There were a lot of metal clanking sounds coming from behind him but he didn't turn around.

You are a man who strives for the power to control other people, he said.

But why do you think that is?

I would say it is because the striving and the power keep you from realizing just how helpless you really are. It protects you from facing the fact that others are manipulating you, that regardless of what you might claim, your philosophy is simply a way to rationalize what you do for others too afraid to do their own dirty work; that you are in a way also a victim of the apartheid state.

You are wrong about me, Sunil. Unlike men like you and even Dante here who have wandered into the dark forest of error unknowingly and who now desperately want to return to their joy, kept from it by your own demons, your ferocious beasts of worldliness, I came here to this hell by choice. Those beasts that are your terrors are my constant companions, sometimes my pets, sometimes my leaders, but never ever the source of terror. I have no terror, you see. I'm not like Dante, who has come upon the sign that asks all who enter to abandon hope. I came here to find hope. I know that I have done bad things, that I must continue to do bad things, but I do so for the ideal. For the utopia that this land was and will remain—we drove the blacks from it and we drove the British from it, and I will be damned if I will let any Afrikaner destroy it. Do you understand? This is the only thing that will last, this land, long after those fools and incontinent cowards and liars in Pretoria and Bloemfontein have been driven from power. Let me tell you, it is hard to tell sometimes who is being controlled and who is doing the controlling, and so the only way forward is to have purpose, and purpose is an ideal. That ideal can be found in heroes like Arjuna. Do you know what Arjuna means?

Sunil shook his head.

Do you know who he was?

Sunil shook his head again.

Your father, before he died, was Indian, right? You of all people should know about the hero of the *Bhagavad Gita*.

My father was Sikh.

Arjuna means light, white, shining, bright, Eugene continued, as though Sunil had not spoken. Arjuna is a peerless archer and a reluctant hero who doesn't want to go to war at first because he loathes having to kill his own relatives who share a different ideology. But Krishna comes to convince him of his duty, the warrior's duty. That was his code, which was the ideal that transformed everything Arjuna did to an act of God, to an act of the highest ethical order.

Do you think you are Arjuna, Sunil asked.

My friend, a tracker who taught me how to love this land, a Zulu, told me that there are two kinds of people in the world, farmers and warriors. You are clearly a farmer. Listen, I don't think the blacks are savages like my friends over there by the fire. I think that they are honorable people, but in the hierarchy of food, they are wildebeests and we are lions. The lion doesn't hate the wildebeest; he just knows he is the better. I'm not a racist, *ja?* Just a pragmatist.

Sunil said nothing.

Let's get on with it! Eugene yelled at the men. Pack up the food first.

The sun was beginning to dip behind the hilltop to their west, by the river, as the men began to pack up for the night. The food was wrapped carefully, attentively even, and placed into coolers. Then more wood was gathered and the fire in the pit fed until it raged, more bonfire than barbecue. The earlier grill had been removed and from the grass a larger one had been picked up and erected over the fire.

Did you know, Eugene said, that Dante describes hell as a funnel-shaped cone that bores into the center of the Earth? Like a wormhole, no pun intended. I like that image, the idea of descending concentric rings of hell, each ring a different level of sin, each ring its own kind of torture populated by its own depraved souls, and, at the very center, Satan himself. Now that's an interesting being, an angel with a sense of purpose. He doesn't whine like Christ in the garden of Gethsemane when the hard thing has to be done. He just gets on with it. He knows that he is Jesus's dark soul, his unconscious, and his id, that there is no meaning to any of this, no God, without him. Now, that's a sense of purpose.

So you are both Arjuna and Satan, Sunil asked.

Yes, you could say that. They are both balanced between their human ideal and their animal baseness. Nature worships harmony. I told you, this land is my purpose. It has taught me everything; Dante and the *Gita* just provided the language. My father worked as a ranger in Kruger trying to protect wildlife from poachers. He taught me that the only people who really respect and understand this world are the Bushmen; they know everything must live in balance, in harmony with everything else. Have you seen a lion stalk a wildebeest? It does so with respect. It takes its time and tries to make its kills as elegant and efficient as possible. When it kills it doesn't do so for sport or because its feelings have been hurt, it kills for hunger and protection, nothing more. And in this way it brings honor to its victims. And what it doesn't eat of its kill, the land takes back, using scavengers from the four-legged kind down to the microscopic kind. Nature uses everything in a cycle of honor, each thing in its right place. I told you that I am different from these men. When I kill a man, or a woman, it is with regret and honor. I never dispose of their bodies; I return them to the honor of

nature's use. I feed their bodies to the scavengers; I grind
their bones up and fertilize the flowers in the compound. I
pray when I do this, not in a Christian way, but in the way of
Bushmen, I say to the souls of the dead, You can leave this
place now and return in another form because you have been
honored. I am an elegant and efficient killer, and a warrior
with the highest ideals; I take no joy in my work, except
when it is done with honor. This in the end is the truth of
this land.

Sunil swallowed. And these men, he asked. I can't imagine
what they would do that could be worse.

Watch, Eugene said.

The men had gathered axes and machetes and they were
systematically chopping the hooded man into pieces, which
they threw onto the grill.

They are not—

Going to eat him? No, they are disposing of him. They
don't care that he be returned; they care only that he not be
identifiable. It will take about six hours to finish burning his
body; highly inefficient, and what is worse is that there is no
honor in this.

And yet you let it happen.

All great generals know that they must allow their men
sport. All work and no play is bad for morale. This is their
sport.

Sunil watched the policemen drinking as the hooded man
burned, white and black together, united in this terror.

Do you know why that man died, Eugene asked.

I cannot imagine, Sunil said.

He wouldn't give up information about the location of
ANC terrorists that he was known to associate with. That's
why you are here. I want you to find ways with psychology
and drugs to improve the interrogations. I don't want to waste
bodies. I want you to turn prisoners into informants. Only

those who must die will die. I don't enjoy the slaughter; I am a warrior, not a killer.

I traveled from Pretoria with that man, Sunil said. He begged for his life the entire journey.

He wasn't a man to them, Sunil. It's like this: every creation story needs a devil. For the Boer, the blacks are the demons.

The man never confessed, Sunil asked, the fire dancing off his eyes and skin, reflecting in Eugene's glasses.

Never, Eugene breathed, something like respect in his voice.

Then I am just like that man, Sunil said.

How so?

Can I tell you a story?

Sure, Eugene said. I like stories. They help us bond.

Bertolt Brecht told of a European peasant caught by the Nazi invasion. An SS officer commandeers the man's house and tells him, From now on, I will live here and you will serve me and attend to my every need, and if you do not, I will kill you. Do you submit to me? The peasant doesn't answer but spends the next two years serving the SS officer in every way. Then the Russians come and liberate the town. They gather all the Nazis in the square, and just before they are shot, the peasant comes up to the officer and answers the question that he greeted with silence two years before. No, he spits at the officer, I will not submit to you. This is the end that awaits apartheid.

Perhaps, Eugene said, and if I am that officer in your story, I will go happy knowing that all I did was in service of a higher ideal and has already been transformed into God's work. But for now, we need to end some of this killing. Will you help me?

No, but I will help men and women like him, Sunil said, pointing to the burning man. I don't expect it to be transformed into God's work, but only hope that mercy may find me before the end of my life.

Welcome aboard, Eugene said.

Together they stood in silence, for the next six hours, watching the burning man.

MONDAY

Forty-seven

Dawn almost never brings clarity with it, and this morning was no different. It was close to four a.m. when Salazar dropped Sunil off.

One of your guests is still waiting, the doorman said as he let him in.

Guests? There's more than one?

Yes, Dr. Singh, your girlfriend and another woman. An older one.

My girlfriend?

The young lady who is always here. Asia, I think her name is.

Ah, and the older one?

She signed in as Dr. Jackson. She had the same work ID as you. I thought you might be working late, but she left very soon after she arrived.

Huh, thank you, Sunil said. He was unsettled by the idea that Sheila and Asia had met. He didn't understand why Sheila had come, but he didn't like that she knew about Asia.

Oh, also the police were here. Several units were broken into and trashed. We were unable to reach you, so please let us know when you get in if your unit was affected too. I will come up and take pictures and file a report with the police for you. At the moment we think it wasn't a robbery but the work of vandals.

How did vandals get into a secure building, Sunil asked.

The doorman looked down at his shoes. The police and management are investigating, he said.

Sunil contemplated calling Salazar. Fuck, he thought, this is not what I need now. Thank you, he said to the doorman, and crossed to the elevators. As the doors closed, Sunil reached for his phone. Why hadn't anyone tried to call him, he wondered, and then remembered that his phone had been off, and that he still hadn't listened to any of his messages.

Why would vandals break into this building? Fuck, he was too tired for drama. He had barely inserted his key into the lock when the door swung open and Asia stood there, face less swollen than before, but clearly badly bruised. She was wearing his shirt and not much else, and in that moment, Sunil hated himself because he was at once turned on and torn up for her.

Asia, he said.

Sunil.

What happened?

I've missed you, she said, and her voice was very quiet.

They stood there for a while, as though stranded, stuck, as if waiting for directions from someone hidden in the wings. He smiled suddenly and touched her face, and she pulled back, wincing.

Can I come in, he asked, as though he needed permission.

She stepped back and he shut the door behind him, then drew her to him, holding her close, yet gently, so as not to hurt her.

Did the vandals do this to you?

No, she said. They were long gone by the time I got here.

Did a client do it?

She nodded against his shoulder.

Have you been checked out, medically?

I'm fine, really.

Was it, you know—

Rape? No.

What then?

Someone tried to kill me.

Oh baby, he said, and his voice was heavy with sorrow and guilt and despair. I'm so sorry, so sorry. What did the police say?

The casino handled it. You know, it would get awkward with the police; I would be arrested for solicitation. Besides, he got away.

I'm so sorry, Sunil repeated, realizing that, like most people, he kept forgetting that although prostitution was legal in most of Nevada, it was actually illegal in Vegas itself.

I'm okay, Asia said, but her voice was slight, a faint tremolo against his skin.

They stood there for a while in silence, Sunil stroking her hair.

Sheila was here looking for you, she said, trying to keep the jealous bite out of her voice.

Did she say what she wanted?

To see you. Like me, she was worried. We'd both been trying to call you all day.

I'm sorry. My phone was switched off.

I needed you today.

I'm sorry.

She pulled away, wrapping her arms tight around herself. Where were you?

Salazar and I went to chase down a lead in the desert.

Who is Salazar, she asked. She hadn't meant for her voice to be shrill, but it was.

The detective who brought the twins into my institute.

What twins?

The ones you didn't want to talk about, remember, he said.

Right, she said. Of course.

The doorman says the police were here. Did they bother

you, he asked, unconsciously straightening the Kentridge painting, looking things over, trying to tell if anything was missing, wondering if it was too soon to go through his effects.

No, she said. Nobody came here.

Do you need anything, he asked. Something to drink, to eat, or something for pain?

Asia shook her head.

Can you tell me about your attack? Do you know who it was?

She nodded. Yes, she said.

He sat next to her on the couch, noting that the Bible where he'd hidden the hard drive with his research was open, the disk gone. This is not the time, he said to himself, forcing his attention back to the moment, to Asia. He took her hands in his, and something about this moment, about his absence in her time of need, reminded him of Jan and of the whitewashed room in Vlakplaas. He pushed the memory down, but not before he saw a spray of crimson pattern the white walls.

Who was it, a regular?

A new client, relatively new, she said.

As she spoke she saw in his eyes how difficult this conversation was for him, and something inside her took pleasure at that. At the knowledge that even beyond himself, beyond any control he could have, he loved her. And in that moment she knew she couldn't drag the moment out. There was no kindness in protecting him, or herself for that matter, from the terrible truth of it.

It was your friend Eskia.

Sunil, who had been stroking her hair, felt himself stiffen, his hand unconsciously gripping her hair.

Ow, she said, so softly it was barely a sound.

I'm sorry, he said, letting go. Eskia, you said?

Eskia.

He needed to sit down. No, wait, he was sitting down. He didn't know Eskia was in town. What the fuck was going on? Had Eskia broken in here? To harm Sunil or just steal his work?

Why, he asked, not sure what he meant. Did he mean, Why did he hurt you or Why would you sleep with my friend, my rival, my nemesis, even if you are a hooker?

Why what, Sunil?

Why would he try to hurt you, Sunil said, gathering himself, bracing. Why did he do this?

He said he wanted to hurt you the way you hurt him before he kills you.

Kills me?

Yes, he said he was going to kill you.

Sunil got up and walked over to the window.

Why does he want to kill you, Asia asked.

Sunil said nothing, unable to speak for the sheer rage that was burning through him. Why hadn't he seen this coming? The e-mail with Jan's ring should have been enough, but he thought the text was from South Africa. It never even occurred to him that it could have originated in the United States. He knew the only way Eskia could have got that ring was by exhuming Jan's body. And because he had been there, because he had seen what Eugene did to Jan when Sunil couldn't turn her with the drugs and mind-altering methods he was perfecting, he knew that if he hadn't found that ring on the remains—a ring that Sunil had slipped into that anonymous hole in the ground as a kindness, as a way to make sure Jan's spirit could find its way into the underworld—Eskia would never have been able to identify the remains as Jan's. He wouldn't ever have found whatever closure he was trying to create. And now this.

Sunil, why does Eskia want to kill you?

Sunil shook his head. Something that happened a long time ago, he said, barely above a whisper.

Something very bad, she asked, realizing even as the words formed that it was a pointless question. She already knew the answer to it.

Yes, he said. Something very bad.

Did you do it?

It's complicated, he said.

Did you kill someone important to him, she interrupted, impatient.

I didn't kill her, he said.

She let out her breath.

But I did nothing to stop it either, he said.

Who was she?

Jan, he said.

Someone he loved?

Someone we both loved.

Jan. And when Asia said the name it brought an old and yet familiar ache back to Sunil and he stood there, wide open and weak, the light passing through him, refracting nothing.

Asia got up from the couch and approached him. She stood behind him for a while, barely an inch between them, and yet it was the chasm between worlds. She stepped forward and wrapped herself around him. Her feelings confused, churning, unsure whether to be angry with him or to comfort him, but yet wanting desperately to hold on to him.

Tell me everything, she said, afraid to ask, her breath hot on his back through his shirt.

Are you sure, he asked.

Yes, she said, thinking, No, I don't want to hear about her, but knowing this exorcism was the only way forward, for her, for Sunil, for both of them. This woman she knew was still alive for Sunil.

And so he told her.

And in the two hours that he spoke, they went from standing by the window to sharing tea in the kitchen and then finally to intertwining their limbs in bed, where they fell into a fitful sleep.

The shrill ring of a cell phone woke Sunil. In the dark bedroom he fumbled around for it. What, he said.

This is Salazar.

What the fuck, Salazar! What time is it?

Just after six. I'm sorry to wake you.

What is it, Sunil asked, glancing over at Asia as he got out of bed and shuffled into the living room. She was still deep asleep as he shut the door behind him.

I need you to come.

Come where?

I'm out by Lake Mead.

Bodies?

Yes. Several bodies, and there's one we both know.

Who?

I need you to come.

How will I find you?

There's a car waiting downstairs for you.

Okay. Fuck, Sunil muttered as he hung up and pulled some clothes on.

As promised, there was a police car waiting outside. He paused, thinking how much he hated the uniforms. Thinking how impossible it was to explain the sheer terror of a Casspir rolling into Soweto, bigger than a tank, more invulnerable it seemed, a sheer beast.

Is everything all right, Dr. Singh, the doorman asked as he opened the door.

Why don't you worry about doing your job so thieves don't just walk in, Sunil snapped, sliding into the back of the police car. They were already pulling away from the building when Sunil remembered Asia was alone upstairs and in danger from Eskia should he choose to return.

Wait, he said, stop.

And he made the cops wait while he called Salazar. He told him about the break-in and said he would come only if Salazar provided police protection for Asia. He omitted that he knew what she might be in danger from. Salazar made one of the cops from the car stay. The guy didn't look too happy about it, and Sunil made a mental note to come back with coffee and a snack for him. He texted Asia so that when she woke up to the cop outside, she wouldn't be startled, and then he was off.

As the car picked up speed, lights and siren going, the sun was coming up over the Luxor, washing the dark pyramid in gold.

Shit, Sunil thought, I need to check in with the twins and Brewster. Not to mention he had to get a visitor's pass for Fred. One day away from the institute and he was already behind. Whatever Salazar wanted him for had better be fucking incredible, he thought.

He wasn't aware he had fallen asleep until he felt Salazar shake him awake. The police car had arrived at Lake Mead and, from the looks of it, so had half the Las Vegas Police Department.

Forty-eight

The peacocks were screaming again and Water rubbed his eyes as he got out of bed. He shuffled to the window but there were no birds in sight. He yawned and hit the Nurse Call button.

Fire's caul snapped back and he yawned too, breath extra funky from the heat of the caul.

Jesus, those fucking birds! I swear if I could I would kill the entire gaggle, he wheezed.

Ostentation, Water reminded him. Not gaggle, ostentation.

Fuck you too, Fire said. Did you call the nurse? I would kill for a cup of coffee. Or at the very least, break a few knees.

Babies are born without kneecaps, Water said.

Really, Fire said. This early? Fuck, I'm too old for this shit.

"Senectitude" means old age, Water said.

And shut up or I'll fuck you up means shut up or I'll fuck you up.

We shed skin particles as we get older, Water continued, as though Fire hadn't spoken. We shed two pounds a year and by the time we're seventy, we've shed one hundred and five pounds of dead skin.

Jesus, you fucker. I'm trying to think about breakfast.

The food that is digested in your stomach is called chyme.

Fire took a swing at Water's face, but his arms weren't co-ordinated and it just looked like Water was swinging a puppet around.

Good morning, gentlemen, the nurse said, responding to the call button. How can I help?

Coffee and some food, Fire wheezed.

It's too early for breakfast, but I'll rustle up some coffee and see if I can't find a couple of cookies.

Do you all have special courses in talking to patients in a condescending tone?

In 1670, Dorothy Jones of Boston was granted the first American license to sell coffee, Water said.

Why can't you be nice like your brother, the nurse asked, smiling at Water, before shutting the door behind him.

And where the fuck is the doctor, Fire asked. He's been gone a whole day. How are we going to get out of here?

Water smiled. Fred is coming for us, he said.

Forty-nine

The crucified horned figure stopped Sunil.

I know, Salazar said gently, handing him a cup of coffee. It's pretty grim.

Naked except for white boxer shorts, the horned figure was nailed to a rough wooden cross, his tattooed arms spread like wings. His throat had been cut nearly through, so that the horned head dangled dangerously close to falling off.

The cross itself was rising out of a heap of corpses.

What the fuck! Sunil said.

Are you going to be okay?

Yes. Is that Horny Nick?

Yes.

Why would anyone want to do this?

I don't know. You're the expert on sick fucks, Salazar said.

Sunil shook his head, watching as the forensic unit took photos and collected samples as though they were inspecting an elaborate movie set. Shit, he said.

I know, right, Salazar said.

Shaking his head, Sunil tried to focus, forcing himself into damage-control mode.

I'm not sure this killing is related to the ones from two

years ago. For a start, those body dumps weren't ritualized like this; neither was the most recent one you saw two months ago, right? This is so radically different. Completely different pattern, different signature. Serial killers are very fixed in their patterns. If this is a serial killer, then you have two different people, Sunil said.

Don't tell me that, Salazar said. I don't want to have to think that there may be more than one.

Sunil wanted to allay Salazar's fears, to tell him that the killings from two years earlier, as well as these, were the work of the institute. His work. He opened his mouth to speak but shut it again. This wasn't Brewster's work. At least, Horny Nick wasn't. There had to be another killer. Probably the same one who killed that girl two years before.

Anything you want to tell me, he asked.

At least we know the twins aren't the killers you're looking for, Sunil said. They've been locked up.

Why do you think the killer targeted Horny Nick?

I don't know. Are the other kids safe?

Yes.

Good, Sunil said, not knowing why.

Salazar was watching him closely.

What is it, Detective, Sunil asked.

Salazar shrugged. Nothing, he said.

Sunil turned his attention to the crucified kid. Poor devil, he muttered.

Listen, I looked into your situation on your way here.

What situation, Sunil asked.

You know, your concerns about your apartment and your worry about being targeted. I mean, normally I wouldn't do that, but you asked me to assign protection to your girlfriend and I needed to know. Anyway, turns out several apartments in your building were vandalized too, so I don't think you are the target. It was just random. Unless there's something you're not telling me.

You have to trust me on this one, Detective.

See, now, that's the kind of crazy talk that just sends up red flags to old policemen like me. I don't even trust the evidence half the time, so why should I trust you?

There are things I can't tell you.

As they spoke, Horny Nick was taken down from the cross. Sunil watched as the coroner and his officers stood on the other bodies to get him. He was laid out on a stretcher, and slowly the other bodies were laid out too. He and Salazar watched the men work, the careful attention to detail as they dismantled the rise of corpses, as though solving a puzzle, each step carefully photographed, each body systematically mined for evidence. It was slow, the work, and it took nearly an hour for the bodies to be separated. Sunil counted twelve lying there, with Horny Nick making thirteen.

Twelve bodies, Sunil said out loud.

What's that, Salazar asked.

The twelve bodies match the twelve apostles, with the crucified Christ making thirteen. Except this was no Christ but a horned figure, a devil on a cross. The devil and his twelve apostles.

Fuck, that's some dark shit, Salazar said. You have to give me something.

Sunil shook his head. I'm not a profiler, he said. You might need an expert from the FBI. I've given you all I have.

I don't trust the fucking FBI. You helped me two years ago, and I need your help now.

No, I didn't help two years ago. If I had, we wouldn't be here today.

We have to try, Salazar said. He grabbed Sunil by the arm and dragged him over to where Horny Nick lay. Look at him.

That kid didn't deserve to die. Look at him! Now, tell me, do you think you might know who did this?

Sunil stared at the lifeless eyes of the teenager and the jagged line where his throat had been cut.

No, Sunil said. No, I don't know who could have done this.

Fifty

Asia was gone by the time Sunil got back. She had left a note saying she was going home. In that moment he had to confront the fact that he had no idea where Asia lived. It was true that she had always deflected his attempts to come round, but still, in retrospect, he could have tried harder.

He called her. It went straight to voice mail.

Asia, he said. You aren't safe on your own. When you get this, ditch this phone—it can be tracked—and then pack some things and come stay here with me. It was stupid and he knew it. She was no safer with him than at her place. Fuck, he said, and hung up. He had to get to the institute, but first a shower and change of clothing.

On the way out, he stopped by the doorman's desk. There was a new guy, which he didn't mind since he hated the last one.

Good morning, Dr. Singh.

Could you arrange for a reliable service to clean my apartment?

On the way to the institute he called Sheila's cell. It went straight to voice mail.

Sheila, it's Sunil. Call me, he said, trying to sound casual—no need to cause any panic.

Good morning, Dr. Singh, the receptionist said as he walked in, a little too cheerfully.

Sunil smiled. Brewster on the warpath?

The receptionist nodded, her smile frozen.

Good, Sunil said.

And it was good. Dealing with Brewster, and the twins, would be a welcome distraction from the events of the past twenty-four hours. He was about to walk away when he remembered Fred was coming.

Listen, Janice, he said to the receptionist. I'm expecting a visitor today. Fred Jacobs. I'll just fill in this visitor request form with all her information. Please make sure she is shown to my office when she comes.

Of course, Dr. Singh.

Brewster was waiting in Sunil's office, pacing back and forth, taking deep drags on the oxygen canister stuffed into his lab-coat pocket. Sunil stood on the threshold and watched him, thinking it would be relatively easy to kill Brewster. All one would need to do would be to substitute liquid nitrogen for the oxygen.

Dr. Brewster, Sunil said, shutting the door behind him and crossing to his desk. To what do I owe the honor?

Where have you been?

On my day off?

You have no days off until the twins have been dealt with. I thought I made that clear.

No, no, I don't remember us agreeing to that. Still, no harm done, eh? They were busy getting an MRI anyway, as I remember.

Your tone is more confrontational than usual, Dr. Singh, Brewster said, sitting down suddenly.

Are you okay, Sunil asked, wanting to, but not saying: You look closer to death than usual.

Tired, Brewster said.

There have been more body dumps. Another teenager among them. Throat slit. Plus twelve men, Sunil said.

I see. Well, we have the MRIs back, Brewster said.

Sunil sat behind his desk and turned his computer on. With a few clicks, he had accessed the images from the MRI. Did you see these yet, Sunil asked.

The MRIs? Of course.

Doesn't look like they are joined by much. They don't seem to share any vital organs.

No, they don't. We could probably separate them very easily.

Not very easily, no, Sunil said. It's still a risky operation given how long they've been conjoined, and at their age, a separation has never been tried. They could die.

I'm just pointing out that we could if our research depended upon it.

I can't imagine why it would, Sunil said.

Well. It's worth noting, Brewster said.

Did you notice that although Water's brain lights up pretty well, Fire's stays mostly dormant, Sunil asked. That's very strange. These results are accurate, right?

Yes, they are accurate. I noticed that too and I thought it was strange since Fire is the animated one. Of course, since he is smaller they could have overdosed him with the anesthetic.

That wouldn't explain why his brain looks dead, like the only things alive are the instinctual circuitry—like respiration.

I told you these twins would be fascinating for our study.

About that, Sunil said. I don't think I want them in my study. I'm thinking I should just let them go. Let the police and county deal with them. Tomorrow is Tuesday anyway, which is the last day we can keep them without admitting them.

Then admit them.

For what? I don't need them in my study and I don't think they are crazy. Odd, eccentric even, but not crazy.

I wasn't asking.

Sunil looked at Brewster for a minute, sizing him up. We need to talk, he began.

Do we? Think carefully before you speak, Sunil.

I think you've started the trials up again.

That's a serious accusation, Sunil, Brewster said.

And yet you're not denying it.

You're right. I have been running live tests again. Your research is taking too long, particularly the control dose. The military contract that funds you moved the timetable up and I knew that I couldn't depend on you to do the tests. You aren't the risk taker I had hoped for. You are far too deliberate, even for a scientist.

Are you responsible for the dead homeless men?

No, Sunil, Brewster said, smiling. It's your research, your doing, so I would say you are responsible.

I can't believe you would be this irresponsible with my work and my reputation. Do you know this could damage me irrevocably if it gets out, Sunil said, his voice higher than he meant for it to be.

Stop being so excitable. I've made you a very rich man. Not bad for a black from the slums of Soweto. The army likes the tests so far. I told them you could have the antidote ready in a month. They're ready to begin tests on their soldiers.

I need more time, more research. Rage is not just chemical. It might be mimetic, too, do you understand? If we start administering that drug to soldiers, they will go berserk and kill each other. There is no controlling that kind of rage.

Well, the U.S. military is not going to wait.

I am close to a breakthrough. I just need more time and no more distractions. We have everything we need from them. MRIs, DNA, X-rays—

I'm still not convinced.

Well, I will give it one last shot. An interview today and

then if you want them to stay, you'll have to sign the papers, Sunil said.

Brewster got up and walked over to the door. Pausing, he turned. It's nice to have you back on board, Sunil, he said and closed the door behind him.

Fifty-one

Fred parked her jeep in the visitors' lot, mentally noting the rental parked two cars down. She could always spot rentals and cop cars. She could also tell that the guy sitting in the front seat was up to no good. That was her true gift in the carnival, besides running everything. An unerring insight into human nature and a true gift for the con: a formidable combination. She lit a cigarette and walked over to the rental.

Hello, she said.

Hello, Eskia said.

She touched the bridge of his glasses. Anyone ever tell you that you look like Superman with those glasses, she asked.

Superman didn't wear glasses.

Fred smiled. All right, Clark Kent, then.

So who are you?

More important, who the fuck are you? Who do you work for, a rival institute? Are you some kind of industrial spy?

I'm just bird-watching.

I don't need you fucking up my deal here.

And what is your deal?

That is none of your business. What is your business is not fucking up mine. So what are you anyway, some kind of private eye? I know you're not a cop. All I want to know is will you be moving on?

When I'm done, Eskia said, smiling. He wanted to ram his fist into Fred's face. Who did she think she was, coming over to him and talking shit? How did she spot him anyway? That could mean only one thing; she was very well trained. Was she CIA or DOD?

All the time they were talking, Fred was scanning Eskia's car for clues. She noted the laptop and reached into her bag and switched on the hard-drive copier she always carried. She could tell he was spooked that she had spotted him, which meant that his laptop probably didn't have any real firewalls or protection. Copying it would be easy.

Eskia reached into the messenger bag next to him on the seat and took out a gun with a silencer on it. Nothing could jeopardize his mission here. Even as he leveled the barrel at her chest as she leaned in, he was scanning the parking lot to see if it was empty. It was.

Clever, Fred said, seeing the gun. Just what every girl needs. A hole in her breast implants.

Well, I guess that's one way of ending this unpleasant conversation, Eskia said.

I guess, Fred said. What's the other option?

I'm sorry, did I suggest there was another option?

Fred smiled and blew cigarette smoke in his face. I have no idea who you are or what you're about, she said. But I have some business here today that cannot be interrupted. Can you stay out of it for today?

Or I could just shoot you now, Eskia said.

I'm a downwinder and a freak, she said. That means I've been paranoid and driven my whole life.

I don't know what that means, Eskia said, smiling and adjusting his glasses.

Fred watched his finger tighten slowly on the trigger and thought, What a fucker, he is one of those sick puppies who loves killing.

Look at your shirt. It looks like you spilled something, she said.

Eskia looked down and saw the red dot of a laser scope.

Oh no wait, Fred continued, that's my sniper. Silly me. Told you I was paranoid. Now, my advice is to lay low and forget your business here for today. Okay?

With that she was gone, headed for the main entrance to the institute, leaving Eskia to wonder who she was and how she could have one-upped him.

Across the lot, in a blue Volkswagen borrowed from a rookie, Salazar watched Fred. Who is that guy, he thought, and what the fuck was going on? He called in a favor with an old friend in the FBI to run the tags for him. Same guy he had looking into Sunil. He liked Sunil, but something was off about him. Something Salazar couldn't ignore.

Salazar adjusted the telephoto lens of the camera. Was that a targeting dot on the driver's shirt? He swung the camera around, scanning the rows of parked cars for the source. Sure enough, in a black SUV, a midget with a rifle pointed at the silver car was visible in the window. He guessed that was one of Fred's fighting midgets. Why she needed this kind of backup was unclear, but there was nothing he could do about it without compromising his cover in some way. Best to wait. He returned to looking at the rental just in time to see Fred disappear into the institute.

Salazar put down the camera with the telescopic and reached for his coffee. It could be a while. With the air off in the car, he was getting a little too hot. Fuck.

Dr. Singh is expecting you, Janice said, handing Fred her pass. John over here will escort you to his office.

Fred turned to look at John. Clearly security, she thought—black suit, black T-shirt, all a tad too obvious.

Hi, John said. Before we go, I need to look in your bag. Is that okay?

Sure, Fred said, handing over her snakeskin bag. While John expertly went through the bag, Janice tried to make small talk.

On the form Dr. Singh filled out it says you run a carnival, she said.

Yes, Fred said, smiling. That was the snake boy until he displeased me, she said, pointing to her bag.

Janice winced and smiled tightly. John didn't pause in his search. Fred noticed the look on Janice's face and smiled at her sweetly.

This way, please, John said, handing her back her bag. Fred took it, glad that John hadn't thought to take her cell phone apart. If he had, in the place where the battery should be he would have found a small wedge of Semtex flattened and a small detonator that was activated by pushing the Call and pound-sign buttons simultaneously.

The elevator ride up was fast and silent. Like bad sex, Fred thought. The door opened up on the sixth floor.

This way, John said.

Soon they were outside Sunil's door. John knocked.

Enter, Sunil called.

Your guest, John said, leaving them alone.

Sunil crossed from behind his desk.

Welcome, he said, offering Fred his hand. How are you? Good trip?

Yeah, sure, thanks. Hey, nice office.

Thank you. Can I offer you a drink? Coffee?

Something stronger?

Yes, of course, he said, going to fetch the single malt from the sideboard. As he poured, Fred crossed to the wall of photographs.

Why cows, she asked, touching their hides through the frames.

Sunil looked up. Just something from my childhood, he said, handing her a glass.

She clinked it against his and took a swig. Good stuff, she said, *very* good. Is it single malt?

Yes.

So tell me about the cows, she said.

They're nothing, he said.

They take up a whole lot of wall space to be nothing, she said.

They're good photos. That's all it is sometimes, he said.

Yes, she said. Sometimes.

Please sit down, he said.

She sat in an armchair and crossed her legs. In jeans, knee-high boots, white shirt, and a simple necklace of turquoise, pale blue against her tanned chest, she looked casual, relaxed.

Are you married, Dr. Singh, she asked.

Sunil was taken aback by the question, and he mumbled his answer. No, he said, holding up his ring finger as proof, absently wondering to himself why he had bothered to do that.

Why not?

I don't know, he said. Work?

She smiled. Me too. Work.

Why do you ask?

Just making small talk, she said, finishing her drink in one gulp and holding out her glass for a refill.

Of course, he said, taking her glass and getting up. It wasn't clear if he meant of course I'll get you a refill, or of course you're making small talk.

I'm quite anxious to see the twins, she said as he handed her the refilled glass.

Yes. I'll have them brought up. This is going to be my last interview with them. If I sign them out you'll be able to take them home tomorrow. You might want to find a place to stay for the night.

Are you offering?

That would be inappropriate, Sunil said.

Of course, she said, and laughed.

Sunil went to his desk and picked up the telephone and dialed. Bring Fire and Water to my office now, he said.

Fifty-two

Asia was heading west, to the King of Siam, a bordello way out in the desert. The King of Siam looked like an ordinary low-sprawling ranch house nestled among twelve acres of green oasis in the desert. The place boasted a world-class spa; a stable with horse-riding lessons, where the exclusive clientele could ride bareback while fucking, if their tastes ran that way; a Tantra teacher; an Olympic-size swimming pool; tennis courts; and a private airstrip. What wasn't immediately obvious were the guards, who were everywhere.

The King of Siam was an exclusive establishment, a members-only cathouse with a membership fee in the high five figures. Its clientele included senators, congressmen, and CEOs. In addition to a selection of the most gifted, diverse escorts, it prided itself on its discretion. Most of the escorts were well educated, many with graduate degrees, and most spoke at least two languages, a necessity since many clients were international.

In a good week, even with the house taking its percentage, some girls could earn up to twenty thousand dollars. Even girls like Asia who didn't have college degrees and spoke only English could still average five thousand a week. Girls couldn't apply or audition for the King of Siam; Big Bill Brown, the owner, chose each girl usually after a chance encounter and a careful background check. In the ten years that they had been open, no one had ever breached the grounds, not even the most committed paparazzi. The joke was that only Area 51 had better security.

Asia had a standing invitation from Big Bill, ever since she'd spent a night with him in Vegas when she first got there. She had taken him up on the offer only once, for just a week, but she found it difficult to follow the house rules.

Even before Sunil had called her, pretty much as soon as she left his place, she ditched her phone and headed for this sanctuary where she knew she would not only be safe but could earn six figures easily in six months. She had every intention of calling Sunil, in a week or two. She wouldn't give up on him but she couldn't deal with the baggage in his life right now.

The landscape was a blur as she picked up speed on an incline. There wasn't much to see here anyway. Just ostrich and alpaca farms, abandoned malls built to service still-empty developments, the occasional deserted water park, desert, and more desert. Classic Nevada—where dreams died as quickly as they were born.

Genevieve was waiting when Asia arrived. Not much older than Asia, at twenty-eight, Genevieve had the poise of an older, more experienced woman.

Hello, Asia, she said. So Big Bill tells me you'll be staying with us for a while. Do you know how long?

Until I figure out some stuff.

A man, Genevieve asked, her voice soft, the texture somewhere between pity and envy.

Isn't it always, Asia said.

Genevieve smiled. You're welcome as long as you want. You'll be staying in Number 12. As always, the money gets processed through me, tips as well. The house now keeps thirty percent, but you'll find that our new services justify that.

Asia took the electronic key for her room. It felt strange to be back, yet oddly comforting. Here there was no pretense about what the girls did. They weren't escorts or hookers or companions or dates. They were just girls—old-fashioned and classy. A good thing; wholesome, even. As she picked up her bag to head down the hall, Genevieve called after her.

Cocktail hour is six. Prompt.

Okay, Asia said.

Whatever it is that you're running from, you're safe here, Genevieve said.

Asia smiled. I know, she said.

Fifty-three

Salazar yawned and stretched. He was still in the institute's parking lot. Eskia hadn't moved. Salazar lifted his camera to his face and studied him through the zoom. He moved the focus around, but Eskia was too far away to get a clear look at his expression. What does he want, Salazar wondered. His phone vibrated against his leg and he reached for it.

Yeah?

So I've got some information on that guy you asked me to run.

Do I need a notebook?

No. He used to be in the ANC's fighting arm in South Africa back when they still had apartheid, and then after the transition was made, he joined the South African Security Services. His file there is sealed even to Interpol, so I am guessing that means he has had some dealings in black ops.

Why is he here?

Visa says he is on holiday.

So this is personal?

Possibly—of course, he could just be lying.

Yeah, you're right. What about the other name I gave you?

What's all this about, Salazar?

Just a hunch, you know?

Well, his name checks out. Sunil Singh is who he says he is, a South African psychiatrist working here in Vegas on a green card. He has Department of Defense clearance, so he must be working on something important for the military.

Any connection between the two of them?

Nothing official, but I don't have access to that kind of information.

What kind is that?

You know, South Africa before 1990. The police and military systematically destroyed most of the records in South Africa before things were fully handed over to the blacks—

Was Sunil DOD or Special Forces over there?

Not as far as I can tell.

Thanks, I owe you.

You owe me several for this, Salazar. I'll never get to call in any of them, though, will I? I hear you're planning to retire, old man.

Fuck you, you dinosaur, Salazar said, laughing.

Tell you what. My wife loves those crazy boats you make. Give me a nice one for her and we'll call it even.

Come over whenever you like and pick one out.

He hung up.

What do you want, Eskia, Salazar muttered to himself. Are you the killer we're looking for?

He finished his coffee and went back to looking through the telephoto lens. Fuck, he had to pee. He put down the camera, reached for the empty coffee cup, unzipped, and sighed.

As he returned the now warm, half-full cup to the cup holder he made a mental note not to drink it by accident.

Fifty-four

Fred, Water said, and even Sunil could tell that he was in love.

Water, she said, crossing the room to hug him. As unlikely as it seemed, Sunil could tell that Fred loved Water, too.

At least one thing hasn't been a lie, he thought.

Doc, Fire said, where the fuck have you been?

Hello, Fire, Sunil said. Please, guys, sit.

They sat. Fred sat next to them on the couch.

Fred, Sunil said. Do you mind moving to the armchair over there?

Why?

This will go faster and easier if you can remain neutral throughout my interview. Physical space is the first step toward that.

Fred nodded. She squeezed Water's hand and moved. Crossing her legs, she cut a look at Sunil.

Water, how are you today, Sunil asked.

Water shrugged.

So where were you, Doc, Fire asked.

I went to get Fred for you, Water, Sunil said.

Water looked up and smiled shyly. I love Fred, he said. Fred loves Water.

Fred smiled.

Do you know what happened to us yesterday, Fire asked.

Yes, you had an MRI done, Sunil said.

It was an outrage. We were forced to undergo a medical procedure against our will at a zoo, a zoo!

I'm sorry about that. I tried to stop it on principle, Sunil said.

A lot of good your principles did us yesterday, Fire said.

Boys, Fred said, voice soft. Play nice. The doctor is trying to help you.

Water smiled at her, Fire looked away.

So your MRIs revealed something interesting. It seems that you are not conjoined at any vital spots. No major organs, no major arteries.

So, Fire asked.

Did nobody do any tests when you were born? You could have been separated with relative ease, Sunil said.

And what kind of life would I have had, Fire asked. I would be a small, immobile lump with a superior intelligence.

Is the life you have now any better? Stuck as you are to your brother's side? A burden to him?

Doctor, Sunil, please don't talk to them like that, Fred said. Her voice was still soft, but there was a definitive edge to it. The twins trust very few people. The only time they were presented with a chance for separation, as babies, it was by the doctors of Area 51 and there were conditions. Their mother, Selah, declined the offer, she said, riffling in her bag and retrieving her cell phone. She pretended to check it and then slipped it into her shirt pocket.

Look, I understand that they are your friends and you want to protect them, but I have a job to do here. I must ask you to be quiet if you want to remain in the room, and if you cannot be quiet then I will have to ask you to leave.

Fred put up her arms in surrender.

I'm sorry, she said.

Now, where were we, gentlemen?

Discussing the possibility of some Frankensteinian surgery, Fire said.

I never mentioned surgery, Sunil said.

You were talking about removing me from my brother's body, Fire hissed.

If it were removed from the body, the small intestine would stretch twenty-two feet, Water said.

The MRI shows some unusual results in the brain area, Sunil said.

Well, I am a genius, Fire said.

Yes, well, as it happens, this does concern your brain, Fire. You see, when we are at rest, even asleep, there are certain areas of the brain that are lit up, and when we are animated, speak, think, or react emotionally, different parts of the brain light up. Do you follow me?

I just said I was a genius, Doc. Of course I follow you, Fire said.

Well, it seems that your scan revealed something a little disturbing. The only areas that are lit up in your brain are at the old brain; you know, the medulla oblongata, the part that governs your autonomic systems. Your brain, for all other intents and purposes, is dead. The scan suggests that you are brain dead, Sunil said.

What the fuck, Doc, Fire said.

Really, Sunil, Fred began.

Sunil turned to her. Please stay out of this, he said. Now, he continued, turning back to Fire, something tells me you already knew this. So I want you to tell me exactly how can you be both so animated and brain dead at the same time?

I'm a yogi, Fire said, and laughed. Fuck, Doc, I told you when you met us. We are King Kongo, African Witchdoctor. We have strange powers, man. What can I tell you? We should be in a comic book, not a psych ward.

This is serious, Sunil said. I want to release you, but certain people here want to keep you here for tests, particularly given the new information on your brain.

One out of twenty people have an extra rib, Water said.

Here's what I know, Sunil said. Water is completely healthy and his brain is fully functional. In fact, according to his MRI, his brain is fully lit up. It would seem from the MRI that Water is in fact the genius.

The twins looked away.

I would go so far as to say that there is no Fire and Water. Just Water. Here's what I believe, and correct me if I am wrong. Fire was born brain dead, alive mostly because he had autonomic function. When the doctors wanted to remove him, it became clear to Selah that Fire would die very quickly if he were removed from Water, so she decided against the operation, which most mothers would do. Am I right so far?

The twins remained silent, and Fred moved uncomfortably in her chair.

It was bad enough that you were conjoined, but to have a parasitic, brain-dead, half-formed twin was worse, Sunil continued, ignoring Fred. So my guess is that you developed a way to make it appear as though Fire was alive. The bigger you made his character, the more believable he was. It's a very good plan, and I think you are very gifted.

Fuck you, Doc, Fire said. Where do you get off talking to me like that!

I'm sorry, Sunil said, not sounding very sorry at all. Look, I don't want to keep you here. Some things have come to light in the last twenty-four hours that place you very low on my priority list. I would like to establish that you are mentally capable and let you go. Then I can focus on what I want to do. Do you understand?

I don't know what you're talking about, Fire said.

Sunil turned to Water.

No pithy fact from you, Water?

Fact, Water said. Something known to exist, or to have happened, something known to be true. Fire and Water are facts.

Really, Sunil asked.

Dr. Singh, that is enough, Fred snapped.

Gentlemen, I have devised a very simple test to prove the fact of Fire and Water. I would like you both to talk at the same time.

What, Doc, Fire asked.

I've been so stupid, Sunil began.

I could have told you that, Fire said.

Fred smiled.

Remember when I asked you about Water's tongue, the first night I examined you?

No, I don't, Fire said.

I asked you if Water's mouth was always a little parted and his tongue moves and you said yes. I should have known then but I was so wrapped up in my own recent struggles. That's a classic tell for ventriloquism.

There are no classic tells for ventriloquism, Fire said.

Then prove me wrong. Both of you speak at the same time.

May I, Doc, Fred asked, walking over to the twins.

Sure, Sunil said.

Sitting next to the twins, Fred gently touched Water's face and embraced him. As she did so, she slipped her cell phone from her shirt pocket into the generous sweatshirt he had on. Pulling away, she kissed Water gently.

Tell him, she said. It's okay.

Water smiled and nodded. Turning to Sunil, he said, You are right, Doc.

About what, Sunil asked.

About everything.

Sunil sat back and let out his breath. He had been half hoping that he wasn't right. He got up and crossed to his desk, where he'd left the bottle of whiskey, and poured himself a drink. What a weekend. It was hard to believe all that had happened since Friday, and now this revelation. He almost wished the twins hadn't been performing. Before he knew it was true there was the slight chance that he could release them. Now he knew he couldn't. He knew without a shadow of a doubt that they were psychopaths. No, that Water was a psychopath. If he could pull off this act for so many years, then he could do anything. Sunil turned around and sat on the edge of his desk.

What were you doing at the lake with all that blood, he asked.

I really was just swimming. The water of the lake feels good, takes the pressure of Fire off my side. Do you know how much muscle control it takes to hold up a dead twin? Water is so very soothing and it's not like I can take a dip in my local gym's pool.

I suppose not, Sunil said. And the blood?

I knew about the body dumps; I couldn't risk a body.

Smart, Sunil said. Enough theater to attract law enforcement, but I still don't know why.

Sunil, Fred said.

Yes?

Can we cover Fire up, she said. He'll be fine under the sweatshirt. He's used to it. The truth is he freaks me out a bit, those eyes. Always has.

Like Ed Mordake's twin, Sunil said. Cover him up. It's fine. I'm a little freaked out too. Now that I know the truth, it's like having an animated corpse looking at you.

Fred nodded.

Tell me something, Sunil said.

Which of us are you asking, Fred said.

Both of you, either of you. I know you're members of the Downwinder Nation, a radical group. What does the Downwinder Nation do, exactly?

We are committed to the eradication of dangerous military research in Nevada, Arizona, and Utah. We find ways to close down facilities engaged in such research.

After everything that had happened in the last few days, Sunil wasn't as surprised as he might have otherwise been. This new information was just one more piece of a crazy week. And do you intend to close us down? I suppose that's why you are here, right?

We do what we can, Water said.

Why risk telling me all this? What is going to stop me from turning you in? You are threatening to destroy my research.

You won't turn us in, Fred said.

How do you know I won't?

Because you have more pressing matters on your mind, Fred said. I met a man outside who I think is looking for you. He has a gun with a silencer.

That's it. We're done here, Sunil said. I'm calling security to escort you out of the building.

With that, Sunil picked up the receiver and dialed the guard. After hanging up he said to Water: You realize I cannot let you go now.

Water just smiled.

I'll see you soon, my love, Fred whispered to Water, loud enough for Sunil to hear. With that she followed the guard out, without a backward glance.

See you around, Doc, Water said. Or maybe you won't. Remember, we are the witchdoctor. Laughing, he followed the security guard out.

When they left, Sunil walked back to his desk and poured another drink. He carried it over to the wall of zebu. Maybe Asia had been right. Maybe it was some tarot that he had unconsciously assembled. Too bad he couldn't read it.

To you, Asia, he said, raising his glass. I hope you are safe.

He downed the drink, straightened his clothes, and headed

out to see Brewster. As he waited for the elevator, his cell
rang. It was Sheila's number.

Sheila, he said, I've been worried about you.

It's me, Sunil, Eskia said.

You fokker! I'll kill you.

Someone will die today, that's for sure, Eskia said. And if
you don't want it to be Sheila, you had better come downstairs now. I'll be waiting.

Don't harm her, you shit. She had nothing do with this.

And Jan? What did she have to do with anything?

Why now, Eskia?

If you're not here in ten minutes I'm leaving with Sheila.

Don't harm her. I'm getting into the elevator now.

Sunil hung up and rode down to the lobby. In the parking
lot, Salazar watched Eskia start up his car and pull up to the
front of the institute. He saw Sunil come out and get into Eskia's car. As they drove off, Salazar started up the Bug and followed.

By her car, Fred lit up a cigarette and watched the cars
leave. She glanced at her watch. It was midafternoon. It
wouldn't be long now. She'd better get going. She pulled her
car around to the back of the institute, where deliveries were
made. A Dumpster hid her car from view.

She settled down to wait. Water should be out anytime now.

Fifty-five

Behind them, the sun was burning a hole in Vegas with the magnifying glass of the MGM. Sunil's right hand was secured to the door handle with a zip tie.

Just in case you think about escaping, Eskia said.

He did it as soon as Sunil sat down, before he had a moment to realize that Sheila wasn't in the car. As they headed west, Sunil pulled at the door.

Where is Sheila?

I don't have her, Eskia said. She was just the lure.

Where are we going?

For a ride. Somewhere private where we can talk honestly.

You could have just walked up to me and shot me anytime, Sunil said.

And how would that have been any fun?

You stole the disk from my place, Sunil said. Do you plan on selling the contents? If so, good luck with that; it's password protected.

I don't need luck. I have you. I was trained to be like your friend Eugene. You will tell me everything.

Eugene wasn't my friend, Sunil said.

How could you work for him, harming your own people? Give up every last shred of dignity to serve those killers. But you were not alone in that particular weakness, and thanks to the humanity of our leaders like Madiba and Tutu we forgave scum like you. But I will never forgive you for Jan.

Do you think that's what Jan would want?

If you speak her name again I will shoot you right here, so help me God.

Something in his tone told Sunil he wasn't kidding. Fine, he said. But can you at least tell me where we are going?

To your reckoning. Now, shut up while I drive.

Behind them Salazar took swigs from the bottle of whiskey in his jacket pocket. He had to keep reminding himself that the coffee cup, though still warm, was not full of coffee.

Slowly Vegas slid behind them like a mirage and was soon swallowed up by desert and sand. The sun was tilting west.

Fifty-six

Sheila stood by the slot machines as she waited in line for Starbucks. It had never bothered her before, but now the tackiness of Vegas felt like a layer of dirt she couldn't quite wash off.

Really, did there need to be gambling in the airport? But that was the way of Vegas. To wring you dry and then send you off poor and broken but still full of hope—enough so that you would come back to lose, or win, depending on the fates.

While she waited, she listened to Sunil's message again. Typically he waited a full day to return her calls and when he did he tried to make it sound like there was something other than his tardiness involved.

Double macchiato, she said to the overly cheerful barista.

What size?

Medium.

Grande it is.

Sheila smiled. Starbucks Italian—its own special language. She moved down to the other end of the coffee bar. In a few minutes she was shaking fake sugar into her cup.

She should call Sunil. He sounded so worried. But when she dialed, it rang and rang. No answer.

Typical, she thought. She was going to hang up without leaving a message, but at the last minute she changed her mind.

Hi, Sunil, it's Sheila. I'm at the airport. I decided to leave a day early for Cape Town. I met Asia. She seems nice. So, eh, unless there's something that needs my attention, I'm going to be boarding in a couple of hours. Okay, I'm going to stop rambling now. Call me. It'll be nice to hear your voice before I leave.

She hung up. In the corner by the vending machines a woman had just won on the penny slots. Sheila sighed. She'd never felt so alone.

Fifty-seven

You should let me answer my phone, Sunil said. If I don't, it will raise suspicions.

Eskia laughed.

You overestimate your own importance, he said. No one's looking for you. And in a couple of hours I'll be done with you, and by tomorrow the coyotes will have done with you too if you're lucky.

Will killing me change anything? Bring Jan back?

Don't try to work me, Sunil.

The things I did, you did, the people who died, that was a different time, Eskia. We were different people then. Hasn't there been enough unnecessary death? All of us from that time, we have so much to atone for, so much to forgive. Can you really handle any more?

Eskia laughed: You don't understand anything. It didn't stop for me. I still do what I did then. I still clean up the mess of spineless men like you. I am still fighting the war, Sunil. It didn't end just because Madiba was freed and the world congratulated itself. It's still going on; the Boer are still at war with us, and we with them. You will never know the depth of my sacrifice. What I have given up for the ideal of a free and equal South Africa. The sacrifices I made, I made not just for that ideal. I made them for love, for the love of a particular woman. Jan was that woman. And what you and your friends did in Vlakplaas took that away from me, demeaned everything I gave, made all the blood on my hands meaningless. When you took Jan, you took my grace. But your death will buy back my meaning. You should feel honored that you will be my Isaac and I your Abraham.

Listen to yourself, Sunil said, and there was something like pity in his voice.

I think we're being followed, Eskia said, abruptly changing the conversation. Yes, he said, we are. He pulled off onto the shoulder, the tires throwing up small pebbles.

Salazar smiled. That old trick, he thought, shooting by, pretending to go on. When Eskia pulled back onto the road, he could still see him in the rearview mirror. Cat and mouse, Salazar said. He liked that. I can still follow you from up here, he said.

Eskia, Sunil said. There is still time to stop.

Stop?

You can't believe all that juvenile shit about giving so much for South Africa's freedom just so you could be married to a white woman legally? That is the depth of self-delusion. You may have given up a lot for love, but it wasn't for romantic love. It wasn't. And don't you think the rest of us paid a huge price? What is it with all this one-upping of trauma? That's all the new South Africa seems to be about. Who suffered more, those who went to prison or those who stayed out, those who lost loved ones or those who didn't. On and on, tallying an impossible math.

Shut the fuck up, Eskia said. Try to die like a man, with some dignity, not this babbling that you think will save you. Do you think I have forgotten that once, a long time ago, we had a friendship? I never forgot that and yet here I am, re-solved to kill you. No last-minute babbling will shake my resolve—you will die here today, alone, and I will bury you here. So please, if you must speak, make peace with your gods.

Sunil was silent. There was nothing to be said. He was

going to die here. Alone. He wondered if there was something he was supposed to think about, if his entire life was
meant to flash before his eyes. If it was, it wasn't happening to
him. Instead all he felt was an overwhelming fatigue, and a
curious empty detachment. As if he were watching all this in
a movie. He felt only one niggling regret. That he had never
let himself love again, not since Jan. What a waste that had
been. All that guilt, all those years. What would it have felt
like to let himself truly fall in love—with Asia, or Shelia?
Would it have made this moment feel any different, because if
there was any certainty here, it was the inevitability of today?
Of this moment. In a strange, inexplicable way, it felt right.
I'm going to die today, he thought, and it wasn't as scary as he
had expected it to be.

Eskia turned off the freeway and onto a dirt road, headed
for some disused buildings a few miles in the distance, in the
shadow of a huge rock formation. Sunil was oddly impressed
by it all—not only the eternity of the landscape but by the
level of planning and effort and resolve Eskia had put into
this.

Perhaps I should have kept my research in South Africa instead of coming here to Las Vegas, Sunil thought. There
would be no end of damaged people like Eskia that he could
have studied, not to mention the entire Boer nation. Maybe
psychopathy wasn't born in the brain after all. Perhaps it wasn't
a function of which gland was closer to or farther from another. Maybe psychopathy was born in the heart, by shame;
shame and a broken, betrayed heart. He liked this new line of
thought. It didn't lend itself to empirical exploration, but there
was a beauty to it, he thought, something beyond the mecha-
nistic. Perhaps it just means that I still have a heart, which in
itself is no small miracle.

Eskia stopped the car and pulled him out. He threw Sunil
to the dirt and quickly attached a new plastic tie to his wrists

while he lay there, breathing in the dust, feeling it tickle the back of his throat. He looked over to see Eskia pulling a duffel bag from the trunk of the car. Struggling to his knees, he looked around. There was a clump of Joshua trees in the distance and what looked like a flash of blue.

Well, Eskia said. Here we are.

Fifty-eight

Sunil knelt there in the dirt while Eskia put his bag on the closed trunk and began to unpack it. Both of Sunil's hands were securely fastened with zip ties, which were cutting deeply into his skin; still he struggled against them, feeling the sticky warmth of blood on his wrists.

There's no point struggling, Sunil, Eskia said, back turned. No one can get out of a zip tie. Not even Houdini if he were still alive.

Sunil resisted every impulse to scream, to curse, to beg. Instead he mustered all his energy and got up on his feet. He fully intended to ram into Eskia from behind, then head off into the desert, take his chances there. But before he could gather momentum for his charge, Eskia turned and struck him across the face with a crowbar, dropping him to his knees again.

Come on, Sunil, really? Do you know how long I've been doing this? Worked over people like you? I am justice, Eskia said.

You sound like Eugene, Sunil gasped, licking at the blood from his cut lip.

Eskia shrugged. Angels and demons have a lot in common, he said. Except of course to what service they put their powers.

Sunil spat at Eskia, the spittle and blood landing short.

Come now, bruh, Eskia said. Have some dignity. Now, here's what I need from you. The password for the hard drive.

You're going to kill me anyway, so why should I tell you?

I didn't say how I was going to kill you. Sunil, you should know there are things worse than death.

Sunil said nothing, but he was beginning to sweat.

Did I ever tell you that I sent you the telegram announcing your mother's death, Eskia said.

What the fuck are you talking about?

I was with your mother when she died. Or rather, I should say, when she begged me to take her life.

You're lying!

Why would I lie? I have nothing to gain from that. Do you want to hear my story or not? Makes no difference to me.

Fuck you!

Your choice.

Eskia turned and paused before a series of items he had laid out on the trunk lid. The crowbar, a set of pliers, several scalpels, needles in varying sizes, a small blowtorch of the kind chefs use to caramelize a crème brûlée, a piece of rubber six inches long and about as wide, taken from the inner tube of a small tire—from the days when tires still had inner tubes— and a plain jute bag. Everything needed to break a man, to destroy body and soul, was available in most hardware stores or pharmacies.

Sunil glanced at the assemblage of materials and looked away, taking deep breaths, trying to brace himself. He knew only too well what was coming.

Eskia held up the bag.

In the old days, he said, the Afrikaner police would wet a bag like this, force you facedown, and squat on your back. Then they would pull the bag over your head until your lungs began to burn. Sometimes, depending on what they wanted, they would just let your lungs burn out, no questions asked. A fire made of air, or its lack. But I have something different planned for you.

Eskia put the bag down and picked up the piece of rubber.

Do you know what this is?

Sunil looked away.

The Afrikaner police called it the devil's ski mask. Remember how it works.

With a lot of effort, Eskia pulled the piece of rubber down over the struggling Sunil's head until his entire face was covered.

There, there. Now, how long should I leave it on?

Sunil was thrashing around on the ground, trying to use the friction of sand and pebbles to dislodge the mask. He couldn't breathe, or see, or hear, or swallow. He felt like his head was on fire. He heard himself yelling in his head but knew instinctively that he had made no sounds. Just as a warm blackness welcomed him, Eskia pulled the mask up over his mouth, exposing it. Sunil opened his mouth and swallowed air in big wheezing gulps until he began to choke.

Password, Eskia asked, voice casual.

Fuck—

That was all Sunil could say before the rubber covered his mouth again, forcing him to once more thrash around like the chickens he'd seen being killed in the shebeen. Again, just at the threshold of that welcome wet, black blanket, Eskia pulled the mask up a couple of inches. And although he didn't want to, although he wanted not to breathe, to end it now, his mouth and lungs overrode him, taking in deep gulps of air.

When I went to see your mother I worked for a unit of the ANC that was dedicated to killing informants. Killing those who betrayed the cause. To send a warning to others who might be tempted to turn us in. A kind of incentive, you could say. We came to the camp where your mother was being kept. In those days, the republic put black mental patients in camps, temporary shelters in the worst parts of the city, under flyovers or in former dump sites. In your mother's case, she was housed with others in an abandoned mine workers' barracks right in the heart of a township, one big ugly building that housed three hundred crazy people and thirty attendants who treated them worse than dogs. There was not a doctor in sight or a single dose of medication. It was little more than a prison. The worst part was that all those attendants, all thirty of them, were black, just like the patients. There were twenty names on that list. Your mother's was one of them. We knew about White Alice and the deaths of our men in Zimbabwe. There was a lot of debate about your mother, Sunil. Many felt she should be spared because she hadn't really been an informer. That she had paid enough when she sewed her mouth shut, and that even though those scars had long since healed over, she was locked in the hospital. But mercy was in short supply in those days and her name was added to the list. When I came into her room, she knew why I was there, but she said nothing. I'm not saying that it was easy to kill your mother. I stood there a fair while just looking at her. And then she let out this moan. Oh my God, it was awful. Like the sound a dying animal makes, a keening to freeze your blood. So I did the only humane thing I could, I did what I saw her eyes begging for. It was a mercy, you know, that bullet to her head. You should thank me for that. The thing is, Sunil, you and I know that you should have died, not her. It was you who betrayed your father. Johnny Ten-Ten told us everything when he joined. Instead your reward was a job at Vlakplaas. Maybe that was punishment enough.

The sound from Sunil was guttural and now he struggled to his feet, hands still tied behind him, and lunged for Eskia. A short blow from the crowbar brought him down.

I'm getting bored, Sunil, Eskia said.

With that, Eskia pulled the piece of rubber tubing back down over Sunil's mouth and watched him writhe.

In his head, Sunil begged for a quick death. Willed his body, and his mind, to stop fighting, to just give in. Please let me die, Sunil begged his body. Let me die. He couldn't even bring himself to think about his mother, to think about all the ways he had betrayed her. That was too much to contemplate, even now. Instead he forced himself to only think of death, of his dying, of speeding it up. And then there it was, a deep, wet darkness, and it was taking him, like a river of blood, a waterway of oblivion.

But then he was sputtering and his chest hurt and the sun burned his eyes. Words wouldn't come, but he was thinking, No, no, no. Fuck, no!

Slowly his eyes began to focus and he realized he wasn't dead and that there was a new wetness. Salazar was giving him mouth to mouth. Closing his eyes, Sunil bit down on Salazar's lip, forcing him to let go.

What the fuck, you asshole! Salazar screamed, jumping back.

Sunil coughed for a minute and then said: I'm sorry, man, but you were enjoying that a little too much.

Fuck you! I should have let you die.

Sunil struggled up, his hands still tied.

Can you cut me loose?

Salazar pulled a pocketknife and cut the plastic. Sunil rubbed his still-bleeding wrists.

Where is—

Over there, Salazar said, pointing.

Eskia lay a little distance from the rental, his body twisted, glasses in the dirt, one lens broken. But it was the gaping hole in the back of his head that held Sunil's attention.

Had no choice, Salazar said. I had to shoot the fucker.

Yeah, Sunil said, but his voice was sad.

Here, Salazar said, passing Sunil his flask. Drink some of this.

The whiskey burned Sunil's air-deprived throat, but its sting felt good. It was the sting of life. Thanks, he said, passing it back.

Welcome back, Salazar said. Now, wait here, I'm going to fetch my car, then radio the locals to come in. I think we're on reservation grounds so it will have to be the tribal police. But they're fair.

Was that you I saw by the Joshua trees? In a blue car?

Yeah, I borrowed the Bug from a rookie at the precinct.

Hey, Salazar, he called as Salazar began to walk away. There's your killer right there, he said, pointing to Eskia. He is the man who took the lives of all those homeless men.

Yeah, Salazar said. I guess we solved it, then.

Fifty-nine

The security man shoved Water unceremoniously into his room. He sat on the bed for a moment and, lifting his shirt, he stroked Fire's head gently, singing softly under his breath. Half an hour later the door opened. Brewster stood there sucking on his oxygen tank flanked by two security guards.

Water, the man said.

Water said nothing.

It's okay, boys, Brewster said to the guards. I think this one is harmless.

If you say so, Doctor, one of the guards said.

Brewster waved them away. Go, go, he said. Turning back to Water, he said, Don't you think that's creepy, stroking your dead brother's head like that?

How would you know that, Water asked.

Brewster pointed to the ceiling. I have eyes everywhere. Remember me? I believe you belong to me now. Did Sunil explain to you that you are now here for good?

Has anyone ever told you that you have a sort of Dr. Mengele manic look about you?

Dr. Brewster laughed. This is good, he said. You are as feisty as I have been led to believe. I am really looking forward to studying you.

Fuck you, Water said.

No, no, my friend, it's you who's getting fucked. You are

not going anywhere. You don't seem to understand that I have complete power over you. Unlike Sunil, I am not soft, or trying to make restitution for my sins. In my experience, men of science—true men of science, mark you—are like unto the gods. I have no interest in your humanity. No, I am only interested in your monstrosity, and that, my friend, is the medical term for your condition. So if I decide to cut your hands off as part of my exam or dissect you where you stand—

It's vivisect, Water corrected.

What?

Vivisect if alive; dissect if dead, Water said. You should know that, being a doctor and all. Or are you so high off that oxygen tank you've been sucking on?

Why you—

Oh, shut up, Water said. While he spoke, Fire retreated under his caul.

I—, Brewster began.

Fuck this, Water said. He reached forward, ripped Brewster's ID off, and then, wrapping his oxygen line around his neck, he slowly strangled him. It took longer than he expected. It was like Brewster wouldn't die.

He let himself out with Brewster's key and headed to the elevator, which he rode down to the hidden labs in the basement, the ones he knew Sunil had never seen. Selecting one that seemed right in the middle, he gathered all the tanks labeled FLAMMABLE into a pile. Next he took out the cell phone that Fred had given him. He pushed the buttons in sequence and the countdown began. He had five minutes to get out. Best to go, he thought, placing the phone in the middle of the pile of tanks. He took off at a fast trot, and three minutes and fifty seconds later he was out the back door, past the loading dock, and into Fred's car.

Fred gunned it out of the institute's grounds and quickly onto the main road.

Did it go well?

I had a bit of unexpected luck, Water said.

Oh yeah?

Yeah, Brewster came to see me.

Did he?

Yes, with his own oxygen line.

They laughed, and Fred gunned the engine some more, pushing the car even faster. Then she pulled off the road into a strip mall that afforded a perfect view of the institute from its lot, parking right next to the black SUV that held the midgets. They all got out and sat on the roof of the SUV. Fred glanced at her watch.

Not bad, she said, we have ten seconds to spare.

In exactly ten seconds, the institute went up in a ball of fire. It was spectacular, as though the old days of the bomb tests were back. Flames and smoke in a big plume that rose over a hundred feet into the sky, throwing debris everywhere, showering the parking lot of the strip mall with ash.

I told you I was a fire wizard, Water said.

Yes, baby, Fred said, kissing him.

We should have brought Champagne, he said.

You don't drink, remember?

Oh yeah.

I feel bad about all those poor apes still trapped in the building, one of the midgets said.

I know, the other said. I wish it could have been different.

By the time the fire brigade got there, there was nothing left to save. They just concentrated on making sure the fire didn't spread. The entire institute was gone; even the peacocks had gone up in flames.

Spectacular work, Fred said.

Water turned and kissed her deeply.

Where now, he said.

The desert for a while. The carnival has already moved on. We'll catch up later.

And like that, Fred, Fire, Water, and the fighting midgets were gone.

VERB

We are many things—shapeshifters, actresses, mothers, sisters, virgins, whores, homemakers, and home wreckers—but more than anything, prostitutes are mirrors. We reflect only what the john wants, what he has paid to see, to experience. There are many different kinds of johns and a prostitute to match each need. In that way the best prostitutes are those who aren't ever there. Not really. We are only the desire of men slowly taking shape in the muted lights and scented rooms of their shame and need.

I never have figured out why we call them johns. Some say it's because men arrested for soliciting always give their names as John Smith. I don't care much for this stuff. The origin of things is more Sunil's thing.

In fact, it was Sunil who once told me that the word "prostitute" comes from the Latin verb *prostituere*, which means to put forth in public, to expose, to dishonor, to put to unworthy use. I thought it curious that he mentioned it was a verb, and not a noun, because that means we can only exist in the moment, in the doing. We are always prostitutes but since we are not always prostituting, we cannot therefore always exist. A real mind fuck, if you ask me. Like the world truly disappears when we close our eyes. I only exist in the verb of doing the thing, the nasty, so to speak. Shit, I've even started to sound like Sunil, proof that five years with someone you adore but who doesn't really see you will make you mold yourself around your own desire to be seen.

Personally, I think the word john comes from John Doe, as in a person who is and who can never really be there except in body, a need that forms only in the reflection of us. Any true hooker will tell you that this is never really about sex for the men—no matter how horny the john is. Maybe that is why it becomes easier with time, to fuck all those men, this knowledge that you are never really fucking them, you are never really having sex. Some johns come to empty themselves in your mirror, to peel away their own loss, until finally they see what they truly are. The trouble with this kind of john is that they often don't like what they see, because they stunted their own growth so long ago. What is most longed for, their deepest nostalgia, is lost forever—and while that youth they imagine, that virile self who could have taken over the world, is dreamed of, the truth is that in the face of the mirror, they are little more than grotesque dwarves. And then the desire for you turns to hate. These johns vary in tone from the mild asshole to the very dangerous, violent kind. Hookers learn very quickly how to obscure the true face of the monster in the mirror. It can never be fully obfuscated, but it can be mitigated, the john brought back from the edge before it is too late.

The other type of john wants to be kind. He wants to lavish attention on you, gifts even. He will pay you more to let him kiss your lips, your breasts, and your vagina, to trace his breath on your neck in tender arousal, to bury his nose in your hair and nuzzle you. He will try hard to make you come. He will ask you your name, your real name, and he will whisper it as he enters you. He will always be clean when he comes to you. Will always smell good, will never disrespect you, and will always act like he is on a real date with a woman he loves, or can love. But he cannot, and that is why he has chosen you.

Because you will let him love you, but only in the ways he wants to, the ways he thinks you should like, the ways in which he is capable, the ways that make him feel good. For him you reflect how gentle he is, how special, how unlike other men he can be. How he is the man all women dream of. How he is misunderstood, hurt by his own deep tenderness. He is a deeply wounded soul yearning to be beautiful, and there is the danger. Some girls become entranced by him and fall in love: yes, we fall in love.

This kind of john can never love you back. Not in any real way, because not even you, with all the true gifts of the courtesan, can live for any length of time in the illusion that he has of you, wants of you, and even demands of you. You will be too tired to have sex some nights, you will want him to fuck you in ways that you want to be fucked, you will grow tired of always having to reassure him that he is good, that he is loved, that he is everything you don't deserve. So your heart will get broken.

The deeper danger, though, with this kind of john, is that the monster he sometimes glimpses in the mirror of you is so far away from what he can accept of himself. Because unlike the asshole john, this john's vision of himself is not of a virile self who dominates women, it is of a saint. When the saint glimpses the monster, if his will is too weak, he turns not into the enlightened one but into the worst kind of violent man— the kind who will burn the world down.

But in the end, I suppose, hookers are women and so we are drawn to this flame of destruction by our own need, our own fear, our own weakness, which is, I suppose, that we all want to fall in love.

At least, that is what I want. I want Sunil to fall in love with me, to say without reservation, Asia, I love you.

TUESDAY

Sixty

Lake Mead and a gathering dusk, loons coming in to land in the rustling tamarisk, the sun little more than a memory, the foundations of the ghost town, all silent and brooding.

It was quiet when Sunil pulled up. A little too quiet, not even a cicada to be heard. He parked next to Salazar's car and walked down the crunchy, shell-lined path to the edge of the lake.

Salazar was already there. He had come prepared. There were two canvas chairs and a folding table, all of which had been set up. There was a paraffin lamp hissing on the tabletop and two giant cups of coffee.

In the center of the folding table sat the ship. The beauty of it took Sunil's breath away.

When Salazar had rescued him from Eskia, they had talked. And for the first time in more than seven years, Sunil unburdened himself to someone. No secrets, half-truths, no deceptions or deflections, just the whole unadorned story of him. It took longer than he had expected so that it was nearly dark when Salazar called in the tribal police. They examined Eskia and seemed somewhat uninterested since the victim wasn't from the reservation. They wrote up a statement that suggested it was self-defense and then called in the coroner. Still, by the time all the paperwork was done and they drove back, it was quite late.

They heard about the explosion at the institute on the radio.

I knew there was something off about them. I knew it.

I guess they weren't joking about that Downwinder Nation action group, Sunil said.

I should go arrest Fred and the twins myself, Salazar said.

They'll be long gone by now, Sunil said. Then he added: I'm sorry I didn't believe you.

That's okay. You'd better not leave town, though. The police, and maybe even the military, might be looking for you, plenty of questions.

I know, Sunil said. I know. Do you want to go by the institute?

We're never going to solve this case, are we, Salazar asked.

No, we'll never know for sure. But I have a sense that it's over now.

Yeah, you're right.

As he dropped him off that night, Salazar had asked Sunil to join him at dusk the next day by Lake Mead. Same place the twins had been arrested, by the ruins of St. Thomas.

I have this ritual thing that I have to do. A way to let go of all the ghosts. I would be privileged if you'd come.

Sunil liked that. The idea of setting free all the ghosts of his past. As long as no human or animal dies in this ritual, he said.

No animals. I build these model ships for the dead I have known or been touched by. I take them to a large body of water, light them on fire, and set them free, Salazar explained.

That sounds spectacular, Sunil said. I'll be there.

And so here he was. But still, he hadn't expected the ship to be this magnificent. The truth is, he wasn't sure what he'd expected; a paper boat, some facsimile made out of balsa wood, but not this.

This was a perfect replica of a seventeenth-century Spanish galleon, three feet long, about two wide, and with its masts up and sails unfurled, it was at least another three feet tall. The detail was incredible. There was even a masthead with a mermaid.

Wow, Sunil said. This is a beautiful ship.

You came, Salazar said, passing him a cup of coffee. He said the last part as though he was genuinely surprised by Sunil's voice, even though he must have heard him coming.

I brought something for the cold, Sunil said, holding up a bottle of single malt.

Fuck yeah, Salazar said.

So this is the ship you built for that girl from two years ago? The one we never identified.

Yes, yes, this is the one. But you know, it seems like I was building it for more than just her.

I know what you mean, Sunil said, circling the table. It's really, truly exquisite. Are you sure you want to burn it?

It's my swan song, my last ghost. I plan to retire soon. So yes, I'm sure.

What'll you do?

Salazar shrugged. Travel maybe. I've never been to Cuba. Or I may stay here but get close to it, like, say, Florida. Open up a shop and build ships for collectors.

That actually sounds fantastic, Sunil said.

You think so? Fuck, that means a lot coming from you.

Sunil coughed and looked away, taking a sip of coffee.

Look at us, being sentimental like a couple of fucking girls, Salazar growled.

Sunil laughed. There's my Salazar, he said.

He cracked open the bottle, tipping a libation to the ground. Salazar watched.

Force of habit, Sunil said, catching his look.

I was thinking how beautiful it was, Salazar said. My father used to do something similar.

Sunil splashed generous amounts into their coffee cups and took a deep swig from his own.

How's your throat today, Salazar asked.

Better.

Salazar nodded.

So, exactly how do we do this, Sunil asked.

Well, I think we should say a few words, Salazar said. Taking note of the look on Sunil's face, he added: Or we could just think of them.

Yeah, that sounds better. You know, it's just that I'm not that into God.

Salazar nodded. He put his coffee cup down, picked up the bottle of lighter fluid that sat beside the ship, and doused it liberally. Then he delicately lifted the ship and walked over to the water. Sunil followed. By now it was pitch-dark and the only light was the distant glow of Vegas in the background.

The ship bobbed on the water, kept close by Salazar's foot. Sunil thought Salazar was whispering what must be prayers. And then he realized that it wasn't Salazar whispering, but him, and that if anything Salazar was waiting for him. The prayer had been a simple one: Forgive me, Mother, forgive me.

Salazar bent down and lit the tip of one sail. He held the ship back until the flames were steady and then he pushed it off with the tip of his shoe.

Both men watched the flaming ship ride out on the dark water. By the time it was halfway out, the flames had climbed to about six feet and spread out, like a being of light was retreating over the waves.

So what will you do now, Salazar asked.

I really don't know. It seems I do have to go back to South Africa for a while, make amends with my past, my history.

To making peace, Salazar said.

I'll drink to that.

They stood there, watching the ship sail away, each man lost in thought, lost in his own unique release.

A loon took off from the tamarisk and rose toward the sky.